Mark Twain, Alvah C Beecher

Beecher's Recitations and Readings

Humorous, serious, dramatic, including prose and poetical selections in Dutch,

French, Yankee, Irish, Backwoods, Negro, and other dialects

Mark Twain, Alvah C Beecher

Beecher's Recitations and Readings
Humorous, serious, dramatic, including prose and poetical selections in Dutch, French,
Yankee, Irish, Backwoods, Negro, and other dialects

ISBN/EAN: 9783337115616

Printed in Europe, USA, Canada, Australia, Japan

Cover: Foto ©Andreas Hilbeck / pixelio.de

More available books at **www.hansebooks.com**

BEECHER'S

RECITATIONS AND READINGS.

HUMOROUS, SERIOUS, DRAMATIC,

INCLUDING

PROSE AND POETICAL SELECTIONS IN DUTCH, FRENCH,
YANKEE, IRISH, BACKWOODS, NEGRO,
AND OTHER DIALECTS.

EDITED BY

ALVAH C. BEECHER,

CONTENTS.

4 CONTENTS.

BEECHER'S RECITATIONS.

MISS MALONEY GOES TO THE DENTIST.

ANONYMOUS.

Sure, and did I tell yez how I wint to the dintist yisterday? Be aisy now, will yez, and wait a bit, and I'll tell yez all about it. Says I, "Och, docthur, docthur dear, it's me tooth that aches intirely, sure it is, an' I've a mind to have it drawn out, av ye plaze, sur." "Does it hurt ye?" says he till me. "Och, murther, can ye ax me that, now, an' me all the way down here to see yez about it?" says I. "Sure I haven't slept day or night these three days. Bedad, haven't I tried all manes to quiet the jumpin' divil? Sure didn't they tell me to put raw whiskey intil me mouth, but would it stay there, jist tell me now? No, the divil a bit could I kape it up in my mouth, though it's far from the likes o' me to be dhrinkin' the whiskey widout extrame provocation, or by accidint." So thin the docthur took his iron instrumints in a hurry, wid as little consarnment of mind as Barney would swape the knives an' forks from the table.

"Be aisy, docthur," says I, "there's time enough; sure you'll not be in such a hurry," says I, "whin your time comes, I'm thinkin'." "Och, well," says the docthur, "an' av yez not ready now, Miss Maloney, ye may come on the morrow." "Indade, docthur, I'll not sthir from this sate wid this ould dead tooth alive in me jaw," says I, "so ye may jist prepare ; but ye nade not come slashin' at a poor Christian body as av ye would wring her neck off first, an' dhraw her tooth at yez convaynience mebbe a quarther of an hour or so aftherward.

Now clap on yer pinchers, bad luck to thim, but mind ye git hould av the right one—sure, ye may aisily see it by the achin' an' jumpin'," says I. "Och," says he, "I'll git hould av the right one," an' wid that he jabs a small razor-lookin' weapon intil me mouth an' cuts up me gooms as av it was nothin' but cowld mate for hash for breakfast. Says I, "Docthur, thunder an' turf!" for me mouth was full of blood, "fwhat in the divil are ye afther ? D'ye want to make an anatomy av a livin' craythur, ye grave-robber, ye ?" says I. "Sit sthill," says he, jamming something like a corkscrew intil me jowl, an' twisting the very sowl out av me. Sure I sat still, bekase the murther-in' thafe held me down wid his knee and the gripe av his iron in me lug. If you'll belave me, the worrest of all was whin he gave an awful wring, hard enough to wring a wet blankit as dhry as gunpowdher. Arrah! didn't I think the judgmint day had come till me ? Holy fathers! may I niver brathe another breath if I didn't see the red fire in the pit! Sure I felt me head fly off me shoulders, an' lookin' up, saw somethin' monsthrous bloody in the docthur's wrenchin' iron. "Is that me head ye have got thare?" says I. "No, it's only your tooth," says he. "You lie," says I. "God bliss you," says he. "May be it is me tooth," says I, as me eyes began to open, an' by puttin' me hand up, troth I found the outside av me face on, tho' I felt as if all the inside had been hauled out, barrin' the jumpin' pain in the tooth, which had grown to fill the gap.

Och! may the divil take the tooth, an' the bad luck too, if I iver think av it any more. Sure I've had enough of its company, bad cess to the little divil !

LOST AND FOUND.

READ BY J. M. BELLEW.   HAMILTON AIDE

Some miners were sinking a shaft in Wales—
(I know not where,—but the facts have fill'd
A chink in my brain, while other tales

Have been swept away, as when pearls are spill'd,
One pearl rolls into a chink in the floor ;)
—Somewhere, then, where God's light is kill'd,

And men tear in the dark, at the earth's heart-core,
These men were at work, when their axes knock'd
A hole in a passage closed years before.

A slip in the earth, I suppose, had block'd
This gallery suddenly up, with a heap
Of rubble, as safe as a chest is lock'd,

Till these men pick'd it ; and 'gan to creep
In, on all-fours.   Then a loud shout ran
Round the black roof—" Here's a man asleep !"

They all push'd forward, and scarce a span
From the mouth of the passage, in sooth, the lamp
Fell on the upturn'd face of a man.

No taint of death, no decaying damp
Had touch'd that fair young brow, whereon
Courage had set its glorious stamp.

Calm as a monarch upon his throne,
Lips hard clench'd, no shadow of fear
He sat there taking his rest, alone.

He must have been there for many a year.
The spirit had fled ; but there was its shrine,
In clothes of a century old or near!

The dry and embalming air of the mine
Had arrested the natural hand of decay,
Nor faded the flesh, nor dimm'd a line.

Who was he, then? No man could say
When the passage had suddenly fallen in—
Its memory, even, was past away!

In their great rough arms, begrimed with coal,
They took him up, as a tender lass
Will carry a babe, from that darksome hole,

To the outer world of the short warm grass.
Then up spoke one, " Let us send for Bess,
She is seventy-nine, come Martinmass;

Older than any one here, I guess!
Belike, she may mind when the wall fell there,
And remember the chap by his comeliness."

So they brought old Bess with her silver hair,
To the side of the hill, where the dead man lay,
Ere the flesh had crumbled in outer air.

And the crowd around him all gave way,
As with tottering steps old Bess drew nigh,
And bent o'er the face of the unchanged clay.

Then suddenly rang a sharp low cry! . . . .
Bess sank on her knees, and wildly toss'd
Her wither'd arms in the summer sky . . . .

" O Willie! Willie! my lad! my lost!
The Lord be praised! after sixty years
I see you again! . . . . The tears you cost,

O Willie darlin', were bitter tears! . . . .
They never looked for ye underground,
They told me a tale to mock my fears!

They said ye were anver the sea—ye'd found
A lass ye loved better nor me, to explain
How ye'd a-vanish'd fra sight and sound!

O Darlin', a long, long life o' pain
I ha' lived since then! . . . . And now I'm old,
'Seems a'most as if youth were come back again,

LOST AND FOUND.

Seeing ye there wi' your locks o' gold,
And limbs as straight as ashen beams, ...
I a'most forget how the years ha' rolled

Between us ! . . . . O Willie ! how strange it seems
To see ye here as I've seen ye oft, ...
Anver and anver again in dreams !"

In broken words like these, with soft
Low wails she rock'd herself. And none
Of the rough men around her scoff'd.

For surely a sight like this, the sun
Had rarely looked upon.   Face to face,
The old dead love, and the living one !

The dead, with its undimm'd fleshly grace,
At the end of threescore years; the quick,
Pucker'd, and wither'd, without a trace

Of its warm girl-beauty ! A wizard's trick
Bringing the youth and the love that were,
Back to the eyes of the old and sick !

Those bodies were just of one age ; yet there
Death, clad in youth, had been standing still,
While Life had been fretting itself threadbare !

But the moment was come ;—(as a moment will
To all who have loved, and have parted here,
And have toil'd alone up the thorny hill ;

When, at the top, as their eyes see clear,
Over the mists in the vale below,
Mere specks their trials and toils appear,

Beside the eternal rest they know !)
Death came to old Bess that night, and gave
The welcome summons that she should go.

And now, though the rains and winds may rave
Nothing can part them. Deep and wide,
The miners that evening dug one grave.

And there, while the summers and winters glide
Old Bess and young Willie sleep side by side !

GUS WILLIAMS.

Vell, of you'll only lisden, I vill told you aboud dot barty vot Mygel Snyder gife last week at his house. Yah, mine freunds, dot vas a high-doned barty und all de fustglass beoples vas dere. Dere vas Miss Krouse, Misder Bumblestein, Mrs. Dinglebender of Baxter street, Mr. Kansmeyer, Mr. Gimp, Misder und Mrs. Lautenslauger of Soudth Fidth Afenue, und a goot many oders whose names I dond forgot. Miss Krouse had her hair done up in scrambled eggs, und den she vore a dress of blain corded bed-dick. Mr. Bumblestein had on a new segond hand swallow-head coat, und den he vore a vatch-chain made oud of de dail of de cow vot kicged de lamp over in Shicago. Den dere vas nice dances doo ; dere vas Polkers, Valtzes, Les Lunches, Squadrilles, und Succatoshes. Und den afder de dancing ve blayed some games ; ve blayed Buss in Shoes, Bost Office, und Grokenhagens, und Plind Man's Snuff. Und den afder dot a young man got ub to make a sbeech, und he gommenced py saying,—"I am here." In aboud dree minudes he vasn't dere ; he vas drunk, und de gommiddee shucked him oud of de segond sdory vindow, und he valked right off on his ear.

Vell, Mrs. Dinglebender broughd her baby, de sweedest liddle baby vot you efer seen, mit a nose like a chesdnud, (vell, de baby can't helb dot,) und id's head vas as large as a foot-ball, (vell de baby can't helb dot,) und de baby vas yust old enough to grawl around on de garpet, und feed on dacks und hair-bins. Vell, putty guick righd avay ond, dot baby fell in de slob-bail und got choging mit a bod-a-do-sgin.

Id's a nice ding, dough, being a farder, und exbecially gedding ub of a cold vinter's nide, mit your feet on de oilcloth, bouring oud baregoric in a dea-sboon mit der ther-

*By kind permission of the author.

momeder ninedy-nine degrees pelow de cidy-hall py moon-lide; (vell, de baby can't helb dot;) id's a nice ding to dink dot a baby vas going to grow ub und have "mumbs," "measles," " golera infandum," "jim-jams" und dings like dot to dake avay a man's money vot he has laid avay for a new suit of glothes. Bud I subboses dot's all righd, dond it?

Ven subber vas putty guick ready, I sot mineself down to ead dribe, und cakes, und onions, und bodadoes, und pigs feed, und Miss Krouse she ead so hardly dot she got fery sick, und der doctor sait she had der coleric. Yes, Miss Krouse got de coleric. She vas drying to ead a mince-pie mit a doot-prush in id, und id didn't agree vit her.

Bud den dot subber dable vas loaded ub mit all de in-delicacies of de season. Dere vas beanuts und red herrings und boddles of green-zeal soda-vater; und den Oofty Gooft broughd a boddle of Vooster-sdreet sauce, und den dere vas a Christmas dree aboud dwo inches high sed in a spiddoon in de middle of de dable yust for noding put ornamendations.

Afder subber dere vas such nice singing. Vone young man got ub und singed a song vot vent like dis:—"He flies drough de air mit his mout full of cheese, he vas a young man vot chewed ub a drapeze,"—or someding like dot anyhow; den ve all joined in de ghorus. Den dey asged me to sing, und ven I got ub to sing de beoble kepd so sdill you could hear a house fall down. I sung dot song aboud Mary had a leetle lamp, ids vool all over vite—und ven I had sung vone verse, some fellar hollere loud—"Oh! give us a resd." I dold him dot I didnt know de resd of id; of I did I vould give id to him, und den he dold me to "drob of mineself;" but I dond understood Ladin, so I couldn't make oud vot he vas dalking aboud, bud I must have sung nice, for vile I vas singing every vone vent oud of de room. Soon afder dot I vent home, bud venever

I regomember dot vestif night I alvays say to mine-self:

> Oh! vot lods of fun,
> Oh! vot lods of fun,
> Dancing, singing, all de dime,
> Drinking lager-bier und vein;
> At dot barty down at Mygel Snyder's.

----◆◆◆----

MAGDALENA, OR THE SPANISH DUEL.

READ BY J. M. BELLEW.

> Near the city of Sevilla,
>   Years and years ago—
> Dwelt a lady in a villa
>   Years and years ago;—
> And her hair was black as night,
> And her eyes were starry bright;
> Olives on her brow were blooming,
> Roses red her lips perfuming,
> And her step was light and airy
> As the tripping of a fairy;
> When she spoke, you thought, each minute,
> 'Twas the thrilling of a linnet;
> When she sang, you heard a gush
> Of full-voiced sweetness like a thrush;
> And she struck from the guitar
> Ringing music, sweeter far
> Than the morning breezes make
> Through the lime trees when they shake—
> Than the ocean murmuring o'er
> Pebbles on the foamy shore.
> Orphaned both of sire and mother
>   Dwelt she in that lonely villa,
> Absent now her guardian brother
>   On a mission from Sevilla.
> Skills it little now the telling
> How I wooed that maiden fair,

Tracked her to her lonely dwelling
  And obtained an entrance there.
Ah! that lady of the villa!   ·
    And I loved her so,
  Near the city of Sevilla,
    Years and years ago.
Ay de mi!—Like echoes falling
    Sweet and sad and low,
Voices come at night, recalling
    Years and years ago.
Once again I'm sitting near thee,
    Beautiful and bright;
Once again I see and hear thee
    In the autumn night;
Once again I'm whispering to thee
    Faltering words of love;
Once again with song I woo thee
    In the orange grove.
Growing near that lonely villa
    Where the waters flow
Down to the city of Sevilla—
    Years and years ago.

  · 'Twas an autumn eve; the splendor
    Of the day was gone,
And the twilight, soft and tender,
    Stole so gently on
That the eye could scarce discover
How the shadows, spreading over,
    Like a veil of silver gray,
Toned the golden clouds, sun-painted,
Till they paled, and paled, and fainted
    From the face of heaven away.
And a dim light rising slowly
    O'er the welkin spread,
Till the blue sky, calm and holy,
    Gleamed above our head;
And the thin moon, newly nascent,
    Shone in glory meek and sweet,
As Murillo paints her crescent

Underneath Madonna's feet.
And we sat outside the villa
      · Where the waters flow
Down to the city of Sevilla—
      Years and years ago.

There we sate—the mighty river
      Wound its serpent course along·
Silent, dreamy Guadalquiver,
      Famed in many a song.
Silver gleaming 'mid the plain
Yellow with the golden grain,
Gliding down through deep, rich meadows,
      Where the sated cattle rove,
Stealing underneath the shadows
      Of the verdant olive grove;
With its plenitude of waters,
      Ever flowing calm and slow,
Loved by Andalusia's daughters,
      Sung by poets long ago.

Seated half within a bower
      Where the languid evening breeze
Shook out odors in a shower
      From oranges and citron trees,

Sang she from a romancero,
      How a Moorish chieftain bold
Fought a Spanish caballero
      By Sevilla's walls of old.

How they battled for a lady,
      Fairest of the maids of Spain—
How the Christian's lance, so steady,
      Pierced the Moslem through the brain.

Then she ceased—her black eyes moving,
      Flashed, as asked she with a smile,—
"Say, are maids as fair and loving—
      Men as faithful, in your isle?" ·

"British maids," I said, "are ever
      Counted fairest of the fair;

Like the swans on yonder river
Moving with a stately air.

"Wooed not quickly, won not lightly—
But, when won, forever true;
Trial draws the bond more tightly,
Time can ne'er the knot undo.

"And the men?"—"Ah! dearest lady,
Are—quien sabe? who can say?
To make love they're ever ready,
When they can and where they may;

"Fixed as waves, as breezes steady
In a changeful April day—
Como brisas, como rios,
No se sabe, sabe Dios."

"Are they faithful?"—"Ah! quien sabe?
'Who can answer that they are?
While we may we should be happy."—
Then I took up her guitar,
And I sang in sportive strain,
This song to an old air of Spain.

"QUIEN SABE."

I.

"The breeze of the evening that cools the hot air,
That kisses the orange and shakes out thy hair,
Is its freshness less welcome, less sweet its perfume,
That you know not the region from which it is come?
Whence the wind blows, where the wind goes,
Hither and thither and whither—who knows?
Who knows?
Hither and thither—but whither—who knows?

II.

"The river forever glides singing along,
The rose on the bank bends a'down to its song;
And the flower, as it listens, unconsciously dips,
Till the rising wave glistens and kisses its lips.

But why the wave rises and kisses the rose,
And why the rose stoops for those kisses—who knows?
                Who knows?
And away flows the river—but whither—who knows?

III.

"Let *me* be the breeze, love, that wanders along
  The river that ever rejoices in song;
Be *thou* to my fancy the orange in bloom,
The rose by the river that gives its perfume.
Would the fruit be so golden, so fragrant the rose,
If no breeze and no wave were to kiss them?
    Who knows?
             Who knows?
If no breeze and no wave were to kiss them?
    Who knows?"

As I sang, the lady listened,
    Silent save one gentle sigh:
When I ceased, a tear-drop glistened
    On the dark fringe of her eye.

Then my heart reproved the feeling
    Of that false and heartless strain
Which I sang in words concealing
    What my heart would hide in vain.

Up I sprang. What words were uttered
    Bootless now to think or tell—
Tongues speak wild when hearts are fluttered
    By the mighty master spell.

Love, avowed with sudden boldness,
    Heard with flushings that reveal,
Spite of woman's studied coldness,
    Thoughts the heart cannot conceal.

Words half-vague and passion-broken,
    Meaningless, yet meaning all
That the lips have left unspoken,
    That we never may recall.

"Magdalena, dearest, hear me,"
 Sighed I, as I seized her hand—
"Hóla! Senor," very near me,
 Cries a voice of stern command.

And a stalwart caballero
 Comes upon me with a stride,
On his head a slouched sombrero,
 A toledo by his side.

From his breast he flung his capa
 With a stately Spanish air—
[On the whole, he looked the chap a
 Man to slight would scarcely dare.]

" Will your worship have the goodness
 To release that lady's hand ?"—
"Senor," I replied, " this rudeness
 I am not prepared to stand.

"Magdalena, say "—the maiden,
 With a cry of wild surprise,
As with secret sorrow laden,
 Fainting sank before my eyes.

Then the Spanish caballero
 Bowed with haughty courtesy,
Solemn as a tragic hero,
 And announced himself to me.

"Senor, I am Don Camillo
 Guzman Miguel Pedrillo
 De Xymenes y Ribera
 Y Santallos y Herrera
 Y de Rivas y Mendoza
 Y Quintana y de Rosa
 Y Zorilla y'—" No more, sir,
" 'Tis as good as twenty score, sir,"
 Said I to him, with a frown ;
" Mucha bulla para nada,
 No palabras, draw your 'spada
 If you're up for a duelo

You will find I'm just your fellow—
    Senor, I am PETER BROWN!"

By the river's bank that night,
    Foot to foot in strife,
Fought we in the dubious light
    A fight of death or life.
Don Camillo slashed my shoulder,
With the pain I grew the bolder,
    Close, and closer still I pressed;
Fortune favored me at last,
I broke his guard, my weapon passed
    Through the caballero's breast—
Down to the earth went Don Camillo
Guzman Miguel Pedrillo
De Ximenes y Ribera
Y Santallos y Herrera
Y de Rivas y Mendoza
Y Quintana y de Rosa
Y Zorilla y—One groan,
And he lay motionless as stone.
The man of many names went down,
Pierced by the sword of PETER BROWN!

Kneeling down, I raised his head;
The caballero faintly said,
"Signor Ingles, fly from Spain
With all speed, for you have slain
A Spanish noble, Don Camillo
Guzman Miguel Pedrillo
De Ximenes y Ribera
Y Santallos y Herrera
Y de Rivas y Mendoza
Y Quintana y de Rosa
Y Zorilla y"—He swooned
With the bleeding from his wound.
If he be living still, or dead,
    I never knew, I ne'er shall know.
That night from Spain in haste I fled,
    Years and years ago.

Oft when autumn eve is closing,
    Pensive, puffing a cigar,
In my chamber lone reposing,
Musing half, and half a-dozing,
    Comes a vision from afar
Of that lady of the villa
In her satin, fringed mantilla,
And that haughty caballero
With his capa and sombrero,
Vainly in my mind revolving
    That long, jointed, endless name;—
"Tis a riddle past my solving,
    Who he was, or whence he came.
Was he that brother home returned?
Was he some former lover spurned?
Or some family *fiancé*
That the lady did not fancy?
Was he any one of those?
Sabe **Dios**. Ah! God knows.

Sadly smoking my manilla,
    Much I long to know
How fares the lady of the villa
    That once charmed me so,
When I visited Sevilla
    Years and years ago.
Has she married a Hidalgo?
Gone the way that ladies all go
In those drowsy Spanish cities,
Wasting life—a thousand pities—
Waking up for a fiesta
From an afternoon siesta,
To " Giralda " now repairing,
Or the Plaza for an airing;
At the shaded *reja* flirting,
At a bull-fight now disporting;
Does she walk at evenings ever
Through the gardens by the river?
Guarded by an old duenna
Fierce and sharp as a hyena,

With her goggles and her fan
Warning off each rakish man?
Is she dead, or is she living?
Is she for my absence grieving?
Is she wretched, is she happy?
Widow, wife, or maid?   *Quien sabe?*

JIM WOLFE AND THE CATS.

We was all boys, then, an' didn't care for nothin' only heow to shirk school, an' keep up a revivin' state o' devilment all the time. This yah Jim Wolfe I was talkin' about, was the prentice, an' he was the best hearted feller, he was, an' the most forgivin' and ouselfish, I ever see—well, there couldn't be a more bullier boy than what Jim was, take him heow you would; and sorry enough I was when I see him for the last time.

Me an' Henry was allers pesterin' him, an' plasterin hoss bills on his back an' puttin' bumble-bees in his bed, and so on, an' sometimes we'd jist creowd in an' bunk with him, not'standin' his growlin,' and then we'd let on to git mad an' fight acrost him, so as to keep him stirred up like. He was nineteen, he was, an' long, an' lank, an' bashful, an' we was fifteen an' sixteen, an' pretty tolerabul lazy an' wuthless.

So, that night, you know, that my sister Mary gin the candy pullin', they started us off to bed airly, so as the comp'ny could have full swing, and we rung in on Jim tew have some fun.

Wall, our winder looked out onter the ruff of the ell, an' about ten o'clock a couple of old tom cats got to rairin' an' chargin' reound on it, an' carryin' on jist like sin.

There was four inches o' snow on the ruff, and it froze so that there was a right smart crust of ice on it, an' the moon was shinin' bright, an' we could see them cats jist like day-light.

Fust they'd stand off, e-yow-yow-yow, jist the same as if they was a cussin' one another, you know, an' bow up their backs, an' bush up their tails, an' swell around, an' spit, an' then all of a suddin the gray cat he'd snatch a handful of fur off the yaller cat's back, an' spin him around jist like a button on a barn door. But the yaller cat was game, and he'd come an' clinch, an' the way they'd gouge, an' bite, an' howl, and the way they'd make the fur fly, was peowerful.

Wall, Jim he jist got disgusted with the row, and 'lowed he'd climb out there, an' shake 'm off'n that ruff. He hadn't reely no notion o' doin' it, likely, but we everlast-ingly dogged him, an' bullyragged him, an' lowed he'd allers bragged heow he wouldn't take a dare, an' so on, till bimeby he jist histed the winder, an' lo and behold you! he went—went exactly as he was—nothin' on but his shirt. You ought to a seen him! You ought to seen him creepin' over that ice, an' diggin' his toe nails an' finger nails in, fur tew keep him from slippin'; and, 'bove all, you ought to seen that shirt a flappin' in the wind, and them long ridick-lous shanks of his'n a glistenin' in the moonlight.

Them comp'ny folks was down there under the eaves, an' the whole squad of 'em under that ornery shed o' dead Wash'ton Bower vines—all sett'n reound two dozzen sas-sers o' bilin hot candy, which they'd sot in the snow to cool. And they was laughin' an' talkin' lively; but, bless you, they didn't know nothin' 'bout the panorammy that was goin' on over their heads.

Wall, Jim, he jist went a sneakin' an' a sneakin' up un-beknowns to them tom-cats—they was a swishin' their tails, and yow-yowin' an' threatnin' to clinch, you know, an' not payin' any attention—he went a sneakin' an' a sneak-in' right up to the comb of the ruff, till he got in a foot an' a half of 'em, an' then all of a suddin he made a grab fur the

yaller cat! But, by gosh, he missed fire, an' slipped his
holt, an' his heels flew up, an' he flopped on his back, and
shot off'n that ruff jist like a dart!—went a smashin' and a
crashin deown thro' them old rusty vines, an' landid right
in the dead centre of all them comp'ny people!—sot deown
jist like a yearthquake in them two dozzen sassers of red-
hot candy, and let off a howl that was hark from the tomb!
Them gals—wall, they left, you know. They see he warn't
dressed for comp'ny, an' so they left—vamoosed. All done
in a second; it was jist one little war-whoop and a whish
of their dresses, and blame the one of 'em was in sight
anywhere!

Jim, he war in sight. He war gormed with the bilin'
hot molasses candy clean deown to his heels, an' more
busted sassers hangin' to him than if he was a Injun prin-
cess—an' he came a prancin' up stairs jist a whoopin' an' a
cussin', an' every jump he gin he shed some sassers, an'
every squirm he fetched he dripped some candy! an' blis-
tered! why, bless your soul, that pore creetur couldn't reely
set deown comfortable fur as much as four weeks.

THE WOOLEN DOLL.

A MANIAC'S STORY.   GEORGE W. BOWS.

A weary, cowering figure,
     Huddling to the wall,
A mass of golden hair, a sallow face,
     And that is all!
A wretched, blank, lost mind,—
     Whose only thought
Rests in the foolish toy
     The poor, thin hands have wrought.

A simple woolen doll,
     Clasped to her lonely breast,
Gazed wildly on at times,
     Then closer pressed.

The others sneeringly pass by
    While here and there
Stops one more curious,
    To banter or to stare.

" Father is coming, darling,—
    There,—don't cry ;
He won't be gone for long,
    He'll come by and by.
You know he's gone away, my sweet,
    To be a sailor on the sea ;
Gone far away, my pet, with words
    Of love for you and me.

They tell me he is dead, my dear ;
    But never mind,
He wouldn't go up there and leave
    Us here behind.
He told us, darling, when he went,
    He would come back again ;
And he would never break his word,
    The truest, best of men.

Ah, sir ! I see you're smiling,
    And, with alarm,
Draws back the sweet lady
    Hanging on your arm—
Miss, I was handsome once,
    But all this woe,
This misery, and grief, and shame,
    Have brought me low.

Look at me with those large blue eyes,
    That tell of love,—
Such eyes as sometimes beam on me
    From heaven above.
I know your heart is good as is your face,
    And I will tell
To you the sad, sad story,
    They all know so well.

Father was stern, and cold, and proud,
    And when James said—
' Let Rose, sir, be my wife,
    I love the maid,'—
He laughed at him, and, with a sneer,
    Sent him away—
God grant, ma'am, you may never know
    The sorrows of that day.

I loved him with a girl's first love,
    And, when he came
With father's surly message,
    Full of shame,
I cheered him as I best knew how,
    Gave him my hand,
Promised, through life, with him
    Alone I'd stand.

It was in the winter, sir,
    When all was dead,
And snow was on the ground,
    That we two fled.
A good, kind parson married us,
    Dear soul !
I often, often think of him
    In this dark hole.

Then came trouble—no work, no bread ;
    And one October morn,
When all was dark and drear,
    The child was born.
See, he's a pretty boy, sweet pet,
    With just his father's face ;
But, oh ! the good God grant,
    Without poor James' disgrace.

Things went from bad to worse—
    He took to drink,
To gambling, robbery, and shame—
    I cannot think—
Oh, no—he was mad then, I feel
    His was too good a heart

To do aught ever that would
    Make mine smart.

It came at last—the bitter hour—
    Hot words, a blow—
He beat me cruelly—
    So, darling, so—
And then we parted, and he went
    Off on the sea,
Leaving the dark, blank world
    To baby here, and me.

'Heard from him since?' you ask,
    No, ma'am, never,
Yet baby here and I
    Were waiting ever—
Waiting to hear his voice once more.
    To see his face,
To welcome him home again
    With a long, last embrace.

Oh, ma'am, 'tis sad to sit here,
    Far away from home,
Waiting for one perhaps
    Will never come.
They tell me he is dead, these people,
    Then they smile ;
While I can only hope, and clasp
    My child the while.

Father is dead, long since, they say,
    Died of a broken heart ;
Cut from the wretched tragedy
    In which he played a part.
Look, look ! see how the baby smiles !
    Give him a penny, do ;
God grant, ma'am, all such misery
    May never come to you."

Out in the sparkling sunshine,
    In the merry autumn air,
Where the breeze, in gaily passing,
    Kisses a cheek most fair—

Within, four dark and dingy walls,
That sigh with every breath
Of the mother, with her woolen doll,
Dying a living death.

THE CHARITY DINNER.

READ BY J. M. BELLEW.   LITCHFIELD MOSELY.

Time : half-past six o'clock.   Place : The London Tavern.   Occasion : Fifteenth Annual Festival of the Society for the Distribution of Blankets and Top-Boots among the Natives of the Cannibal Islands.

On entering the room, we find more than two hundred noblemen and gentlemen already assembled; and the number is increasing every minute.   The preparations are now complete, and we are in readiness to receive the chairman. After a short pause, a little door at the end of the room opens, and the great man appears, attended by an admiring circle of stewards and toadies, carrying white wands like a parcel of charity-school boys bent on beating the bounds.   He advances smilingly to his post at the principal table, amid deafening and long-continued cheers.

The dinner now makes its appearance, and we yield up ourselves to the enjoyments of eating and drinking.   These important duties finished, and grace having been beautifully sung by the vocalists, the real business of the evening commences.   The usual loyal toasts having been given, the noble chairman rises, and, after passing his fingers through his hair, he places his thumbs in the armholes of his waistcoat, gives a short preparatory cough, accompanied by a vacant stare round the room, and commences as follows :—

"MY LORDS AND GENTLEMEN :—It is with feelings of mingled pleasure and regret that I appear before you this evening : of pleasure, to find that this excellent and world-

wide-known society is in so promising a condition; and of
regret, that you have not chosen a worthier chairman; in
fact, one who is more capable than myself of dealing with
a subject of such vital importance as this. (Loud cheers.)
But, although I may be unworthy of the honor, I am
proud to state that I have been a subscriber to this society
from its commencement; feeling sure that nothing can
tend more to the advancement of civilization, social reform, fireside comfort, and domestic economy among the
Cannibals, than the diffusion of blankets and top-boots.
(Tremendous cheering, which lasts for several minutes.)
Here, in this England of ours, which is an island sur-
rounded by water, as I suppose you all know—or, as our
great poet so truthfully and beautifully expresses the same
fact, 'England bound in by the triumphant sea'—what,
down the long vista of years, have conduced more to our
successes in arms, and arts, and song, than blankets?
Indeed, I never gaze upon a blanket without my thoughts
reverting fondly to the days of my early childhood.
Where should we all have been now but for those warm
and fleecy coverings? My Lords and Gentlemen! Our
first and tender memories are all associated with blankets:
blankets when in our nurses' arms, blankets in our cradles,
blankets in our cribs, blankets to our French bedsteads in
our school-days, and blankets to our marital four-posters
now. Therefore, I say, it becomes our bounden duty as
men—and, with feelings of pride, I add, as Englishmen—
to initiate the untutored savage, the wild and somewhat
uncultivated denizen of the prairie, into the comfort and
warmth of blankets; and to supply him, as far as practi-
cable, with those reasonable, seasonable, luxurious, and
useful appendages. At such a moment as this, the lines of
another poet strike familiarly upon the ear. Let me see,
they are something like this—ah—ah—

" Blankets have charms to soothe the savage breast,
  And to—to do—a—"

I forget the rest. (Loud cheers.) Do we grudge our money for such a purpose? I answer, fearlessly, No! Could we spend it better at home? I reply, most emphatically, No! True, it may be said that there are thousands of our own people who at this moment are wandering about the streets of this great metropolis without food to eat or rags to cover them. But what have *we* to do with them? Our thoughts, our feelings, and our sympathies are all wafted on the wings of charity to the dear and interesting Cannibals in the far-off islands of the great Pacific Ocean. (Hear, hear.) Besides, have not our own poor the workhouses to go to; the luxurious straw of the casual wards to repose upon, if they please; the mutton broth to bathe in; and the ever toothsome, although somewhat scanty allowance of " toke " provided for them! If people choose to be poor, is it our business? And let it ever be remembered that our own people are not savages and man-eaters; and, therefore, our philanthropy would be wasted upon them. (Overwhelming applause.) To return to our subject. Perhaps some person or persons here may wonder why we should not send out side-springs and bluchers, as well as top-boots. To those I will say, that top-boots alone answer the object desired—namely, not only to keep the feet dry, but the legs warm, and thus to combine the double uses of shoes and stockings. Is it not an instance of the remarkable foresight of this society, that it purposely abstains from sending out any other than top-boots? To show the gratitude of the Cannibals, for the benefits conferred upon them, I will just mention that, within the last few weeks, his illustrious Majesty, Hokee Pokey Wankey Fum the First—surnamed by his loving subjects 'The Magnificent,' from the fact of his wearing, on Sundays, a shirt-collar and an eye-glass as full court costume—has forwarded the president of the society a very handsome present, consisting of two live alligators, a boa constrictor, and three pots of preserved

Indian, to be eaten with toast; and I am told, by competent judges, that it is quite equal to Russian caviare.

"My Lords and Gentlemen—I will not trespass on your patience by making any further remarks; knowing how incompetent I am—no, no! I don't mean that—knowing how incompetent you all are—no! I don't mean that either—but you all know what I mean. Like the ancient, Roman lawgiver, I am in a peculiar position; for the fact is, I cannot sit down—I mean to say, that I cannot sit down without saying that, if there ever *was* an institution, it is *this* institution; and, therefore, I beg to propose, 'Prosperity to the Society for the Distribution of Blankets and Top-Boots among the Natives of the Cannibal Islands."

The toast having been cordially responded to, his lordship calls upon Mr. Duffer, the secretary, to read the report. Whereupon that gentleman, who is of a bland and oily temperament, and whose eyes are concealed by a pair of green spectacles, produces the necessary document, and reads in the orthodox manner—

"Thirtieth Half-yearly Report of the Society for the Distribution of Blankets and Top-Boots to the Natives of the Cannibal Islands.

"The society having now reached its fifteenth anniversary, the committee of management beg to congratulate their friends and subscribers on the success that has been attained.

"When the Society first commenced its labors, the generous and noble-minded natives of the islands, together with their King—a chief whose name is well known in connection with one of the most sterling and heroic ballads of this country—attired themselves in the light but somewhat insufficient costume of their tribe—viz., little before, nothing behind, and no sleeves, with the occasional addition of a pair of spectacles; but now, thanks to this useful association, the upper classes of the Cannibals seldom appear in public without their bodies being enveloped in blankets, and their feet encased in top-boots.

"When the latter useful articles were first introduced into the islands, the society's agents had a vast amount of trouble to prevail upon the natives to apply them to their proper purpose; and, in their work of civilization, no less than twenty of its representatives were massacred, roasted, and eaten. But we persevered; we overcame the natural antipathy of the Cannibals to wear any covering to their feet; until, after a time, the natives discovered the warmth and utility of boots; and now they can scarcely be induced to remove them until they fall off through old age.

"During the past half-year, the society has distributed no less than 71 blankets and 123 pairs of top-boots; and your committee, therefore, feel convinced that they will not be accused of inaction. But a great work is still before them; and they earnestly invite co-operation, in order that they may be enabled to supply the whole of the Cannibals with these comfortable, nutritious and savory articles.

"As the balance sheet is rather a lengthy document, I will merely quote a few of the figures for your satisfaction. We have received, during the last half-year, in subscriptions, donations, and legacies, the sum of 5,403*l.* 6*s.* 8¾*d.* We have disbursed for advertising, &c., 222*l.* 6*s.* 2*d.* Rent, rates, and taxes, 305*l.* 10*s.* 0¼*d.* Seventy-one pairs of blankets, at 20*s.* per pair, have taken 71*l.* exactly; and 123 pairs of top-boots, at 21*s.* per pair, cost us 134*l.* some odd shillings. The salaries and expenses of management amount to 1,307*l.* 4*s.* 2¼*d.*; and sundries, which include committee meetings and traveling expenses, have absorbed the remainder of the sum, and amount to 3263*l.* 9*s.* 1¼*d.* So that we have expended on the dear and interesting Cannibals the sum of 205*l.* and the remainder of the sum—amounting to 5,198*l.*—has been devoted to the working expenses of the society."

The reading concluded, the secretary resumes his seat, amid hearty applause, which continues until Mr. Alderman

Gobbleton rises, and, in a somewhat lengthy and discursive speech—in which the phrases,·· the **Corporation of the City of London,"** "suit and service," **"ancient guild,"** "liberties and **privileges,"** and **" Court of Common Council,"** figure frequently, states **that he agrees with everything the** noble chairman **has said ; and has, moreover, never** listened to a more comprehensive and exhaustive document than the one just read ; which is calculated to satisfy even the most obtuse and hard-headed of individuals.

Gobbleton is a great man in the city. He has either been lord mayor, or sheriff, or something of the sort ; and, as a few words of his go a long way with his friends and admirers, his remarks are very favorably received.

"Clever man, Gobbleton !" says a common councilman, sitting near us, to his neighbor, a languid swell of the period.

"Ya-as, vewy ! Wemarkable style of owatowy— gweat fluency," replies the other.

But attention, if you please !—for M. Hector de Longnebeau, the great French writer, is on his legs. He is staying in England for a short time, to become acquainted with our manners and customs.

"MILORS AND GENTLEMANS !" commences the Frenchman, elevating his eyebrows and shrugging his shoulders. "Milors and Gentlemans—You excellent chairman, M. le Baron de Mount–Stuart, he have say to me, 'Make de toast.' Den I say to him dat I have no toast to make ; but he nudge my elbow ver soft, and say dat dere is von toast dat nobody but von Frenchman can make proper ; and, derefore, wid your kind permission, I vill make de toast. 'De brevete is de sole of de feet,' as you great philosophere, Dr. Johnson, do say, in dat amusing little vork of his, de Pronouncing Dictionnaire ; and, derefore, I vill not say ver moch to de point. Ven I vas a boy, about so moch tall, and used for to promenade de streets

of Marseilles et of Rouen, vid no feet to put onto my shoe,
I nevare to have exposé dat dis day vould to have arrivé.
I vas to begin de vorld as von garçon—or, vat you call in
dis countrie, von vaitaire in a café—vere I vork ver hard,
vid no habillemens at all to put onto myself, and ver little
food to eat, excep' von old bleu blouse vat vas give to me
by de proprietaire, just for to keep myself fit to be showed
at; but, tank goodness, tings dey have changé ver moch
for me since dat time, and I have rose myself, seulement
par mon industrie et perseverance. (Loud cheers.) Ah!
mes amis! ven I hear to myself de flowing speech, de ora-
tion magnifique of you Lor' Maire, Monsieur Gobbledown, I
feel dat it is von great privilege for von étranger to sit at
de same table, and to eat de same food, as dat grand, dat
majestique man, who are de terreur of de voleurs and de
brigands of de metropolis; and who is also, I for to sup-
posé, a halterman and de chef of you common scoundrel.
Milors and gentlemans, I feel dat I can perspire to no
greataro honneur dan to be von common scoundrelman
myself; but, hélas! dat plaisir are not for me, as I are
not freeman of your great cité, not von liveryman servant
of von of you compagnies joint-stock. But I must not forget de toast. Milors and Gentlemans! De immortal
Shakispeare he have write, 'De ting of beauty are de joy
for nevermore.' It is de ladies who are de toast. Vat is
more entrancing dan de charmante smile, de soft voice, de
vinking eye of de beautiful lady! It is de ladies who do
sweeten de cares of life. It is de ladies who are de guiding
stars of our existence. It is de ladies who do cheer but
not inebriate, and, derefore, vid all homage to dere sex,
de toast dat I have to propose is, 'De Ladies! God bless
dem all!'"

And the little Frenchman sits down amid a perfect
tempest of cheers.

A few more toasts are given, the list of subscriptions is
read, a vote of thanks is passed to the noble chairman;

and the Fifteenth Annual Festival of the Society for the Distribution of Blankets and Top-Boots among the Natives of the Cannibal Islands is at an end.

———————

GO-MORROW, OR LOT'S WIFE.

As I approached a pond, a few days ago, where some negroes were cutting ice, I chanced to hear the conclusion of a conversation between two of the hands on the subject of religion.

"What do you know 'bout 'ligion? You don't know nuthin' 'tall 'bout 'ligion."

"I know a heap 'bout 'ligion; ain't I bin done read de Bible?"

"What you read in de Bible? I say you can't tell me nuthin' what you read iu de Bible?"

"But I kin, dough. I read 'bout 'Morro."

"What sort-o' Morrow—to-morrow?"

"No, Go-Morrow."

"Well, whar he go, and what he go fur?"

"Shoh, man! he didn't go nowhar, 'cuz he was a town."

"Dar! didn't I tell you you didn't know nuthin' 'bout nuthin'? You read de Bible! Hoccum (how come) de town name 'Morro, and how de town gwine to go anywhar? Town haint got no legs."

"Man, you's a born fool, sho'. De town named Go-Morrow, but dey call it 'Morro, 'cuz they didn't have no time to stay talkin' long talk."

"Debbil dey didn't! Ef dey stay dar to-day, why can't dey stay dar to-morrow? 'Splain me dat."

"But dey all gone, and de town too. All done bu'n up."

"Ef dere ain't no pepul, and dere ain't no town, how de town name 'Morro? G'long, nigger! Didn't I know you didn't know nuthin' 'tall 'bout 'ligion ?   But (sarcastically) tole me some mo' what you read in de Bible ?"

" Well, 'Morro was a big town—'bout mighty nigh's big as Washington city—and de pepul wat live dar was de meannes' pepul in de whole worl'.   Dey was dat mean dat de Lord he couldn't abear 'em, and he make up his min' dat he gwine bu'n de town clear up.   But dar was one good man dar—member uv de church, a p'sidin elder—named Lot."

" Yaas, I know'd him !"

" Whar you know him ?"

" On de cannell (canal).   He owned a batto, and dror it hisself."

" Heist, man ! I talkin' sensé now.   Den de Lord he came to Lot, and he say, ' Lot, I gwine bu'n dis town. You and you wife git up and gether you' little alls and put out fo' de crack o' day, coz I certn'ly gwine bu'n dis town and de pepul to-morrow.'   Den Lot he and his wife riz and snatched up their little alls and traveled soon in de mornin'.   And de Lord he tuk two light 'ud (light wood) knots and some shavin's, and he set fire to dat ar town uv 'Morro, and he bu'n it spang up clear down to the groun'."

" What 'come o' Lot ?"

" He and he wife dey went and dey went and dey went t'well pres'n'ly he wife say, ' Lord ! ef I ain't gone and lef de meal-sifter and de rollin' pin I wish I may die,' and she turn round, and—and—she dar now !"

" What she doin' now ?"

" Nuthin ."

" Must be mons'us lazy woman."

" No, she ain't.   De Lord he tu'n her to pillow uv salt, 'cos she too 'quisitive."

" Dar ! ev'rybody know 'bout sack o' salt ; but who ever hear 'bout pillow o' salt ?   But what come o' Lot ?"

" Lot, he weren't keerin' 'tall 'bout no rollin' pin and no meal-sifter, so he kept straight 'long, 'thout turnin' uv he head to the right, neither to the left."

"And lef de ole 'oman dar?"

"Yass."

"In de middle of de road?"

"Yaas?"

"Must keered mighty little fur her—want to git married to sec'n wife I spec'. But de fus man come 'long and want to git some salt to bake ash-cake, he gwine to bust a piece out'n Lot's wife, and 'stroy her; and what you think o' dat? call dat 'ligion? And de ole man lef her? and you read dat—

Here a peremptory order from the foreman to "go to work" broke short the conversation.

THE WIND AND THE MOON.

GEORGE MACDONALD.

Said the Wind to the Moon, "I will blow you out.
   You stare
   In the air
   Like a ghost in a chair,
Always looking what I am about;
I hate to be watched; I will blow you out."

The Wind blew hard, and out went the Moon.
   So, deep
   On a heap
   Of clouds, to sleep,
Down lay the Wind, and slumbered soon—
Muttering low, "I've done for that Moon."

He turned in his bed; she was there again!
   On high
   In the sky,
   With her one ghost eye,
The Moon shone white and alive and plain.
Said the Wind—"I will blow you out again."

The Wind blew hard, and the Moon grew dim.
> "With my sledge
> And my wedge
> I have knocked off her edge!
If only I blow right fierce and grim,
The creature will soon be dimmer than dim."

He blew and he blew, and she thinned to a thread.
> "One puff
> More's enough
> To blow her to snuff!
One good puff more where the last was bred,
And glimmer, glimmer, glum will go the thread!"

He blew a great blast, and the thread was gone;
> In the air
> Nowhere
> Was a moonbeam bare;
Far off and harmless the shy stars shone;
Sure and certain the Moon was gone!

The Wind he took to his revels once more;
> On down,
> In town,
> Like a merry mad clown,
He leaped and hallooed with whistle and roar,
What's that?"   The glimmering thread once more!

He flew in a rage—he danced and blew;
> But in vain
> Was the pain
> Of his bursting brain;
For still the broader the Moon-scrap grew,
The broader he swelled his big cheeks and blew.

Slowly she grew—till she filled the night,
> And shone
> On her throne
> In the sky alone,
A matchless, wonderful, silvery light,
Radiant and lovely, the queen of the night.

Said the Wind—"What a marvel of power am I!
> With my breath,
> Good faith!
> I blew her to death—
First blew her away right out of the sky—
Then blew her in; what a strength am I!"

But the Moon she knew nothing about the affair,
> For, high
> In the sky,
> With her one white eye,
Motionless, miles above the air,
She had never heard the great Wind blare.

———————•◆•———————

DYIN VORDS OF ISAAC.

ANONYMOUS.

Vhen Shicago vas a leedle villages, dherein lifed dherein,
py dot Clark Sdhreet out, a shentlemans who got some
names like Isaacs; he geeb a cloting store, mit goots dot
vit you yoost der same like dhey vas made. Isaacs vas a
goot fellers, und makes goot pishness on his hause. Vell,
thrade got besser as der time he vas come, und dose leetle
shtore vas not so pig enuff like anudder shtore, und pooty
gwick he locks out und leaves der pblace.

Now Yacob Schloffenheimer vas a shmard feller, und he
dinks of he dook der olt shtore he got good pishness und
dose olt coostomers von Isaac out. Von tay dhere comes
a shentlemans on his store, und Yacob quick say of der
mans, "How you vas, mein freund; you like to look of
mine goots, aind it?" "Nein," der mans say. "Vell,
mein freund, it makes me notting troubles to show dot
goots." "Nein; I dond vood buy sometings to tay."
"Yoost come mit me vonce, mein freund, und I show you
sometings, und, so hellub me gracious, I dond ask you to
buy dot goots." "Vell, I told you vat it vas, I dond vood

look at some tings yoost now; I keebs a livery shtable,
und I likes to see mein old freund, Mister Isaacs, und I
came von Kaintucky out to see him vonce." "Mister
Isaacs? Vell, dot ish pad; I vas sorry von dot. I dells
you, mein freund, Mister Isaacs he vas died. He vas mein
brudder, und he vas not mit us eny more. Yoost vhen he
vas on his deat-ped, und vas dyin, he says of me, 'Yacob;
(dot ish mine names,) und I goes me ofer mit his peteide,
und he poods his hands of mine, und he says of me,
'Yacob, ofer a man he shall come von Kaintucky out, mit
ret hair, und mit plue eyes, Yacob, sell him dings cheab,'
und he lay ofer und died his last."

MAUD MULLER IN DUTCH.

Maud Muller, von summer afternoon
 Vas dending bar in her fadder's saloon.
She solt dot bier, und singed "Shoo Fly,"
 Und vinked at der men mit her lefd eye.
Bud ven she looked oud on der shdreed,
 Und saw dem gals all dressed so shweed,
Her song gifed out on a nbber note,
 Cause she had such a hoss in her troat;
Und she vished she had shdamps to shbend,
 So she might git such a Grecian Bend.
Hans Brinker valked shlowly down der shdreed,
 Shmilin at all der gals he'd meed;
Old Hans vas rich—as I've been dold,—
 Had hoases und lots, und a barrel of gold.
He shdopped py der door, und pooty soon
 He valked righd indo dot bier saloon.
Und he vinked at Maud, und said "My Dear,
 Gif me, of you pblease, a glass of bier."
She vend to der pblace vere der bier keg shtood,
 Und pringed him a glass dot vas fresh und goot.

" Dot's goot," said Hans, "dot's a better drink
　As offer I had in mine life, I dink."
He dalked for a vhile, den said, " Goot day."
　Und up der shdreet he dook his vay.
Maud hofed a sigh, and said, " Oh how
　I'de like to been dot olt man's frow,
Such shplendid close I den vood vear,
　Dot all the gals around vood shdare.
In dot Union Park I'd drive all tay,
　Und efery evenin go to der blay.
Hans Brinker, doo, felt almighty gweer,
　(But dot mite peen von trinkin beer.)
Und he says to himself, as he valked along,
　Hummin der dune of a olt lofe song,
" Dot's der finest gal I efer did see,
　Und I vish dot she my wife cood be."
But here his solillogwy came to an end,
　As he dinked of der gold dot she might shbend ;
Und he maked up his mind dot as for him,
　He'd marry a gal mit lots of " din."
So he vent righd off dot fery day,
　Und married a rooman olt und gray.
He vishes now, but all in vain,
　Dot he vas free to marry again ;
Free as he vas dot afdernoon,
　Ven he med Maud Muller in der bier saloon.
Maud married a man without some " soap"—
　He vas lazy doo—but she did hope
Dot he'd get bedder when shildren came ;
　But vhen dey had, he vas yoost der same.
Und ofden now dem dears vill come
　As she sits alone ven her day's vork's done,
Und dinks of der day Hans called her " my dear,"
　Und asked her for a glass of bier ;
But she don'd comblain, nor efer has,
　Und oney says, " Dot coodn't vas."

MOSES, THE SASSY; OR, THE DISGUISED DUKE.

CHAPTER I.

ELIZY.

My story opens in the classic presinks of Bostin. In the parler of the bloated aristocratic mansion on Bacon street sits a luvly young lady, whose hair is covered ore with the frosts of between 17 Summers. She has just sot down to the piany, and is warblin the popler ballad called "Smells of the Notion," in which she tells how, with pensiv thought, she wandered by a C beat shore. The son is settin in its horizon, and its gorjus light pores in a golden meller flud through the winders, and makes the young lady twict as beautiful nor what she was before, which is onnecessary. She is magnificently dressed up in a Berage basque, with poplin trimmins, More Antique, Ball Morals and 3 ply carpeting. Also, considerable gauze. Her dress contains 16 flounders and her shoes is red morocker, with gold spangles onto them. Presently she jumps up with a wild snort, and pressin her hands to her brow, she exclaims, "Methinks I see a voice!"

A noble youth of 27 summers enters. He is attired in a red shirt and black trowsis, which last air turned up over his boots; his hat, which it is a plug, being cockt onto one side of his classical head. In sooth, he was a heroic lookin person, with a fine shape. Grease, in its barmiest days, near projuced a more hefty cavileer. Gazin upon him admirinly for a spell, Elizy (for that was her name) organized herself into a tabloo, and stated as follers:

"Ha! do me eyes deceive me earsight? Is it some dreams? No, I reckon not! That frame! them store close! those nose! Yes, it is me own, me only Moses!"

He (Moses) folded her to his hart, with the remark that he was "a hunkey boy."

Chapter II.

WAS MOSES OF NOBLE BIRTH?

Moses was foreman of Engine Co. No. 40. Forty's fellers had just bin havin an annual reunion with Fifty's fellers on the day I introjuce Moses to my readers, and Moses had his arms full of trofees, to wit: 4 scalps, 5 eyes, 3 fingers, 7 ears (which he chawed off), and several half and quarter sections of noses. When the fair Elizy recovered from her delight at meetin Moses, she said:—"How hast the battle gonest? Tell me!"

"We chawed 'em up—that's what we did!" said the bold Moses.

"I thank the gods!" said the fair Elizy. "Thou did'st excellent well. And, Moses," she continnered, layin her hed confidinly agin his weskit, "dost know I sumtimes think thou istest of noble birth?"

"No!" said he, wildly ketchin hold of hisself. "You don't say so!"

"Indeed do I! Your dead grandfather's sperrit comest to me the tother night."

"Oh no, I guess it's a mistake," sed Moses.

"I'll bet two dollars and a quarter he did!" replied Elizy. "He said, 'Moses is a Disguised Juke!'"

"You mean Duke," said Moses.

"Dost not the actors all call it Juke?" said she.

That settled the matter.

"I hev thought of this thing afore," said Moses, abstractedly. "If it is so, then thus must it be! 2 B or not 2 B! Which? Sow, sow! But enuff. O life! life!—*you're too many for me!*" He tore out some of his pretty yeller hair, stampt on the floor sevril times, and was gone.

Chapter III.

THE PIRUT FOILED.

Sixteen long and weary years has elapst since the seens narrated in the last chapter took place. A noble ship, the

Sary Jane, is a-sailin from France to Ameriky via the
Wabash Canal. The pirut ship is in hot pursoot of the
Sary. The pirut capting isn't a man of much principle,
and intends to kill all the people on bored the Sary and
confiscate the wallerbles. The capting of the S. J. is on
the pint of givin in, when a tine lookin feller in russet
boots and a buffalo overcoat rushes forored and observes:

"Old man! go down stairs! Retire to the starbud bulk-
hed! I'll take charge of this Bote!"

"Owdashus cuss!" yelled the capting, "away with thee,
or I shall do mur-rer-der-r-r!"

"Skurcely," observed the stranger, and he drew a dia-
mond-hilted fish-knife and cut orf the capting's hed. He
expired shortly, his last words bein, "We are governed
too much."

"People!" sed the stranger, "I am the Juke d'Moses!"

"Old hoss!" sed a passenger, "methinks thou art
blowin!" wharenpon the Juke cut orf his hed also.

"Oh that I should live to see myself a ded body!"
screamed the unfortunit man. "But don't print any verses
about my deth in the newspapers, for if you do I'll haunt
ye!"

"People!" sed the Juke, "I alone can save you from
yon bloody pirut!• Ho! a peck of oats!" The oats was
brought, and the Juke, boldly mountin the jibpoop,
throwed them onto the towpath. The pirut rapidly approached, chucklin with fiendish delight at the idee of in-
creasin his ill-gotten gains. But the leadin hoss of the pirut ship stopt suddent on comin to the oats, and commenst
for to devour them. In vain the piruts swore and throwed
stones and bottles at the hoss—he wouldn't budge an inch.
Meanwhile the Sary Jane, her hosses on the full jump,
was fast leavin the pirut ship!

"Onct again do I escape deth!" said the Juke between
his clencht teeth, still on the jibpoop.

CHAPTER IV.

THE WANDERER'S RETURN.

The Juke was Moses the Sassy! Yes, it was!

He had bin to France, and now he was home agin in Bostin, which gave birth to a Bunker Hill! He had some trouble in gitting hisself acknowledged as Juke in France, as the Orleans Dienasty and Borebones were fernest him, but he finely conkered. Elizy knowed him right off, as one of his ears and a part of his nose had bin chawed off in his fights with opposition firemen durin boyhood's sunny hours. They lived to a green old age, beloved by all, both grate and small. Their children, of which they have numerous, often go up onto the Common and see the Fountain squirt.

This is my 1st attemt at writin a Tail & it is far from bein perfeck, but if I have indoosed folks to see that in 9 cases out of 10 they can either make Life as barren as the Dessert of Sarah, or as joyous as the flower garding, my objeck will have been accomplished, and more too.

THE YARN OF THE "NANCY BELL."

READ BY J. M. BELLEW. W. H. GILBERT.

'Twas on the shores that round our coast
　From Deal to Ramsgate span,
That I found alone on a piece of stone
　An elderly naval man.

His hair was weedy, his beard was long,
　And weedy and long was he,
And I heard this wight on the shore recite
　In a singular minor key:

"Oh, I am a cook, and a captain bold,
　And the mate of the *Nancy* brig,
And a bo'sun tight, and a midshipmite,
　And the crew of the captain's gig!"

And he shook his fists, and he tore his hair,
  Till I really felt afraid,
For I couldn't help thinking the man had been drinking,
  And so I simply said:

" Oh, elderly man, it's little I know
  Of the duties of men of the sea,
And I'll eat my hand if I understand
  How you can possibly be

" At once a cook and a captain bold,
  And the mate of the *Nancy* brig,
And a bo'sun tight, and a midshipmite,
  And the crew of the captain's gig."

Then he gave a hitch to his trousers, which
  Is a trick all seamen larn,
And having got rid of a thumpin' quid,
  He spun this painful yarn:

'Twas in the good ship *Nancy Bell*
  That we sailed to the Indian sea,
And there on a reef we come to grief,
  Which has often occurred to me.

" And pretty nigh all o' the crew was drowned,
  (There was seventy-seven o' soul),
And only ten of the *Nancy's* men
  Said ' Here !' to the muster roll.

" There was me, and the cook, and the captain bold,
  And the mate of the *Nancy* brig,
And the bo'sun tight, and a midshipmite,
  And the crew of the captain's gig.

" For a month we'd neither wittles nor drink,
  Till a-hungry we did feel,
So we drawed a lot, and accordin' shot
  The captain for our meal.

" The next lot fell to the *Nancy's* mate,
  And a delicate dish he made;
Then our appetite with the midshipmite
  We seven survivors stayed.

" And then we murdered the bo'sun tight,
 And he much resembled pig;
Then we wittled free, did the cook and me,
 On the crew of the captain's gig.

" Then only the cook and me was left,
 And the delicate question, 'Which
Of us two goes to the kettle f' arose,
 And we argued it out as sich.

" For I loved that cook as a brother, I did,
 And the cook he worshiped me;
But we'd both be blowed if we'd either be stowed
 In the other chap's hold, you see.

" ' I'll be eat if you dines of me,' says Tom
 ' Yes, that,' says I, ' you'll be.'
 ' I'm boiled if I die, my friend,' quoth I ;
 And ' Exactly so,' quoth he.

" Says he, ' Dear James, to murder me
 Were a foolish thing to do,
For don't you see that you can't cook me
 While I can—and will—cook *you* ?'

" So he boils the water, and takes the salt
 And the pepper in portions true
(Which he never forgot), and some chopped shalot
 And some sage and parsley too.

" ' Come here,' says he, with a proper pride,
 Which his smiling features tell,
 ' 'Twill soothing be if I let you see
 How extremely nice you'll smell.'

" And he stirred it round and round and round,
 And he sniffed at the foaming froth—
When I ups with his heels, and smothers his squeals
 In the scum of the boiling broth.

" And I eat that cook in a week or less,
 And—as I eating be
The last of his chops, why, I almost drops,
 For a wessel in sight I see.

*   *   *   *   *   *

" And I never grieve, and I never smile,
    And I never larf nor play,
  But I sit and croak, and a single joke
    I have—which is to say:

" Oh, I am a cook, and a captain bold,
    And the mate of the *Nancy* brig,
  And a bo'sun tight, and a midshipmite,
    And the crew of the captain's gig!"

PADDY THE PIPER.

SAMUEL LOVER.

I'll tell you, sir, a mighty quare story. 'Twas afther nightfall, and we wor sittin' round the fire, and the pratees was boilin', and the noggins of butthermilk was standin' ready for our suppers, whin a knock kem to the door. "Whist," says my father, "here's the sojers come upon us now," says he. "Bad luck to thim, the villains; I'm afeard they seen a glimmer of the fire through the crack in the door," says he.

"No," says my mother, "for I'm afther hanging an ould sack and my new petticoat agin it, a while ago."

"Well, whist, anyhow," says my father, "for there's a knock agin;" and we all held our tongues till another thump kem to the door.

"Oh, it's folly to purtind any more," says my father; "they're too cute to be put off that-a-way," says he. "Go, Shamus," says he to me, "and see who's in it."

"How can I see who's in it in the dark?" says I.

"Well," says he, "light the candle, thin, and see who's in it. But don't open the door for your life, barrin' they break it in," says he, "exceptin' to the sojers; and spake them fair, if it's thim."

So with that I wint to the door, and there was another knock.

" Who's there ?" says I.

" It's me," says he.

" Who are you ?" says I.

" A friend," says he.

" *Baithershin* !" says I ; " who are you, at all ?"

" Arrah ! don't you kuow me ?" says he.

" Divil a taste," says I.

" Sure I'm Paddy the Piper," says he.

" Oh, thundher and turf !" says I; " is it you, Paddy, that's in it ?"

" Sorra one else," says he.

" And what brought you at this hour ?" says I.

" By gar," says he, " I didn't like goin' the roun' by the road," says he, " and so I kem the short cut, and that's what delayed me," says he.

* * * * * * *

" Faix, then," says I, " you had betther lose no time in hidin' yourself," says I, " for troth I tell you, it's a short thrial and a long rope the Husshians would be afther givin' you—for they've no justice, and less marcy, the villains !"

" Faith, thin, more's the raison you should let me in, Shamus," says poor Paddy.

" It's a folly to talk," says I; " I darn't open the door."

" Oh then, millia murther !" says Paddy, " what'll become of me at all, at all ?" says he.

" Go aff into the shed," says I, " behind the house, where the cow is;" but instead of going to the cow-house, he set off to go to the fair, and he wint meandherin' along through the fields, but he didn't go far, until climbin' up through a hedge, when he was coming out at t'other side, he kem plump agin somethin' that made the fire flash out iv his eyes. So with that he looks up—and what do you think it was, Lord be marciful unto uz! but a corpse hangin' out of a branch of a three ? " Oh, the top of the mornin' to you, sir," says Paddy ; " and is that the way with you, my poor fellow ? Throth you took a start out

o' me," says poor Paddy; and 'twas thrue for him, for it
would make the heart of a stouter man nor Paddy jump to
see the like, and to think of a Christian cratbur being
hanged up, all as one as a dog.

*   *   *   *   *   *   *

Says Paddy, eyein' the corpse, "By my sowl thin, but
you have a beautiful pair of boots an you," says he, "and
it's what I'm thinkin' you won't have any great use for
thim no more; and shure it's a shame to see the likes o'
me," says he, "the best piper in the sivin counties, to be
trampin' wid a pair of ould brogues not worth three *tra-
neens*, and a corpse wid such an illigant pair o' boots, that
wants some one to wear thim." So with that Paddy laid
hould of him by the boots, and began a pullin' at thim,
but they wor mighty stiff; and whether it was by rayson
of their bein' so tight, or the branch of the tree a-jiggin'
up and down, all as one as a weighdee buckettee, and not
lettin' Paddy cotch any right hoult o' thim, he could get
no *advantuge* o' thim at all; and at last he gev it up, and
was goin' away, whin, lookin' behind him agin, the sight of
the illigant fine boots was too much for him, and he turned
back . . . . . . outs with his knife, and what does
he do, but he cuts off the legs av the corpse; and says he,
"I can take aff the boots at my convanyience." And
throth it was, as I said before, a dirty turn.

Well, sir, he tucked up the legs undher his arm, and
walked back agin to the cow-house, and hidin' the corpse's
legs in the sthraw, Paddy wint to sleep. But what do you
think? the divil a long Paddy was there antil the sojers
kem in airnest, and, by the powers, they carried off Paddy;
and faith it was only sarvin' him right for what he had
done to the poor corpse.

Well, whin the morning kem, my father says to me,
"Go, Shamus," says he, "to the shed, and bid poor Paddy
come in, and take share o' the pratees; for I go bail he's
ready for his breakquest by this, anyhow."

Well, out I wint to the cow-house, and called out "Paddy!" and afther callin' three or four times, and gettin' no answer, I wint in, and called agin, and divil an answer I got still. "Blood-an-agers!" says I, "Paddy, where are you, at all, at all?" and so, castin' my eyes about the shed, I seen two feet sticking out from undher the hape o' straw. "Musha! thin," says I, "bad luck to you, Paddy, but you're fond of a warm corner; and maybe you havn't made yourself as snug as a flay in a blanket? But I'll disturb your dhrames, I'm thinkin'," says I, and with that, I laid hould of his heels (as I thought), and givin' a good pull to waken him, as I intindid, away I wint, head over heels, and my brains was a'most knocked out agin the wall. Well, whin I recovered myself, there I was, on the broad o' my back, and two things stickin' out o' my hands, like a pair of Husshian's horse-pistils; and I thought the sight 'd lave my eyes whin I seen they wor two mortial legs. My jew'l, I threw thim down like a hot pratee, and jumpin' up, I roared out millia murther. "Oh, you murtherin' villain," says I, shaking my fist at the cow—"Oh, you unnath'ral baste," says I; "you've ate poor Paddy, you thievin' cannable; you're worse than a neyger," says I. "And bad luck to you, how dainty you are, that nothin' 'd serve you for your supper but the best piper in Ireland!"

* * * * * * *

With that I ran out, for throth I didn't like to be near her; and goin' into the house, I tould them all about it.

"Arrah! be aisy," says my father.

"Bad luck to the lie I tell you," says I.

"Is it ate Paddy?" says they.

"Divil a doubt of it," says I.

"Are you sure, Shamus?" says my mother.

"I wish I was as sure of a new pair of brogues," says I. "Bad luck to the bit she has left iv him but his two legs."

"And do you tell me that she ate the pipes too?" says my father.

"By gar, I b'lieve so," says I.

"Oh, the divil fly away wid her," says he; "what a cruel taste she has for music!"

"Arrah!" says my mother, "don't be cursing the cow that gives milk to the childer."

"Yis, I will," says my father; "why shouldn't I curse sitch an unnath'ral baste?"

"You oughtn't to curse any livin' that's undher your roof," says my mother.

"By my sowl, thin," says my father, "she shan't be undher my roof any more; for I'll send her to the fair this minit," says he, "and sell her for whatever she'll bring. Go aff," says he, "Shamus, the minit you've ate your breakquest, and dhrive her to the fair."

"Troth, I don't like to dhrive her," says I.

"Arrah, don't be makin' a gommagh of yourself," says he.

"Faith, I don't," says I.

"Well, like or no like," says he, "you must dhrive her."

*   *   *   *   *   *   *

Well, away we wint along the road, and mighty throng'd it wuz wid the boys and the girls, and, in short, all sorts, rich and poor, high and low, crowdin' to the fair.

"God save you," says one to me.

"God save you, kindly," says I.

"That's a fine beast you're dhrivin'," says he.

"Troth she is," says I; though God knows it wint agin my heart to say a good word for the likes of her. . . . I dhriv her into the thick av the fair, whin all of a suddint, as I kem to the door av a tint, up sthruck the pipes to the tune av 'Tattherin' Jack Walsh,' and my jew'l, in a minit, the cow cock'd her ears, and was makin' a dart at the tint.

"Oh, murther!" says I to the boys standin' by; "hould her," says I, "hould her—she ate one piper already, the vagabone, and bad luck to her, she wants another now."

"Is it a cow for to ate a piper?" says one o' thim.

"Divil a word o' lie in it, for I seen it's corpse myself,

and nothin' left but the two legs," says I; "and it's a folly
to be sthrivin' to hide it, for I *see* she'll never lave it
off—as Poor **Paddy Grogan** knows to his cost, Lord be marciful to him."

" Who's **that takin' my name in vain ?**" says a voice in
the crowd; and with that, shovin' **the throng a one side,**
who **the** divil should **I see but Paddy Grogan, to all ap-**
pearance.

" Oh, hould him **too,**" says I; "keep him aff me, for
it's not himself at all, **but his ghost,**" says I; " for he was
kilt last night, to my sartin knowledge, **every inch av him,**
all to his legs."

Well, sir, with **that, · Paddy—for it was Paddy himself,**
as it **kem** out afther—fell a laughin' **so that you'd think**
his sides 'ud split. **And whin he kem to himself, he ups**
and he tould uz how it was, as I tould **you** already. **And**
av coorse the poor **slandered cow was dhruv home agin,**
and many a quiet day she had wid uz afther that; and
whin she died, **throth, my father had sich a regard for the**
poor thing that **he had her skinned, and an illigant**
pair of breeches **made out iv her hide, and it's in the**
fam'ly to this day. **And isn't it** mighty remarkable, what
I'm goin' to tell you now, but it's **as thrue as** I'm here,
that from that out, **any one that has thim breeches an, the**
minit a pair o' pipes sthrikes **up, they can't rest, but** goes
jiggin' and jiggin' in their sate, and never stops as long as
the pipes is playin—and there, there is the very breeches
that's an me now, and a fine pair they are this minit.

SCHNEIDER SEES LEAH.

UNCLE SCHNEIDER.

I vant to dold you vat it is, dots a putty nice play. De
first dime dot you see Leah, she runs cross a pridge, mit
some fellers chasin her mit putty **big** shties. Dey *ketch*
her right in de middle of der edge, und der leader, (dot's

de villen) he sez of her, "Dot its better ven she *dies*, und dot he coodent allow it dot she can *lif.*" Und de *oder* fellers hollers out "So ve vill ;" "Gife her some deth ;" "Kill her putty quick ;" "Shmack her of der jaw," und such dings; und chust as dey vill kill her, de priest says of dem, "Dond you do dot," und dey shtop dot putty quick. In der nexd scen, dot Leah meets Rudolph (dots her feller) in de voods. Before dot he comes in, she sits of de bottom of a cross, und she dond look pooty *lifely*, und she says, "Rudolph, Rudolph, how is dot, dot you dond come und see aboud me ? You didn't shpeak of me for tree days long. I vant to dold you vot it is, dot ain't some luf. I dond like dot." Vell, Rudolph he dond vas dere, so he coodent sed something. But ven he comes in, she dells of him dot she lufs him *orful*, und he says dot he guess he lufs her orful too, und vants to know vood she leef dot place, und go oud in some oder country mit him. Und she says, "I told you, I vill ;" und he says, "Dots all right," und he tells her he vill meet her soon, und dey vill go vay dogedder. Den he *kisses* her und goes oud, und she feels honkey dorey boud dot.

Vell, in der nexd scen, Rudolph's old man finds oud all aboud dot, und he don'd feel putty *goot* ; und he says of Rudolph, "Vood you leef *me*, und go mit dot gal ?" und Rudolph feels putty bad. He don'd know vot he shall do. Und der old man he says "I dold you vot I'll do. De skoolmaster (dot's de villen) says dot she mighd dook some money to go vay. Now, Rudolph, my poy, I'll gif de skoolmaster sum money to gif do her, und if she don'd dook dot money, I'll let you marry dot gal." Ven Rudolph hears dis, he chumps mit joyness, und says " Fader, fader, dot's all righd. Dot's pully. I baed you anydings she voodent dook dot money." Vell, de old man gif de skoolmaster de money, und dells him dot he shall offer dot of her. Vell, dot pluddy skoolmaster comes back und says dot Leah dook dot gold righd avay ven she didn't do dot.

Den de old man says, "Didn't I told you so?" und **Rudolph** gits so vild dot he **svears** dot she can't haf someding more to do mit him. So ven Leah vill meet him in de voods, he don'd vas dere, und she feels orful, und goes avay. Bime-by she comes up to Rudolph's house. She feels putty bad, und she knocks of de door. De old man comes oud, und says, "Got out of dot, you orful vooman. Don'd you come round after my boy again, else I put you in de dooms." Und she says, "Chust let me see Rudolph vonce, und I vill vander avay." So den Rudolph comes oud, und she vants to rush of his arms, but dot pluddy fool voodent allow dot. He chucks her avay, und says, "Don'd you touch me, uf you please, you deceitfulness gal." I dold you vot it is, dot looks *ruff* for dot poor gal. Und she is extonished, und says, "Vot is dis abound dot?" Und Rudolph, orful mad, says, "Got oudsiedt, you ignomonous vooman." Und she feels so orful she coodent said a vord, und she goes oud.

Afterwards, Rudolph gits married to anoder gal in a shurch. Vell, Leah, who is vandering eferyveres, happens to go in dot shurchyard to cry, chust at de *same* dime of Rudolph's marriage, vich she don'd know someding abound. Putty soon she hears de organ, und she says dere is some beeples gitten married, und dot it vill do her unhappiness goot if she sees dot. So she looks in de vinder, und ven she sees who dot is, my graciousness, don'd she holler, und shvears vengeance. Putty soon Rudolph chumps oud indo der shurchyard to got some air. He says he don'd feel putty good. Putty soon dey see each oder, und dey had a orful dime. He says of her, "Leah, how is dot you been here?" Und she says mit big scornfulness, "Got oud of dot, you beat. How is dot, you got cheek to talk of me after dot vitch you hafe done." Den he says, "Vell, vot for you dook dot gold, you false-hearded leetle gal?" und she says, "Vot gold is dot? I didn't dook some gold." Und he says, "Don'd you dold a lie abound dot!" She says slowfully, " I told you I didn't dook some gold. Vot gold is dot?" Und den Rudolph tells her all abond dot, und she says, "Dot is a orful *lie*. I didn't seen some gold;" und she adds mit much sarkasmness, " Und you beliefed I dook dot gold. Dot's de vorst I efer heered. Now, on account of dot, I vill gif you a few gurses." Und den she svears mit orful voices dot Mister Kain's gurse should git on him, und dot he coodent never git any happiness efery-vere, no matter vere he is. Den she valks off. Vell, den a long dime passes avay, und den you see Rudolph's farm. He has got a nice vife, und a putiful leetle child. Purty soon Leah comes in, being shased, as ushual, by fellers mit shticks. She looks like she didn't cad someding for two monds. Rudolph's vife sends off dot mop, und Leah gits avay again. Den dot nice leedle child comes oud, und Leah comes back ; und ven she sees dot child, don'd she feel orful aboud dot, und she says mit affectfulness, " Come here, leedle child, I voodn'd harm you ;" und dot nice lee-dle child goes righd up, und Leah chumps on her, und grabs her in her arms, und gries, und kisses her. Oh ! my graciousness, don'd she gry aboud dot. You got to blow your noses righd avay. I vant to dold you vat it is, dot looks pully.

Und den she says vile she gries, " Leedle childs, don'd you got some names ?" Und dot leedle child shpeaks oud so nice, pless her leedle hard, und says, " Oh ! yes. My name dot's Leah, und my papa tells me dot I shall pray for you efery nighd." Oh ! my goodnessness, don'd Leah gry orful ven she hears dot. I dold you vat it is, dot's a shplaindid ding. Und quick comes dem tears in your eyes, und you look up ad de vall, so dot noboby can'd see dot, und you make oud you don'd care aboud it. But your eyes gits fulled up so quick dot you couldn'd keep dem in, und de tears comes down of your face like a shnow storm, und den you don'd care a tarn if efery body sees dot. Und Leah kisses her und gries like dot her heart's broke, und she dooks off dot gurse from Rudolph und goes avay. De child den dell her fader und muder aboud dot, und dey pring her back. Den dot mop comes back und vill kill her again but she exposes dot skoolmaster, dot villain, und dot fixes him. Den she falls down in Rudolph's arms, und your eyes gits fulled up again, und you can'd see someding more. I like to haf as many glasses of beer as dere is gryin chust now. You couldn't help dot any vay. Und if I see a gal vot don'd gry in dot piece, I voodn't marry dot gal, efen if her fader owned a pig prewery. Und if I see a feller vot don'd gry, I voodn't dook a trink of lager bier mit him. Vell, afder de piece is oud, you feel so bad, und so goot, dot you must ead a few pieces of hot stuff do drife avay der plues. But I told you vat it is, dot's a pully piece, I baed you, don'd it?

CALDWELL OF SPRINGFIELD.

BRET HARTE.

Here's the spot. Look around you. Above, on the height,
Lay the Hessians encamped. By that church on the right
Stood the gaunt Jersey farmers. And here ran a wall—
You may dig anywhere and you'll turn up a ball.
Nothing more. Grasses spring, waters run, flowers blow,
Pretty much as they did ninety-three years ago.

Nothing more, did I say? Stay, one moment; you're heard
Of Caldwell, the parson, who once preached the Word
Down at Springfield? What! no? Come, that's bad; why he had
All the Jerseys aflame! and they gave him the name
Of "the rebel high priest." He stuck in their gorge,
For he loved the Lord God, and he hated King George!

He had cause, you might say! When the Hessians that day
Marched up with Knyphausen, they stopped on their way
At the "Farms," where his wife, with a child in her arms,
Sat alone in the house. How it happened, none knew
But God, and that one of the hireling crew
Who fired the shot. Enough! there she lay,
And Caldwell, the chaplain, her husband, away!

Did he preach—did he pray ? Think of him, as you stand
By the old church, to-day ; think of him, and that band
Of militant plowboys ! See the smoke and the heat
Of that reckless advance—of that straggling retreat !
Keep the ghost of that wife, foully slain, in your view—
And what could you, what should you, what would you do ?

Why, just what he did ! They were left in the lurch
For the want of more wadding. He ran to the church,
Broke the door, stripped the pews, and dashed out in the road
With his arms full of hymn-books, and threw down his load
At their feet ! Then, above all the shouting and shots,
Rang his voice—" Put Watts into 'em, boys ! give 'em Watts !

And they did. That is all. Grasses spring, flowers blow,
Pretty much as they did ninety-three years ago.
You may dig anywhere and turn up a ball,
But not always a hero like this—and that's all.

ARTEMUS WARD'S PANORAMA.—"AMONG THE MORMONS."

ARTEMUS WARD.

Ladies and Gentlemen : Should you be dissatisfied with anything here to-night, I will admit you all free when I show in New Zealand—if you will come to me there for the passes.

I am not an artist. I don't paint myself, though perhaps if I were a middle-aged single lady of some forty-five summers, I should ; yet I have a passion for pictures. I have had a great many pictures—photographs—taken of myself. Some of them are very pretty—rather sweet to look at—for a short time—and wear a look of moral turpentine that is worth an independent fortune to me. I have an uncle who takes photographs, and I have a servant who—takes anything he can get his hands on. I once undertook to be a sculptor—and was often two weeks on a bust—but finding it wearing upon me, I gave it up.

I like music—I can't sing. As a singist I am not a success. I am saddest when I sing—so are those who hear me.

This picture is a great work of art. It is an oil-painting painted in oil—done in petroleum. It is by the Old Masters. It was the last thing they did before dying. They did this and then expired. Some of the greatest artists in New York come here every morning before daylight, with lanterns, to look at it. Some say they never saw anything like it before—others, going farther, say they hope they never may again. When I first exhibited this picture in New York, the audience were so enthusiastic in their admiration, that they called for the artist—and when he appeared, they—threw—things—at him.

Owing to a slight indisposition we will now have an intermission of fifteen minutes. But, ah—during the intermission I will go on with my lecture!

This benevolent looking old gentleman you see in the foreground is second in authority to Brigham Young. One day he came to me with tears in his eyes. I said: "Why this thusness? Why these weeps?" He told me he had a mortgage on his farm—and wanted to borrow $1,000. I lent him the money—and he went away. Some time after he returned with more weeps. He said he must leave me forever. I ventured to remind him of the money he had borrowed. He was much cut up. I thought I would not be hard upon him, so told him I would throw up $500. He brightened—shook my hand—and said—"Old friend, I won't allow you to outdo me in generosity—I will throw up the other five hundred."

This building on the right is the Mormon theatre, and it was here I made my first appearance as an actor—and made the great hit of my life. I wish you could have seen me—I have a fine education—you may have noticed it—and chew tobacco in fourteen different languages. The play was the "Ruins of Pompeii"—I played the Ruins. I rashly gave a leading Mormon an order admitting himself and family.—I knew he was married—but did not know he was so much married—he brought 84 wives and 987 children—and they filled the room to overflowing. It was a great success—but no money. The next night we played the beautiful domestic tragedy of Romeo and Juliet—but it did not go down. The audience thought it made altogether too much fuss over one woman. The third night I played Romeo to 15 Juliets and it went down very well.

These animals that look like rocks—are horses. I know they are, because my artist says so. For two years before I discovered this fact I exhibited them as cows. The artist came to me about six months ago, and said, " It is useless to disguise it from you any longer—they are horses." In painting them he fractured his right trachea, which brought on an attack of—new-mown hay.

This road which you see, leading over the mountains, is one thousand miles in length—I traveled the whole distance in a stage-coach, but am happy to state that since that time a railroad has been built. The length of the railroad is ten miles—thus leaving only nine hundred and ninety miles to be traveled by stage—which breaks the monotony of the journey.

SORROWFUL TALE OF A SERVANT GIRL.

JOHN QUILL.

Mary Ann was a hired girl.

She was called " hired," chiefly because she always objected to having her wages lowered.

Mary Ann was of foreign extraction, and she said she was descended from a line of kings. But nobody ever saw her descend, although they admitted that there must have been a great descent from a king to Mary Ann.

And Mary Ann never had any father and mother. As far as it could be ascertained, she was spontaneously born in an intelligence office.

It was called an intelligence office because there was no intelligence about it, excepting an intelligent way they had of chiseling you out of two-dollar bills.

The early youth of Mary Ann was passed in advertising for a place, and in sitting on a hard bench, dressed in a bonnet and speckled shawl and three-ply carpeting, sucking the end of a parasol.

Her nose began well, and had evidently been conceived in an artistic spirit, but there seemed not to have been stuff enough, as it was left half finished, and knocked upwards at the end.

She said she would never live anywhere where they didn't have Brussels carpet in the kitchen, and a family that would take her to the sea-shore in summer. And as she knew absolutely nothing, she said she must have five dollars a week as a slight compensation for having to take the trouble to learn.

Mary Ann was eccentric, and she would often boil her stockings in the tea-kettle, and wipe the dishes with her calico frock.

Her brother was a bricklayer, and he used to send her letters sealed up with a dab of mortar, and it was thus, perhaps, she conceived the idea that hair was a good thing to mix in to hold things together, and so she always introduced some of her own into the biscuit.

But Mary Ann was fond—yes, passionately fond—of work. So much did she love it that she dilly-dallied with it, and seemed to hate to get it done. She was often very much absorbed in her work. In fact, she was an absorbing person, and many other things were absorbed besides Mary Ann. Butter, beef, and eggs, were all absorbed, and nobody ever knew where they went to.

And whenever Mary Ann had to make boned turkey, she used to bone the turkey so effectually that nobody could tell what had become of it.

And if she so much as laid her little finger on a saucer,

that identical saucer would immediately fall on the floor and be shattered to atoms.

But Mary Ann would merely say that if the attraction of gravitation was very powerful in that spot she was not to blame for it, for she had no control over the laws of nature.

Uncles seem to have been one of Mary Ann's weaknesses; for she had some twenty or thirty cousins, all males, who came to see her every night, and there was a mysterious and inexplicable connection between their visits and the condition of the pantry, which nobody could explain. There was something shadowy and obscure about it, for whenever Mary's cousins came, there was always a fading away in the sugar-box, and low tide in the flour-barrel. It was strange—but true.

Mary Ann was troubled with absence of mind, but this was not as strong a suit with her as absence of body, for her Sunday out used to come twice a week, and sometimes three times a week.

But she always went to church, she said, and she thought it was right to neglect her work for her faith, for she believed that faith was better than works.

But if the beginning of Mary Ann was strange, how extraordinary was her ending! She never died—Mary Ann was not one of your perishable kind. But she suddenly disappeared. One day she was there full of life and spirits and hope and cooking wine, and the next day she wasn't, and the place that once knew her knew her no more.

Where she went to, how she went, by what means she went, no one could tell; but it was regarded as a singular coincidence that eight napkins, a soup-ladle, five silver spoons, a bonnet, two dresses, two ear-rings, and a lot of valuable green-backs melted away at the same time, and it is supposed that the person who stole Mary Ann away must have captured these also.

HOW A FRENCHMAN ENTERTAINED JOHN BULL.

In years by-gone, before the famous Rockaway Pavilion was built, the Half-way-House, at Jamaica, Long Island, used to be filled with travelers to the sea-shore, who put up there, and visited the beach either in their own or in hired vehicles, during the day. One warm summer evening, when the house was unusually crowded, an Englishman rode up in a gig, and asked for accommodation for the night. The landlord replied that all his rooms were taken, and all his beds, except one, which was in a suite of rooms occupied by a French gentleman. "If you and Monsieur can agree to room together," said the landlord, "there is an excellent vacant bed there."

The traveler replied, "No, I cannot sleep in the same room with a devil of a Frenchman," and off he rode with all the grum looks of a real John Bull.

In about half an hour, however, he came back, saying that as he could find no other lodgings, he believed he would have to accept the Frenchman as a room-mate. Meantime his first ill-natured remark had somehow reached the French gentleman's ears, and he resolved to pay off Johnny in his own coin.

On being shown to the apartment, the Englishman stalked in in his accustomed haughty manner, while the Frenchman, as is usual with his nation, rose and received him with smiles and bows—in short, he was more precisely polite than usual—sarcastically so, a keen observer would have thought. Not a word passed between the two, but soon the Englishman gave a pull at the bell-cord. The Frenchman quietly rose from his seat and gave the string two pulls. On the appearance of the waiter, Bull said— "Waiter, I want supper; order me a beefsteak and a cup of tea."

The Frenchman instantly said—"Vataire, ordaire two cup tea and two bifsteak; I vant two suppaire!"

Bull started and looked grum, but said nothing. The Frenchman elevated his eyebrows, and took a huge pinch of snuff. When supper was ready, the two sat down, and ate for a while in silence, when the Englishman said—

"Waiter, bring me a bottle of Burgundy."

The waiter started on his errand, but before reaching the door, the Frenchman called to him—"Vataire, come back here! you bring me two bottle Burgundy."

Bull knit his brows; Monsieur · elevated his, shrugged his shoulders, and took another pinch of snuff. The wine was brought, and while quaffing it, the Englishman said—

"Waiter, bring me an apple-tart, and a what d'ye call it, there—a Charlotte de Russe."

Monsieur then called to the waiter—"Bring me two of de apple tart, and two vat de diable you call him—Sh-Sh-Sharlie-de-Ross."

Bull's patience was now exhausted, and before the last order could be executed, he started from his seat and rung the bell. The Frenchman went to the string and gave it two violent pulls. The waiter (who was almost convulsed with laughter) came hurrying back, when Bull roared out,

"Waiter, never mind the Charlotte-de-Russe; bring me up a boot-jack and a pair of slippers."

The Frenchman responded—"Vataire, you no mind to bring two of de Sharlie-de-Ross, but you bring two slip-paire, and two shack-boot."

Before there was time to bring these articles, Bull had thoroughly lost his temper, and when the waiter appeared with them, he thundered out—

"Waiter, bring me a candle; and if you have no room in the house with a bed in it, besides this, show me a set-tee, or a lounge, or a couple of chairs, or, in short, any place where I can rest in peace by myself."

· Monsieur instantly called out—"Stop, vataire; you sall bring me two candle, and if you have no room with two bed in him, you sall bring me two lounge, two settee, and two chair! by gar, I vill rest in two pieces!"

Bull could stand it no longer. He kicked the boot-jack out of the way and made a rush for the door, banged his head in an attempt to open it, ran against the waiter at the head of the stairs, when both tumbled to the bottom, darted into the bar-room, paid his bill, and ordered up his horse and gig, swearing he would never sleep in the house with a mad Frenchman.

TIAMONDTS ON DER PRAIN.

Hans —— geebs a millinery shtore py Shtate shtreet out, und vas hereditary on der soopject of dhem tiamondts. Ofer a mans comes on his hause mit shooelry of efery kindts, Hans vas got some affecktions about him. Von tay dhere comes py his pblace von Mister Shmid. Now, dot shendlemans vears py his bosom a tiamondt bin, und von of der bulliest kindt. Hans shpeaks mit him und says: "Vell, Mister Shmid, how you vas? Dot ish a nice tay pehindt noon, Mister Shmid." "Yah, Hans; id vas shure a goot tay." "You dond vas pooty goot lookin to-day, Mister Shmid. You got some mellongholly. Aind it? Vat ish der tifficuldy?" "Vell, Hans, dot ish recht. I have some mellongholly py me. No longer as von veek ago mine sister she vas dook sick und died, und now I got some sad indelligence dot mine mudder she vas on her death-ped." "Ish dot so, Mister Shmid? Vell, I dhruly sympadises mit you. Some dime ago mine brodder vas gone died, und I feel fery pad now. I yoost got some indelligences, too, dot mine leetle cousin vas been dookin sick und vood die. I lofes dot leedle cousin und dot cousin lofes me, und efery time vhen I goes me of her hause, vhen der nito he vas comes, she says of me, "Goot nacht, cousin Hans, und dhen goes on der fhloor, py her petside, und, mit her leedle hands togedder, she brays to der Great Got Almighdy,— Ish dot a tiamondt you vear on your bosom, Mister Shmid?"

KING ROBERT OF SICILY.

READ BY J. M. BELLEW.   H. W. LONGFELLOW.

Robert of Sicily, brother of Pope Urbane
And Valmond, Emperor of Allemaine,
Appareled in magnificent attire,
With retinue of many a knight and squire,
On St. John's eve, at vespers, proudly sat
And heard the priests chant the Magnificat.
And as he listened, o'er and o'er again
Repeated, like a burden or refrain,
He caught the words, " *Deposuit potentes*
De sede, et exaltavit humiles ;"
And slowly lifting up his kingly head,
He to a learned clerk beside him said,
" What mean those words ?" The clerk made answer meet,
" He has put down the mighty from their seat,
And has exalted them of low degree."
Thereat King Robert muttered scornfully,
" 'Tis well that such seditious words are sung
Only by priests, and in the Latin tongue ;
For unto priests and people be it known,
There is no power can push me from my throne !"
And leaning back, he yawned and fell asleep,
Lulled by the chant monotonous and deep.

When he awoke, it was already night ;
The church was empty, and there was no light,
Save where the lamps that glimmered, few and faint,
Lighted a little space before some saint.
He started from his seat and gazed around,
But saw no living thing and heard no sound.
He groped towards the door, but it was locked ;
He cried aloud, and listened, and then knocked,
And uttered awful threatenings and complaints,
And imprecations upon men and saints.
The sounds re-echoed from the roof and walls
As if dead priests were laughing in their stalls.

At length the sexton, hearing from without
The tumult of the knocking and the shout,
And thinking thieves were in the house of prayer,
Came with his lantern, asking, " Who is there ?"
Half choked with rage, King Robert fiercely said,
"Open ; 'tis I, the King!   Art thou afraid ?"
The frightened sexton, muttering with a curse,
" This is some drunken vagabond, or worse !"
Turned the great key and flung the portal wide ;
A man rushed by him at a single stride,
Haggard, half naked, without hat or cloak,
Who neither turned, nor looked at him, nor spoke,
But leaped into the blackness of the night,
And vanished like a spectre from his sight.

Robert of Sicily, brother of Pope Urbane
And Valmond, Emperor of Allemaine,
Despoiled of his magnificent attire,
Bare-headed, breathless, and besprent with mire,
With sense of wrong and outrage desperate,
Strode on and thundered at the palace gate ;
Rushed through the court-yard, thrusting in his rage
To right and left each seneschal and page,
And hurried up the broad and sounding stair,
His white face ghastly in the torches' glare.
From hall to hall he passed with breathless speed ;
Voices and cries he heard, but did not heed,
Until at last he reached the banquet-room,
Blazing with light, and breathing with perfume.
There on the dais sat another king,
Wearing his robes, his crown, his signet-ring—
King Robert's self in features, form, and height,
But all transfigured with angelic light !
It was an angel ; and his presence there
With a divine effulgence filled the air,
An exaltation, piercing the disguise,
Though none the hidden angel recognize.

A moment speechless, motionless, amazed,
The throneless monarch on the angel gazed,
Who met his looks of anger and surprise

With the divine compassion of his eyes!
Then said, "Who art thou and why com'st thou here?"
To which King Robert answered with a sneer,
"I am the king, and come to claim my own
From an impostor, who usurps my throne!"
And suddenly, at these audacious words,
Up sprang the angry guests, and drew their swords;
The angel answered, with unruffled brow,
"Nay, not the king, but the king's jester; thou
Henceforth shalt wear the bells and scalloped cape,
And for thy counselor shalt lead an ape;
Thou shalt obey my servants when they call,
And wait upon my henchmen in the hall!"

Deaf to King Robert's threats and cries and prayers,
They thrust him from the hall and down the stairs;
A group of tittering pages ran before,
And as they opened wide the folding-door,
His heart failed, for he heard, with strange alarms,
The boisterous laughter of the men-at-arms,
And all the vaulted chamber roar and ring
With the mock plaudits of "Long live the King!"
Next morning, waking with the day's first beam,
He said within himself, "It was a dream!"
But the straw rustled as he turned his head,
There were the cape and bells beside his bed;
Around him rose the bare, discolored walls,
Close by the steeds were champing in their stalls,
And in the corner, a revolting shape,
Shivering and chattering, sat the wretched ape.
It was no dream; the world he loved so much
Had turned to dust and ashes at his touch!

Days came and went; and now returned again
To Sicily the old Saturnian reign;
Under the angel's governance benign
The happy island danced with corn and wine.
Meanwhile King Robert yielded to his fate,
Sullen and silent and disconsolate.
Dressed in the motley garb that jesters wear,

With looks bewildered, and a vacant stare,
Close shaven above the ears, as monks are shorn,
By courtiers mocked, by pages laughed to scorn,
His only friend the ape, his only food
What others left—he still was unsubdued.
And when the angel met him on his way,
And half in earnest, half in jest, would say,
Sternly, though tenderly, that he might feel
The velvet scabbard held a sword of steel,
"Art thou the king?" the passion of his woe
Burst from him in resistless overflow,
And lifting high his forehead, he would fling
The haughty answer back, " I am, I am the king!"

Almost three years were ended, when there came
Ambassadors of great repute and name
From Valmond, Emperor of Allemaine,
Unto King Robert, saying that Pope Urbane
By letter summoned them forthwith to come
On Holy Thursday to his city of Rome.
The angel journeyed with them o'er the sea
Into the lovely land of Italy.

And lo! among the menials, in mock state,
Upon a piebald steed, with shambling gait,
His cloak of foxtails flapping in the wind,
The solemn ape demurely perched behind
King Robert rode, making huge merriment
In all the country towns through which they went.

The Pope received them with great pomp, and blare
Of bannered trumpets, on St. Peter's Square,
Giving his benediction and embrace,
Fervent, and full of apostolic grace.
While with congratulations and with prayers
He entertained the angel unawares,
Robert, the jester, bursting through the crowd,
Into their presence rushed, and cried aloud:
"I am the king! Look and behold in me
Robert, your brother, King of Sicily!
This man, who wears my semblance to your eyes,

Is an impostor in a king's disguise.
Do you not know me?   Does no voice within
Answer my cry, and say we are akin?"
The Pope in silence, but with troubled mien,
Gazed at the angel's countenance serene ;
The Emperor, laughing, said, " It is strange sport
To keep a madman for thy fool at court !"
And the poor, baffled jester, in disgrace
Was hustled back among the populace.

In solemn state the holy week went by,
And Easter Sunday gleamed upon the sky ;
The presence of an angel, with its light,
Before the sun rose, made the city bright,
And with new fervor filled the hearts of men,
Who felt that Christ indeed had risen again.
Even the jester, on his bed of straw,
With haggard eyes the unwonted splendor saw ;
He felt within, a power unfelt before,
And, kneeling humbly on his chamber floor,
He heard the rushing garments of the Lord
Sweep through the silent air, ascending heavenward.

And now the visit ending, and once more
Valmond returning to the Danube's shore,
Homeward the angel journeyed, and again
The land was made resplendent with his train.
And when once more within Palermo's wall,
And, seated on his throne in his great hall,
He heard the Angelus from convent towers,
As if the better world conversed with ours,
He beckoned to King Robert to draw nigher,
And with a gesture bade the rest retire.
And when they were alone, the angel said,
" Art thou the king?"   Then bowing down his head,
King Robert crossed both hands upon his breast,
And meekly answered him, " Thou knowest best !
My sins as scarlet are ; let me go hence,
And in some cloister's school of penitence,
Across those stones that pave the way to heaven
Walk barefoot till my guilty soul is shriven !"

The angel smiled, and from his radiant face
A holy light illumined all the place,
And through the open window, loud and clear,
They heard the monks chant in the chapel near,
Above the stir and tumult of the street,
"He has put down the mighty from their seat,
And has exalted them of low degree!"
And through the chant a second melody
Rose like the throbbing of a single string:
"I am an angel, and thou art the King!"

King Robert, who was standing near the throne,
Lifted his eyes, and lo! he was alone!
But all appareled as in days of old,
With ermined mantle and with cloth of gold;
And when his courtiers came, they found him there,
Kneeling upon the floor, absorbed in silent prayer.

GLOVERSON, THE MORMON.

ARTEMUS WARD.

CHAPTER I.

THE MORMON'S DEPARTURE.

The morning on which Reginald Gloverson was to leave Great Salt Lake City with a mule-train dawned beautifully.

Reginald Gloverson was a young and thrifty Mormon, with an interesting family of twenty young and handsome wives. His unions had never been blessed with children. As often as once a year he used to go to Omaha, in Nebraska, with a mule-train, for goods; but although he had performed the rather perilous journey many times with entire safety, his heart was strangely sad on this particular morning, and filled with gloomy forebodings.

The time for his departure had arrived. The high-spirited mules were at the door, impatiently champing their bits. The Mormon stood sadly among his weeping wives.

"Dearest ones," he said, "I am singularly sad at heart

this morning, but do not let this depress you. The journey
is a perilous one, but—pshaw! I have always come back
heretofore, and why should I fear? Besides, I know that
every night, as I lay down on the broad, starlit prairie,
your bright faces come to me in my dreams, and make my
slumbers sweet and gentle. You, Emily, with your mild
blue eyes; and you, Henrietta, with your splendid black
hair; and you, Nelly, with your hair so brightly, beautifully
golden; and you, Molly, with your cheeks so downy ; and
you, Betsey, with your wine-red lips—far more delicious,
though, than any wine I ever tasted; and you, Maria, with
your winsome voice ; and you, Susan, with your—with your
—that is to say, Susan, with your—and the other thirteen
of you, each as good and beautiful, will come to me in sweet
dreams, will you not, dearestists?"

"Our own," they lovingly chimed, "we will!"

"And so farewell!" cried Reginald.   "Come to my arms,
my own!" he said—"that is, as many of you as can do it
conveniently at once, for I must away."

He folded several of them to his throbbing breast and
drove sadly away.

But he had not gone far when the traces of the off-hind
mule became unhitched. Dismounting, he essayed to ad-
just the trace; but ere he had fairly commenced the task,
the mule, a singularly refractory animal, snorted wildly and
kicked Reginald frightfully in the stomach. He arose with
difficulty and tottered feebly towards his mother's house,
which was near by, falling dead in her yard, with the remark, "Dear mother, I've come home to die."

"So I see," she said ; "where's the mules?"

Alas! Reginald Gloverson could give no answer In vain
the heart-stricken mother threw herself upon his inanimate
form, crying, "Oh, my son, my son! only say where the
mules is, and then you may die if you want to !" In vain,
in vain !

Reginald had passed on.

CHAPTER II.

FUNERAL TRAPPINGS.

The mules were **never found.**

Reginald's heart-**broken mother took the body home to** her unfortunate son's **widows.** But before her arrival she discreetly sent a boy **to bust the** news gently to the afflicted wives, which he did by informing them **in a hoarse whisper** that "their old man had gone **in."**

The wives felt very badly **indeed.**

" He was devoted **to me," sobbed Emily.**

" And to me," **said Maria.**

" Yes," said **Emily, "he thought considerably of you,** but not so much as he did of me."

" I say he did."

" And I say he didn't."

" He did."

" He didn't."

" Don't look at **me** with your squint eyes !"

" Don't shake your red head at me !"

" Sisters," **said** the black-haired Henrietta, " **cease this** unseemly wrang**ling. I, as** Reginald's first wife, shall **strew** flowers on his grave !"

" No, you won't," said Susan ; " I, as his last wife, shall strew flowers on his grave. It is my business to strew."

" You shan't ; so there !" said Henrietta.

" You bet I will !" said Susan, with a tear-suffused cheek.

" Well, as for me," said the practical Betsey, " I ain't on the strew much, **but I** shall **ride** at the head of the funeral procession !"

" Not if I've ever **been** introduced to myself, you won't," said the **golden-**haired Nelly ; " **that's** my position. You bet your bonnet-strings it is."

" Children," said Reginald's mother, " you must do some crying, you know, on the day **of** the funeral ; and how many pocket-handkerchiefs will **it** take to go round ?

Betsey, you and Nelly ought to make one do between you."

"I'll tear her eyes out if she perpetrates a sob on my handkerchief," said Nelly.

"Dear daughters-in-law," said Reginald's mother, "how unseemly is this anger! Mules is five hundred dollars a span, and every identical mule my poor boy had has been gobbled up by the red men. I knew when my Reginald staggered into the door-yard that he was on the die; but if I'd only thunk to ask him about them mules ere his gentle spirit took flight, it would have been four thousand dollars in our pockets, and no mistake. Excuse these real tears, but you've never felt a parent's feelin's."

"It's an oversight," sobbed Maria. "Don't blame us."

CHAPTER III.

DUST TO DUST.

The funeral passed off in a very pleasant manner, nothing occurring to mar the harmony of the occasion. By a happy thought of Reginald's mother, the wives walked to the grave twenty abreast, which rendered that part of the ceremony thoroughly impartial.

*　　*　　*　　*　　*　　*　　*

That night the twenty wives, with heavy hearts, sought their twenty respective couches. But no Reginald occupied those twenty respective couches—Reginald would nevermore linger all night in blissful repose on those twenty respective couches—Reginald's head would nevermore press the twenty respective pillows of those twenty respective couches—never, nevermore!

*　　*　　*　　*　　*　　*　　*

In another house, not many leagues from the house of mourning, a gray-haired woman was weeping passionately. "He died," she cried—"he died without sigerfyin', in any respect, where them mules went to!"

CHAPTER IV.

MARRIED AGAIN.

Two years are supposed to have elapsed between the third and fourth chapters of this original American romance.

A manly Mormon, one evening, as the sun was preparing to set among a select apartment of gold and crimson clouds in the western horizon—although, for that matter, the sun has a right to "set" where it wants to, and so, I may add, has a hen—a manly Mormon, I say, tapped gently at the door of the mansion of the late Reginald Gloverson.

The door was opened by Mrs. Susan Gloverson.

"Is this the house of the widow Gloverson?" the Mormon asked.

"It is," said Susan.

"And how many is there of she?" inquired the Mormon.

"There is about twenty of her, including me," courteously returned the fair Susan.

"Can I see her?"

"You can."

"Madame," he softly said, addressing the twenty disconsolate widows, "I have seen part of you before. And although I have already twenty-five wives, whom I respect and tenderly care for, I can truly say that I never felt love's holy thrill till I saw thee! Be mine—be mine!" he enthusiastically cried, "and we will show the world a striking illustration of the beauty and truth of the noble lines, only a good deal more so—

Twenty-one souls with a single thought,
Twenty-one hearts that beat as one.

They were united, they were.

Gentle reader, does not the moral of this romance show that however many there may be of a young widow woman, or rather does it not show that whatever number of persons one woman may consist of—well, never mind what it shows.

DE PINT WID OLE PETE.

ANONYMOUS.

Upon the hurricane deck of one of our gunboats, an elderly darkey, with a very philosophical and retrospective cast of countenance, squatted on his bundle, toasting his shins against the chimney, and apparently plunged into a state of profound meditation. Finding, upon inquiry, that he belonged to the Ninth Illinois, one of the most gallantly behaved and heavy losing regiments at the Fort Donelson battle, I began to interrogate him upon the subject.

"Were you in the fight?"

"Had a little taste of it, sa."

"Stood your ground, did you?"

"No, sa; I runs."

"Run at the first fire, did you?"

"Yes, sa; and would hab run soona, had I knowd it war comin'."

"Why, that wasn't very creditable to your courage."

"Massa, dat isn't my line, sa; cookin's my profeshun."

"Well, but have you no regard for your reputation?"

"Yah, yah; reputation's nuffin to me by de side ob life."

"Do you consider your life worth more than other people's?"

"It is worth more to me, sa."

"Then you must value it very highly?"

"Yes, sa, I does; more dan all dis world, more dan a million ob dollars, sa; for what would dat be wuth to a man wid de bref out ob him? Self-preserbation am de fust law wid me."

"But why should you act upon a different rule from other men?"

"Because different men set different values upon their lives; mine is not in de market."

"But if you lost it, you would have the satisfaction of knowing that you died for your country."

"What satisfaction would dat be to me when de power ob feelin' was gone?"

"Then patriotism and honor are nothing to you?"

"Nuffin whatever, sa; I regard them as among the vanities."

"If our soldiers were like you, traitors might have broken up the government without resistance."

"Yes, sa; dar would hab been no help for it."

"Do you think any of your company would have missed you, if you had been killed?"

"Maybe not, sa; a dead white man ain't much to dese sogers, let alone a dead nigga; but I'd a missed myself, and dat was de pint wid me."

PAT AND THE PIG.

ANONYMOUS.

We have read of a Pat so financially flat
    That he had neither money nor meat,
And when hungry and thin, it was whispered by sin
    That he ought to steal something to eat.

So he went to the sty of a widow near by,
    And he gazed on the tenant—poor soul!
"Arrah now," said he, "what a trate that'll be,"
    And the pig of the widow he stole.

In a feast he rejoiced; then he went to a Judge;
    For, in spite of the pork and the lard,
There was something within that was sharp as a pin,
    For his conscience was pricking him hard.

And he said with a tear, "Will your Riverence hear
    What I have in sorrow to say?"
Then the story he told, and the *tale* did unfold
    Of the pig he had taken away.

And the Judge to him said, "Ere you go to your bed,
    You must pay for the pig you have taken,
For 'tis thus, by my soul, you'll be saving your soul,
    And will also be saving your bacon."

"Oh, be jabers," said Pat, " I can niver do that—
    Not the ghost of a hap'orth have I—
And I'm wretched indade, if a penny it nade
    Any pace for me conscience to buy."

Then in sorrow he cried, and the Judge he replied,
    " Only think how you'll tremble with fear
When the Judge you shall meet at the great judgment seat
    And the widow you plundered while here."

" Will the widow be there ?" whispered Pat, with a stare,
    " And the pig ? by me sowl, is it thrue ?"
" They will surely be there," said the Judge, " I declare,
    And, oh Paddy ! what then will you do ?"

" Many thanks," answered Pat, " for your telling me that ;
    May the blessings upon you be big !
On that sittlemint day to the widow I'll say,
    ' Mrs. Flannegan, here is your pig !' "

THE WIDOW BEDOTT'S LETTER TO ELDER SNIFFLES.

F) M. WHITCHER.

Sence the first time I heered you preach, I've had an undiscribable desire to have some privit conversashun with you in regard to the state of my mind—your discourse was so wonderful sarchin that I felt to mourn over my back-slidden state of stewpidity, and my consarn increased every time I've set under the droppins of your sanctuery. Last night, when I heered of your sickness, I felt wonderful overcome ; onable to conseal my aggitation, I retired to my chamber, and bust into a flood of tears. I felt for you, elder Sniffles—I felt for you. I was wonderful exercised in view of your lone condition.

Oh, it's a terrible thing to be alone in the world ! I know all about it by experience, for I've been pardnerless for nigh twelve year ; it's a trying thing, but I thought 'twas better to be alone than to run enny risk—for yer know it's runnin' a great risk to take a second companion, espeshelly if they ain't decidedly pious—and them that's tried to perswade me to change my condition, dident none of 'em give very satisfactory evidence of piety—'taint for me to say how menny I've refused on account of their want of religion accordin' to my notions, riches and grander ain't to be compared to religion, no how you can fix it, and I always told 'em so.

But I was tellin' how overcome I was when I heered of your being attacked with influenzy. I felt as if I must go right over and take care of you. I wouldent desire no better intertainment than to nuss you up, and if it 'twant for the speech of peeple, I'd fly to your relefe instanter, but I know 'twould make talk, and so I'm necessitated to stay away.

But I felt so consarned about you that I couldn't help writin' these few lines to you to let you know how anxious I be on your account, and to beg of you to take care of yourself. Oh elder, do be careful—the influenzy's a dangerous eppidemik, if you let it run on without attendin' to it in season—do be careful—consider what a terrible thing 'twould be for you to be took away in the height of yer yusefulness; and oh, elder, nobody wouldn't feel yer loss with more intensitude than what I should, though mebby I hadent oughter say so.

Oh, elder Sniffles, I do feel as if I couldent part with you no how. I'm so interested in your preachin, and it's had such a wonderful attendency to subdew my prejudishes agin' your denominashun, and has sot me considerin' whether or no there aint good christuns in all denominashuns, 'cept, of course, the unevarsellers.

Oh, reverend elder, I intreat you to take care of your preshus health. I send you herewith a paper of boneset; you must make some good stiff tea on't and drink about a quart to-night afore you retire. Molasses or vinegar's a good thing, too, for a cold or coff; jest take about a pint of molasses and bile it down with a teacup of vinegar and a hunk of butter as big as a hen's egg, and stir in about a half a teacup full of peppersass, and eat it down hot jest afore bedtime—and take a strip of flannil, and rub some hog's lard on't—though goose ile's about as good—and pin it round yer throat rite off; and I send likewise a bag of hops—you must dip it in bilin' hot water with some red peppers in it; now don't forgit nothin' I've proscribed.

But I was a tellin' how exercised I was when I heerd of your sickness. I went immejitly to my chamber, and gin away to a voiellent flud of tears. I retired to my couche of repose, but my aggetashun prevented my sleepin' I felt quite a call to express my feelins in poitry—I'm very apt to when ennything comes over me—so I riz and lited my candle, and composed these ere stanzys, which I hope will be aggreible to you.

> O reverend sir I do declare,
>   It drives me a'most to frenzy,
> To think of you a lyin thero
>   Down sick with influenzy.

> A body'd a thought it was enough
>   To mourn yer wife's departer,
> Without sech trouble as this 'ere
>   To come a follerin' arter.

> But sickness and affliction is trials sent
>   By the will of a wise creation,
> And always ought to be underwent
>   With fortytude and resignashun.

> Then mourn not for your pardner's deth,
>   But tew submit endever ;
> ·For sposin she hadent a died so soon,
>   She couldn't a lived forever.

> Oh, I could to your bedside fly,
>   And wipe your weepin' eyes,
> And try my best to cure you up,
>   If 'twouldent create surprize.

It's a world of trouble we tarry in—
　　But elder don't dispair;
That you may soon be movin' agin,
　　Is constantly my prayer.

Both sick and well, you may depend
　　Youle never be forgot,
By your faithful and affectionate friend,
　　Priscilla Pool Bedott.

THE CRY OF THE CHILDREN.

ELIZABETH BARRETT BROWNING.

Do ye hear the children weeping, O my brothers,
　　Ere the sorrow comes with years?
They are leaning their young heads against their mothers—
　　And *that* cannot stop their tears.
The young lambs are bleating in the meadows,
　The young birds are chirping in the nest,
The young fawns are playing with the shadows,
　The young flowers are blowing toward the west—
But the young, young children, O my brothers,
　　They are weeping bitterly!—
They are weeping in the playtime of the others,
　　In the country of the free.

They look up with their pale and sunken faces,
　　And their looks are sad to see,
For the man's hoary anguish draws and presses
　　Down the cheeks of infancy—
"Your old earth," they say "is very dreary;"
　"Our young feet," they say, "are very weak!"
Few paces have we taken, yet are weary—
　　Our grave-rest is very far to seek.
Ask the aged why they weep, and not the children,
　　For the outside earth is cold,
And we young ones stand without, in our bewildering,
　　And the graves are for the old.

"True," say the children, "it may happen
　　That we die before our time.

Little Alice died last year—the grave is shapen
    Like a snowball, in the rime.
We looked into the pit prepared to take her—
    Was no room for any work in the close clay :
From the sleep wherein she lieth none will wake her,
    Crying, ' Get up, little Alice ! it is day !'
If you listen by that grave, in sun and shower,
    With your ear down, little Alice never cries !—
Could we see her face, be sure we should not know her,
    For the smile has time for growing in her eyes !
And merry go her moments, lulled and stilled in
    The shroud, by the kirk-chime !
It is good when it happens," say the children,
    " That we die before our time."

Alas alas, the children ! they are seeking
    Death in life as best to have !
They are binding up their hearts away from breaking,
    With a cerement from the grave.
Go out, children, from the mine and from the city—
    Sing out, children, as the little thrushes do—
Pluck you handfuls of the meadow-cowslips pretty—
    Laugh aloud, to feel your fingers let them through !
But they answer, " Are your cowslips of the meadows
    Like our weeds anear the mine ?
Leave us quiet in the dark of the coal shadows,
    From your pleasures fair and fine !

" For oh," say the children, " we are weary,
    And we cannot run or leap —
If we cared for any meadows, it were merely
    To drop down in them and sleep.
Our knees tremble sorely in the stooping—
    We fall upon our faces, trying to go;
And, underneath our heavy eyelids drooping,
    The reddest flower would look as pale as snow.
For, all day, we drag our burden tiring
    Through the coal-dark underground—
Or, all day, we drive the wheels of iron
    In the factories round and round.

" For, all day, the wheels are droning, turning-
    Their wind comes in our faces,—
Till our hearts turn—our head, with pulses burning,
    And the walls turn in their places—
Turns the sky in the high window blank and reeling,
    Turns the long light that drops adown the wall—
Turn the black flies that crawl along the ceiling—
    All are turning, all the day, and we with all.
And all the day, the iron wheels are droning!
    And sometimes we could pray,
'O ye wheels,' (breaking out in a mad moaning),
    'Stop! be silent for to-day!'"

Ay! be silent! Let them hear each other breathing
    For a moment mouth to mouth—
Let them touch each other's hands, in a fresh wreathing
    Of their tender human youth!
Let them feel that this cold metallic motion
    Is not all the life God fashions or reveals—
Let them prove their living souls against the notion
    That they live in you, or under you, O wheels!—
Still, all day, the iron wheels go onward,
    Grinding life down from its mark;
And the children's souls, which God is calling sunward,
    Spin on blindly in the dark.

Now tell the poor young children, O my brothers,
    To look up to Him and pray—
So the blessed One, who blesseth all the others,
    Will bless them another day.
They answer, " Who is God that He should hear us,
    While the rushing of the iron wheels is stirred?
When we sob aloud, the human creatures near us
    Pass by, hearing not, or answer not a word;
And we hear not (for the wheels in their resounding)
    Strangers speaking at the door;
Is it likely God, with angels singing round him,
    Hears our weeping any more?

" Two words, indeed, of praying we remember,
    And at midnight's hour of harm,

'Our Father,' looking upward in the chamber,
    We say softly for a charm.
We know no other words, except 'Our Father,'
    And we think that, in some pause of angel's song,
God may pluck them with the silence sweet to gather,
    And hold both within His right hand, which is strong.
'Our Father!' If He heard us, He would surely
    (For they call Him good and mild)
Answer, smiling down the steep world very purely,
    'Come and rest with me, my child.'

" But no!" say the children, weeping faster,
    " He is speechless as a stone ;
And they tell us, of His image is the master
    Who commands us to work on.
Go to !" say the children—"Up in Heaven,
    Dark, wheel-like, turning clouds are all we find.
Do not mock us; grief has made us unbelieving—
We look up for God, but tears have made us blind."
Do you hear the children weeping and disproving,
    O my brothers, what ye preach ?
For God's possible is taught by His world's loving—
    And the children doubt of each.

They look up with their pale and sunken faces,
    And their look is dread to see,
For they mind you of their angels in their places,
    With eyes turned on Deity ;—
" How long," they say, " how long, O cruel nation,
    Will you stand, to move the world, on a child's heart,—
Stifle down with a mailed heel its palpitation,
    And tread onward to your throne amid the mart ?
Our blood splashes upward, O gold-heaper,
    And your purple shows your path !
But the child's sob curses deeper in the silence
    Than the strong man in his wrath !"

THE DUTCHMAN WHO GAVE MRS. SCUDDER
THE SMALL-POX.

ANONYMOUS.

Some years ago, a droll sort of a Dutchman was the driver of a stage in New Jersey, and he passed daily through the small hamlet of Jericho. One morning, just as the vehicle was starting from Squash Point, a person came up and requested the driver to take in a small box, and "leave it at Mrs. Scudder's, third house on the left after you get into Jericho."

"Yaas, oh yaas, Mr. Ellis, I knows der haus," said the driver, "I pleeve der voman dakes in vashin', vor I always sees her mit her clothes hung out."

"You're right, that's the place," said Ellis, (for that was the man's name,) "she washes for one of the steamboats."

The box was thereupon duly deposited in the front boot, the driver took his 'levenpennybit for carrying it, and the stage started on its winding way. In an hour or two, the four or five houses comprising the village of Jericho hove in sight. In front of one of them, near the door, a tall muscular woman was engaged at a wash-tub, while lines of white linen, fluttering in the wind, ornamented the adjoining lawn. The stage stopped at the gate, when the following ludicrous dialogue, and attendant circumstances, took place:

Driver—Is dis Miss Scutter's haus?

Woman [looking up, without stopping her work,]—Yes, I'm Mrs. Scudder.

Driver—I'fe got der small pox in der stage; vill you come out and dake it?

Woman [suddenly throwing down the garment she was washing] Got the small-pox! mercy on me, why do you stop here, you wicked man? you'd better be off, quick as you can. [Runs into the house.]

Driver mutters to himself—I vonder vat's der matter mit der fool; I'fe goot mind to drow it over der fence.

Upon second thought, he takes the box, gets off the stage, and carries it into the house. But in an instant he reappears, followed by a broom with an enraged woman at the end of it, who is shouting in a loud voice—

"You git out of this! clear yourself quicker!—you've no business to come here exposing decent people to the small-pox; what do you mean by it?"

"I dells you it's der shmall *pox!*" exclaimed the Dutch-man, emphasising the word box as plainly as he could— "Ton't you verstch?—der shmall *pox* dat Misther Ellis sends to you."

But Mrs. Scudder was too much excited to comprehend this explanation, even if she had listened to it. Having it fixed in her mind that there was a case of small-pox on the stage, and that the driver was asking her to take into the house a passenger thus afflicted, her indignation knew no bounds. "Clear out!" exclaimed she, excitedly, "I'll call the men folks if you don't clear!" and then shouting at the top of her voice, "Ike! you Ike! where are you?" Ike soon made his appearance, and inquired—

"W-what's the matter, mother?"

The driver answered—"I dells you now onct more, for der last time, I'fe got der shmall pox, and Misther Ellis he dells me to gif it to Miss Scutter, and if dat vrow ish Miss Scutter, vy she no dake der pox?"

By this time several of the passengers had got off the stage to see the fun, and one of them explained to Mrs. Scudder that it was a box, and not small-pox, that the driver wished to leave with her.

The woman had become so thoroughly frightened that she was still incredulous, until a bright idea struck Ike.

"Oh, mother!" exclaimed he, "I know what 'tis—it's Madame Ellis's box of laces, sent to be done up."

With this explanation the affair was soon settled, and Mistress Scudder received the Dutchman's "shmall pox" amidst the laughter and shouts of the occupants of the old stage coach. The driver joined in, although he had not the least idea of what they were laughing at, and as the vehicle rolled away, he added not a little to the mirth by saying, in a triumphant tone of voice, "I vas pound ter gif der old vomans der shmall pox, vether she vould dake it or not!"

SCULPIN.

ANONYMOUS.

It may not be amiss to remark that it was the identical "Greek Slave" concerning which the ensuing colloquy took place, between the sculptor himself and a successful Yankee speculator, who had " come over to see Eu-rope."

Scene—Power's studio at Florence. Enter stranger, spitting, and wiping his lips with his hand: "Be yeou Mister Powers, the skulpture ?"

"I am a sculptor, and my name is Powers."

"Y-e-a-s; wall, I 'spected so; they tell'd me yeou was —y-e-a-s. Look a here—drivin' a pritty stiff bizness, eh ?"

"Sir ?"

"I say, plenty to du, eh ? What d's one o' them air fetch ?"

"Sir ?"

"I ask't ye what's the *price* of one of them, sech as yeou're peekin' at neow."

"I am to have three thousand dollars for this when it is completed."

"W-h-a-t !—heow much ?"

"Three thousand dollars."

"T-h-r-e-e t-h-o-u-s-a-n-d d-o-l-l-a-r-s ! Han't statewary *riz* lately ! I was cal'latin' to buy some; but it's *tew* high. Heow's paintin's ? Guess I must git some paintin's. T-h-r-e-e t-h-o-u-s-a-n-d d-o-l-l-a-r-s ! Wall, it *is* a trade, sculpin is; that's sartain. What dew they make yeou pay fur your *tools* and *stuff* ? S'pect my oldest boy, Cephas

could skulp; *fact*, I *know* he could. He is allers whittlin'
reound, an' cuttin' away at things. I jist wish yeou'd
'gree to take him prentice, an' let him go at it full chisel.
D' you know where I'd be liable to put him eout? He'd
cut stun a'ter a while with the best of ye, he would; and
make money, tew, at them prices. T-h-r-e-e t-h-o-u-
s-a-n-d d-o-l-l-a-r-s! Wall, guess I won't take enny of
your stone gals tew-day at *them* prices. *Jewhitaker!*"

RATS.

JOHN McINTOSH.

A rat! a rat! dead for a ducat!
Killed with a broom behind a bucket;
Dead as a herring as soon as I struck it.
      Nothing so horribly mean as rats;
Quite as great a nuisance as cats;
Bothered us had they for more than a year,
Gnawing the boards, so very near;
Trundling about at dead of night,
Scurrying round, but seldom in sight;
            Trundling,
            Bundling,
            Hurrying,
            Scurrying,
Rattlety bang! off in a jiffy,
Making a fellow feel ever so "miffy."
Pop she goes, never say die,
Round the barrels I madly fly,
Hoping to catch 'em; all in my eye;
            Off to each hole,
            The villains stole,
Soon as they heard my footsteps nigh.

Went to bed one night in wrath,
After I thought I discovered the path
They gen'rally took to go their rounds;
Heard them skittle behind the lath;
Vowed that night I'd cut a swath,

Killing and mangling and giving wounds;
Put the broom in a handy place,
Chuckled to think of the bloody chase
I'd have with the sport of their losing race ;
      Never a wink,
      Nary a blink
Of sleep had I.   I rose at one,
   Lighted a lamp and roused my wife ;
She woke with a y-a-w-n.
  "Hush," said I, " no noise, on your life ;
Rats," I whispered, "more than a dozen;
Don't you hear 'em ?   Listen !   Was'n
   That a stunner that jumped just now ?
   Forward, march !   Confound the row !"
" Hadn't you better put on your boots ?
  They bite sometimes, the saucy brutes,"
      Wife whispered low ;
     " Consarn them, no ;
  Ain't to be scared so," answered I ;
   " Bite, and says I the fur will fly."
  " We'd better call aunt Polly's cat,"
   She whispered again.   I said to that,
     " Drat the cats !
     At the rats "—
   Quoting a word from Coriolanus—
     Alone I go ;
    " If you are afraid,
    Go back to bed ;
     This I know,
And swear by the bulk of huge Uranus,
This night by the broom
They meet their doom ;
Steal along with a velvet tread ;
No more, keep dark, and imagine them dead."

   Into the kitchen we went with a bounce,
   Seizing my broom like a spear at once,
    I charged amain ;
     Scamper, flit,
     Sudden noise,

" Why don't you hit ?"
    My good wife cries,
      " Hit what ?"
          " Goose ! the rat."
            Slam !
            Jam !
        Over the room
        Slathered the broom ;
              Crack !
              Whack !
But never a one of them went to doom ;
Stealing away like guilty souls,
I heard them squeaking a laugh in their holes.
        I made a vow—
        This was the how :
  Raising my broom as high as the ceiling,
  I thought for a moment of swearing kneeling ;
  And but that 'twould have a ridiculous look,
        I'd done it there ;
  But, goodness me !   I thought, as I took
          A passing glance
          At the circumstance—
          My legs were bare,
    A night-shirt only enveloped my form,
          And then my wife,
          Upon my life,
I knew she would raise such a deuce of a storm
          Of laughter and fun,
          I cut and run.

  I vowed in my heart that night no sleep
  Over my senses numb should creep,
          Or eyes should touch—
          I hadn't much
            For a month before—
          Until a rat,
          Untouched by a cat,
            Should lie on the floor,
            Outstretched in its gore,

And slain by me with my warlike broom;
All this I repeated again in my room.
Wife said but little, my back was riz;
It was well for her that she had the wis-
dom to say little to me that night;
I think, however, she gave a snicker—
Which I ignored, for I dread a bicker
With her, for the reason, she's always right.

Engaugh! She snores. I'm wide awake,
　　Thinking of rats—
　　Of rats, not cats;
　　In fancy, a score
　　I've killed, and more.
　Innocent she of the lives I take
　　In my broom's wild sweep;
　　I will show her the heap
　In the morning, slain for her dear sake.

　　Hark! that was a rat!
　　At once I sat
Up in the bed, to hear it once more;
It skittles across the kitchen floor—
It! thunder! there must be a hundred or more;
Creaking again goes the bedroom door,
But all unheard in their wild uproar.
Soon with Tarquin's ravishing stride
Down the stairs like a ghost I glide;
And I said in my vengeance, woe betide
The sleek mad roystering villain's hide,
That comes as a salve to my wounded pride.
　I place my lamp in the passage there;
　I know that its bright petroleum glare
　Over the kitchen floor will flare;
　I handle my broom *à la militaire.*
　　Bang flies the door. By Jove, there's three!
　　Double quick, forward! Hurrah for me!
Over the tables, clearing the chairs—
　Smash went a couple of window panes—
　Two have escaped, one still remains;

Into a basket of clothes he tears;
　Still for his beggarly life he strove;
　Over the wood-box, under the stove;
　Scampering over the breakfast plates,
　　Jingletywhop went all the spoons;
Soon, on the window-sill he skates,
　　Hi! Look out! I vow, the loon's
　Almost along with his thievish mates.
　Hit him! Co-whollop! I've got you now!
　Thud! and co-whop! Hi! that's the how!
A rat! A rat! dead for a ducat!
Killed with a broom behind a bucket,
Dead as a herring as soon as I struck it.

AN INTRODUCTION.

MARK TWAIN.

"Ladies—and—gentlemen: By—the request of the—
Chair-man of the—Commit-tee—I beg leave to—intro—
duce—to you—the reader of the eve-ning—a gentleman
whose great learning—whose historical ac-curacy—whose
devotion—to science—and—whose veneration for the truth
—are only equalled by his high moral character— and—his
—majestic presence. I allude—in these vague general
terms—to my-self. I—am a little opposed to the custom of
ceremoniously introducing a reader to the audience, because
it seems—unnecessary—where the man has been properly
advertised! But as—it is—the custom—I prefer to make
it myself—in my own case—and then I can rely on getting
in—all the facts! I never had but one introduction—that
seemed to me just the thing—and the gentleman was not
acquainted with me, and there was no nonsense. 'Ladies
and gentlemen, I shall waste no time in this introduction.
I know of only two facts about this man; first, he—has
never been in state prison, and second, I can't—imagine
why.'"

A DUTCHMAN'S DOLLY VARDEN. ·

ANONYMOUS.

Vell, mine freund, you know dat I hav on my het dat leedle bump der frenollogiggers say dat I hav great like for de ladies, aind it ? Vell, I vas goin down de shtreet der tay after yesterday, und ven I comes to der blace vat dey calls der corner, so der shtreet mit anoder shtreet makes a nice leetle cross oder der leetle saw-buck, you know vat dat is. So soon I comes to der blace, vot you tink ? a nice leetle poy mit great many papers in der hand goes by, and shust so soon as he goes by he gifs me von leetle paper mitout notings. But it vas padder as vorse vot I took dot leetle paper, and den I goes and makes me von mineself von great pig fool. Vat you tink I on dot paper find—you no guess dot in swelve tousand year. I dell you vot I see on dot. It vas like diss. " Come und see your Dolly Varden. She is lovely, she is putiful, she is rich ! You can she hav for most notings." Den der leetle paper gives der number von der shtreet vare I could she find. It vas said Mr. Shteward, py Proatvay oud. So soon I reads dot petter as goot mine heart makes me von pitty-pat, knock-knock. You know vat dat is. I no more knows vare I lif oder var I vas goin. Dolly Varden ! She vas rich ; she vas lovely ; she vas putiful ; und Dolly, dot vas shust so nice names, aind it ? Und der leetle poy dat me dot paper gives, made he on dot paper say dot I can she hav for most notings. Der firsht ding vot mine eye come against vas von dose leetle shticks mit der great American flag round him, vot says dot dere viskers be taken off dere, und der hair be so bright and shining made, also der placking boots. Denn I goes right dere, und I pays dot man fifteen cent— fifteen cent ! mind you dot ! vile dot he make mine hair der vay vot I shpeak von. Den, mit mine het up, feeling dot I shust so pig as Carl Schurz, I goes after der shtreet for to git me mine Dolly Varden. I vonders so soon I comes to der blace und sees der pig shtore shop of Mister Shteward, vedder or not she owns all dot nice buildings. Anoder leetle poy opens dot door so nicely, unt he looks me in der face so shmilings dot I tinks praps it vos Dolly's brudder; und mine heart he goes so hot like fire; most like der pig plazing Shecawgo fire. Und I says to der poy so shweet I could you know, "You hav der sister here, aint it?" Denn der poy he look me mit vonder, und he make dot het go so, like dot. I shpeaks no more mit der poy, but I goes to der shtand, vare I sees von fine gentleman, und I says, "I vould dot young lady see, vot der leetle poy givs me paper von." "Vot is dot?" says der shentlemans. Denn I says, "I vants mine Dolly Varden!" Und der man says, "Dolly Varden! come dis vay venn you blease." Und I follows dot man mit mine heart full von great tremblings unt joy put togedder, shust like der apple und meat in der mince pie. Put vat is dot he do now? He go und show me a leetle piece von cloth mit great many putiful color. Denn I say "You nixverstay me. I no vant to see her dress. I vould see Dolly Varden she self." Dere goes more vunder donn der poy hat over der face von der shentlemans, und he say "Dis is Dolly Varden." Denn I say "Dolly Varden! Dolly Varden! Oh! I no vant such voomans as dot." Und mine mind runs vay mit mine het, unt mine het runs vay mit mine bodies, und mine bodies runs vay mit mine feet, und der shtore is vay on der odder side von me. Und ven I see again on der shtreet dot leetle poy I vould him pants make varm for dot he gif me so much heart-ache.

Und denn ven I tinks on vot I pees und vat I used to vas, I feels I trow fifteen cent avay mitout sufficient cause. Den I feels mit mineselfs so mad to trow avays fifteen cents—tree glass lager—for notinks, dat I go very queeck and trown mineself in de try-tock, till I vas vashit ashore mit a bar of soft-soap.

"ROCK OF AGES."

ANONYMOUS.

" Rock of ages, cleft for me,"
   Thoughtlessly the maiden sung,
  Fell the words unconsciously
   From her girlish, gleeful tongue,
  Sung as little children sing,
   Sung as sing the birds in June;
  Fell the words like light leaves sown
   On the current of the tune—
" Rock of ages, cleft for me,
   Let me hide myself in Thee."

  Felt her soul no need to hide—
   Sweet the song as song could be
  And she had no thought beside;
   All the words unheedingly
Fell from lips untouched by care,
   Dreaming not that each might be,
On some other lips, a prayer—
   " Rock of Ages, cleft for me,
    Let me hide myself in Thee."

" Rock of Ages, cleft for me—"
   'Twas a woman sung them now,
  Pleadingly and prayerfully ;
   Every word her heart did know.
  Rose the song as storm-tossed bird
   Beats with weary wing the air,
  Every note with sorrow stirred,
   Every syllable a prayer—
" Rock of Ages, cleft for me,
  Let me hide myself in Thee."

" Rock of Ages, cleft for me—"
   Lips grown aged sung the hymn
  Trustingly and tenderly,
   Voice grown weak and eyes grown dim—
" Let me hide myself in Thee."
   Trembling through the voice, and low,

Rose the sweet strain peacefully
  As a river in its flow;
Sung as only they can sing,
  Who life's thorny paths have pressed;
Sung as only they can sing
  Who behold the promised rest.

" Rock of Ages, cleft for me,"
  Sung above a coffin-lid;
Underneath, all restfully,
  All life's cares and sorrows hid.
Never more, O storm-tossed soul,
  Never more from wind or tide,
Never more from billows' roll
  Wilt thou need thyself to hide.
Could the sightless, sunken eyes,
  Closed beneath the soft gray hair,
Could the mute and stiffened lips,
  Move again in pleading prayer,
Still, aye still the words would be,
" Let me hide myself in Thee."

FEEDING THE BLACK FILLIES.

ANONYMOUS.

Kitchen maids are so often bothered in their household duties by the gallantries of the men servants, that my wife had selected one from the Congo race of negroes, ugly to look at, but good-tempered, and black as your hat. Phillis was her name, and a more faithful, devoted, and patient creature we never had around us. I have thus introduced her to my hearers, because she was a conspicuous personage in some of the droll incidents connected with my taking into service a queer specimen of a Patlander, by name Peter Mulrooney.

Mulrooney applied to me for a situation as groom, in the place of one I had just dismissed; and on my inquiring if he could give me a reference as to his character and qualifications, he mentioned the name of Mr. David Urban (a personal friend of mine), with whom he had lived. "An' sure," said he with enthusiasm, "there isn't a dacenter jintleman in all Ameriky."

"I am happy to hear him so well spoken of," said I, "but if you were so much attached to him, why did you quit his service?"

"Sorra one o' me knows," said he, a little evasively, as I thought. "Ayeh! but 'twasn't his fault, anyhow."

"I dare say not; but what did you do after you left Mr. Urban?"

"Och, bad luck to me, sir! 'twas the foolishest thing in the world. I married a widdy, sir."

"And became a householder, eh?"

"Augh!" he exclaimed, with an expression of intense disgust, "the house wouldn't hould me long; 'twas too hot for that, I does be thinkin'."

"Humph! You found the widow too fond of having her own way, I suppose?"

"Thrue for you, sir; an' a mighty crooked way it was, that same, an' that's no lie."

"She managed to keep you straight, I dare say."

"Straight! Och, by the powhers, Misther Stanley, yo may say that! If I'd swallowed a soger's ramrod, 'tisn't straighter I'd have been!"

"And the result was, that, not approving the widow's discipline, you ran away and left her?"

"Sure sir, 'twas asier done nor that. Her first husband, betther luck to him, saved me the throuble."

"Her first husband! had she another husband living?"

"Oh, yis, sir; one Mike Connolly, a sayfarin' man who was reported dead; but he came back one day, an' I resthored him his wife and childher. Oh, but 'twas a proud man I was to be able to comfort poor Mike by givin' him his lost wife—an' he so grateful, too! Ah, sir, he had a ra'al Irish heart."

Being favorably impressed with Peter's genuine good humor, I concluded to take him at once into my service. Nor was I mistaken in his character, for he took excellent care of my horses, and kept everything snug around the stables. One day I thought I would test his usefulness in doctoring, so I sent for him to the house.

"Peter," said I, "do you think I could trust you to give the black filly a warm mash this evening?"

As he stared at me for a minute or two without replying, I repeated the question.

"Is it a mash, sir?" said he. "Sure, an' I'd like to be plasin' yer honor any way, an' that's no lie."

As he spoke, however, I fancied I saw a strange sort of puzzled expression flit across his face.

"I beg pardin, sir," continued he, "but 'tis bothered I am; will I be afther givin' her an ould counthry mash, or an Ameriky mash?"

"I don't know if there is any difference between them," I answered, rather puzzled at what he was aiming, but I found afterwards that he didn't know what a mash was.

"Arrah, 'tis rasonable enough ye shouldn't," said Peter, "considerin' that yer honor niver set fut in ould Ireland."

"Look here, Mulrooney," said I, impatiently, "I want you to put about two double handfuls of bran into a pail of warm water, and, after stirring the mixture well, give it to the black filly. That is what we call a bran mash in this country. Now, do you perfectly understand me?"

"Good luck to yer honor!" replied Peter, looking much relieved; for he had got the information he was fishing for. "Good luck to yer honor! what 'ud I be good for, if I didn't? sure, 'tis the ould counthry mash afther all."

"Perhaps so; but be sure you make no mistake."

"Oh, niver fear, sir, I'll do it illegant; but about the warm wather?"

"There's plenty to be had in the kitchen."

"An' the naygur? Will I say till her it's yer honor's orthers?" inquired Peter, earnestly.

"Certainly; she'll make no difficulty."

"Oh, begorra! 'tisn't a tranen I care for that; but will I give her the full ov the bucket, sir?"

"'Twill do her no harm," said I, carelessly. With that Peter made his best bow and left my presence.

It might have been some fifteen minutes after this that my wife, who was a little unwell that day, came into the sitting-room, saying, "I wish you'd go into the kitchen, George, and see what's the difficulty between that Irishman and Phillis; I am afraid they are quarreling."

At that moment we heard a crash and a suppressed shriek. I hurried from the room, and soon heard, as I passed through the hall, an increasing clamor in the kitchen beyond. First came the shrill voice of Phillis.

"You jess lebe me 'lone, now, will yer? I won't hab nuffin to do wid de stuff, nairaway."

"You ugly an' conthrary ould nayger, don't I tell ye 'tis the masther's ordhers?" I heard Peter respond.

"Taint no sech ting. Go way, you poor white Irish trash! who ebber heard ob 'spectable color'd woman a takin' a bran mash, I'd like to know."

The reality of Peter's ridiculous blunder flashed upon me at once, and the fun of the thing struck me so irresistibly, that I hesitated for a moment to break in upon it.

"Arrah, be aisy, can't ye? an' be afther takin' it down like a dacent naygur," I heard Peter say.

"Go way, you feller," screamed Phillis, "or I'll call missis, dat I will."

"Och, be this an' be that!" says Peter, resolutely, "if 'tis about to frighten the beautiful misthress ye are, and she sick, too, at this same time, I'll be afther puttin' a shtop to that."

Immediately afterwards came a short scuffle, and then a stifled scream. Concluding that it was now time for me to interfere, I moved quickly on, and just as the scuffling gave way to smothered sobs and broken ejaculations, I flung open the door and looked in. The first thing that caught my eye was Phillis seated in a chair, sputtering and gasping; while Mulrooney, holding her head under his left arm, was employing his right hand in conveying a tin cup of bran mash from the bucket at his side to her upturned mouth.

"What in the name of all that is good are you doing now, Peter?" said I.

"Sure, sir, what wud I do but give black Phillis the warm mash, accordin' to yer honor's ordhers? Augh! the haythen. Bad cess to her! 'tis throuble enough I've had to make her rasonable and obadient, au' that's no lie—the stupid ould thafe of a naygur."

The reader may imagine the finale to so rich a scene; even my wife, sick as she was, caught the infection, and laughed heartily. As for Peter, the last I heard of him that evening was his muttering, as he walked away—

"Ayeh! why didn't he tell me? If they call naygurs fillies, and horses fillies, sure an' how the divil should I know the differ?"

Peter remained in my service five years, during which period he treated Phillis with great deference.

THE HORNET.

JOSH BILLINGS.

The hornet is an inflammibel buzzer, sudden in hiz impreshuns and hasty in hiz conclusion, or end.

Hiz natral disposishun iz a warm cross between red pepper in the pod and fusil oil, and hiz moral bias iz, "git out ov mi way."

They have a long, black boddy, divided in the middle by a waist spot, but their phisikal importance lays at the terminous of their subberb, in the shape ov a javelin.

This javelin iz alwuz loaded, and stands reddy to unload at a minnit's warning, and enters a man az still az thought, az spry az litening, and az full ov melankolly az the tooth-ache.

Hornets never **argy a case**; they settle awl ov their dif-ferences ov opinyon by letting their javelin fly, and are az certain to hit **az a** mule **iz.**

This testy **kritter** lives in congregations numbering about 100 souls, but whether they iz mail or female, or conservative, or matched in bonds of wedlock, or whether they iz Mormons, and a good many ov them kling together and keep one husband to save expense, I don't kno nor don't kare.

I never have examined their habits much, I never kon-sidered it healthy.

Hornets build their nests wherever they take a noshun to, and seldom are disturbed, for what would it profit a man tew kill 99 hornets and hav the 100th one hit him with hiz javelin?

They bild their nests ov paper, without enny windows to them or back doors. They hav but one place ov admis-sion into the family cirkul, and the nest iz the shape ov an overgrown pineapple, and iz cut up into just as many bed-rooms as there iz hornets.

It iz very simple to make a hornet's nest—if you kan—but i will wager enny man 300 dollars he kant bild one that he could sell to a hornet for half price.

They hav found out, by trieing it, that all they can git in this world, and brag on, is their vittles and clothes, and yu never see one standing on the corner ov a street, with a twenty-six inch face on, bekause sum bank had run oph and took their money with them.

I suppose this uneasy world would grind around on its le-tree onst in 24 hours, even ef thare want enny hor-nets, but hornets must be good for sumthing, but I can't think just now what it iz.

Thare haint been a bug made yet in vain, nor one that wants a good job; there is ever lots of human men loafing around black-smith's shops, and cider-mills, and gin-mills, all over the country, that don't seem to be nessesary for anything but to beg plug tobacco and swear, and steal water melons, but you let the cholera break out once, and then you will see the wisdom of having jist sich men lay-ing around ; they help count.

The hornet iz an unsoshall ████, he iz a thorough-bred bug, but his breeding and refinement has made him like sum other folks I know ov, dissatisfied with himself and every boddy else; too much good breeding ackts this way sometimes.

Hornets are long-lived—I kant state jist how long their lives are, but I know from instinkt and observashen that enny krittur, be he bug or be he devil, who iz mad *all* the time, and stings every good chance he kan git, generally outlives all his nabers.

The only good way tew git at the exact fiteing weight of the hornet is tew tutch him up ; jist let him hit you once with his javelin, and you will be willin to testify in court that somebody run a one-tined pitchfork into yer ; and as for grit, i will state, for the informashun of thoze who haven't had a chance tew lay in their vermin wisdom az freely az I hav, that one single hornet, who feels well, will brake up a large camp-meetin.

THE GLOVE AND THE LIONS.

READ BY J. M. BELLEW.   LEIGH HUNT.

King Francis was a hearty king, and loved a royal sport,
And one day, as his lions strove, sat looking on the court;
The nobles fill'd the benches round, the ladies by their side,
And 'mongst them Count de Lorge, with one he hoped to make
    his bride :
And truly 'twas a gallant thing to see that crowning show,
Valor and love, and a king above, and the royal beasts below.

Ramped and roared the lions, with horrid laughing jaws;
They bit, they glared, gave blows like beams, a wind went with
    their paws;
With wallowing might and stifled roar they rolled one on another,
Till all the pit, with sand and mane, was in a thund'rous smother;
The bloody foam above the bars came whizzing through the air;
Said Francis then, "Good gentlemen, we're better here than
    there!"

De Lorge's love o'erheard the king—a beauteous, lively dame,
With smiling lips, and sharp bright eyes, which always seem'd
    the same:
She thought, "The Count, my lover, is as brave as brave can be;
He surely would do desperate things to show his love of me!
King, ladies, lovers, all look on; the chance is wondrous fine;
I'll drop my glove to prove his love; great glory will be mine!"

She dropp'd her glove to prove his love: then looked on him and
    smiled;
He bowed, and in a moment leaped among the lions wild!
The leap was quick; return was quick; he soon regained his
    place;
Then threw the glove, but not with love, right in the lady's face!
"Well done!" cried Francis, "bravely done!" and he rose from
    where he sat:
"No love," quoth he, "but vanity, sets love a task like that!"

I VANT TO FLY.

NONYMOUS

Shortly before the conclusion of the war with Napoleon
there were a number of French officers in an inland town
on their parole of honor. Now, one gentleman being tired
with the usual routine of eating, drinking, gambling, smoking, &c., therefore, in order to amuse himself otherwise,
resolved to go a-fishing. His host supplied him with rod
and line, but being in want of artificial flies, went in search
of a fishing tackle maker's shop. Having found one, kept by
a plain pains-taking John Bull, our Frenchman entered,

and, with a bow, a cringe, and a shrug of the shoulders, thus began :—

"Ah, Monsieur Anglaise, comment vous portez-vous !"

"Eh, that's French," exclaimed the shopkeeper; "not that I understand it, but I'm very well, if that's what you mean."

"Bon, bon, ver good; den, saire, I sall tell you, I vant deux fly."

"I dare say you do, Mounseer," replied the Englishman, "and so do a great many more of your outlandish gentry; but I'm a true-born Briton, and can never consent to assist the enemies of my country to leave it—particularly when they cost us so much to bring them here."

"Ah, Monsieur, you no comprehend ; I shall repeate, I vant deux fly, on the top of de vater."

"Oh! what, you want to fly by water, do you ? then I'm sure I can't assist you, for we are at least a hundred miles from the sea-coast, and our canal is not navigable above ten or twelve miles from here."

"Diable! sare, you are un stup of the block. I sall tell you once seven times over again—I vant deux fly on the top of de vater, to dingle dangle at the end of de long pole."

"Ay, ay! you only fly, Mounseer, by land or water, and if they catch you, I'll be hanged if they won't dingle dangle you, as you call it, at the end of a long pole."

"Sacre un de dieu! la blas! vat you mean by dat, enfer diable ? you are un bandit jack of de ass, Johnny de Bull. Ba, ba, you are effrontee, and I disgrace me to parley vid you. I tell you, sare, dat I vant deux fly on the top of de vater, to dingle dangle at the end of the long pole, to la trap poisson."

"What's that you say, you French Mounseer—you'll lay a trap to poison me and all my family because I won't assist you to escape ? why, the like was never heard. Here, Betty, go for the constable."

The constable soon arrived, who happened to be as ignorant as the shopkeeper, and of course it was not expected that a constable should be a scholar. Thus the man of office began :—

"What's all this? Betty has been telling me that this here outlandish Frenchman is going to poison you and all your family? Ay, ay, I should like to catch him at it, that's all. Come, come to prison, you delinquent."

"No, sare, I sall not go to de prison; take me before de what you call it—de ting that nibble de grass?"

"Nibble grass? You mean sheep?"

"No, I mean de—de—"

"Oh, you mean the cow."

"No, sare, not the cow; you stup Johnny bœuf—I mean de cheval, vat you ride. [Imitating.] Come, sare, gee up. Ah, ha."

"Oh, now I know, you mean a horse."

"No, sare, I mean de horse's vife."

"What, the mare?"

"Oui, bon, yes, sare, take me to de mayor."

This request was complied with, and the French officer soon stood before the English magistrate, who, by chance, happened to be better informed than his neighbors, and thus explained the dilemma of the unfortunate Frenchman, to the satisfaction of all parties—

"You have mistaken the intention of this honest gentleman; he did not want to fly the country, but to go a-fishing, and for that purpose went to your shop to purchase two flies, by way of bait, or, as he expressed it, to la trap la poisson. Poisson, in French, is fish."

"Why, aye," replied the shopkeeper, "that may be true; you are a scholard, and so you know better than I. Poison, in French, may be very good fish, but give me good old English roast beef."

MARK TWAIN.

Did I ever tell you about Smiley's dog? Well, he had
a little small bull pup, that to look at him you'd think he
wan't worth a cent, but to set around and look ornery, and
lay for a chance to steal something. But as soon as money
was up on him, he was a different dog; his under jaw'd
begin to stick out like the fo'castle of a steamboat, and
his teeth would uncover and shine savage like the furnaces.
And a dog might tackle him, and bully-rag him, and bite
him, and throw him over his shoulder, two or three times,
and Andrew Jackson—which was the name of the pup—
Andrew Jackson would never let on but what *he* was satisfied, and hadn't expected nothing else—and the bets
being doubled and doubled on the other side all the time,
till the money was all up; and then all of a sudden he
would grab that other dog jest by the j'int of his hind leg
and freeze to it—not chaw, you understand, but only jest
grip and hang on till they throwed up the sponge, if it was
a year. Smiley always come out winner on that pup, till
he harnessed a dog once that didn't have no hind legs,
because they'd been sawed off by a circular saw, and when
the thing had gone along far enough, and the money was
all up, and he come to make a snatch for his pet holt, he
saw in a minute how he'd been imposed on, and how the
other dog had him in the door, so to speak, and he 'peared
surprised, and then he looked sorter discouraged like, and
didn't try no more to win the fight, and so he got shucked
out bad. He give Smiley a look, as much as to say his
heart was broke, and it was *his* fault, for putting up a dog
that hadn't no hind legs for him to take holt of, which was
his main dependence in a fight, and then he limped off a
piece and laid down and died. It was a good pup, was
that Andrew Jackson, and would have made a name for
hisself if he'd lived, for the stuff was in him, and he had

genius—I know it, because he hadn't had no opportunities to speak of, and it don't stand to reason that a dog could make such a fight as he could under them circumstances, if he hadn't no talent. It always makes me feel sorry when I think of that last fight of Andrew Jackson's, and the way it turned out.

THE STORY OF THE FAITHFUL SOUL.

READ BY J. M. BELLEW.   ADELAIDE PROCTER.

The fettered spirits linger
  In purgatorial pain,
With penal fires effacing
  Their last faint earthly stain,
Which Life's imperfect sorrow
  Had tried to cleanse in vain.

Yet, on each feast of Mary,
  Their sorrow finds release,
For the Great Archangel Michael
  Comes down and bids it cease ;
And the name of these brief respites
  Is called " Our Lady's Peace."

Yet once—so runs the legend—
  When the Archangel came,
And all these holy spirits
  Rejoiced at Mary's name,
One voice alone was wailing,
  Still wailing on the same.

And though a great Te Deum
  The happy echoes woke,
This one discordant wailing
  Through the sweet voices broke :
So when St. Michael questioned,
  Thus the poor spirit spoke :

" I am not cold or thankless,
  Although I still complain ;

I prize our Lady's blessing,
   Although it comes in vain
To still my bitter anguish,
   Or quench my ceaseless pain.

" On earth a heart that loved me
   Still lives and mourns me there,
And the shadow of his anguish
   Is more than I can bear ;
All the torment that I suffer
   Is the thought of his despair.

" The evening of my bridal,
   Death took my life away ;
Not all love's passionate pleading
   Could gain an hour's delay,
And he I left has suffered
   A whole year since that day.

" If I could only see him—
   If I could only go
And speak one word of comfort
   And solace—then I know
He would endure with patience,
   And strive against his woe."

Thus the Archangel answered :
   " Your time of pain is brief,
And soon the peace of Heaven
   Will give you full relief;
Yet if his earthly comfort
   So much outweighs your grief,

" Then, through a special mercy
   I offer you this grace—
You may seek him who mourns you,
   And look upon his face,
And speak to him of comfort
   For one short minutes' space.

" But when that time is ended,
   Return here, and remain

A thousand years in torment,
  A thousand years in pain;
Thus dearly must you purchase
  The comfort he will gain."

*   *   *   *   *   *

The lime-trees' shade at evening
  Is spreading broad and wide;
Beneath their fragrant arches,
  Pace slowly, side by side,
In low and tender converse,
  A Bridegroom and his Bride.

The night is calm and stilly,
  No other sound is there
Except their happy voices;
  What is that cold bleak air
That passes through the lime-trees,
  And stirs the Bridegroom's hair?

While one low cry of anguish,
  Like the last dying wail
Of some dumb, hunted creature,
  Is borne upon the gale—
Why does the Bridegroom shudder
  And turn so deathly pale?

*   *   *   *   *   *

Near Purgatory's entrance
  The radiant Angels wait;
It was the great St. Michael
  Who closed that gloomy gate,
When the poor wandering spirit
  Came back to meet her fate.

"Pass on," thus spoke the Angel;
  "Heaven's joy is deep and vast;
Pass on, pass on, poor spirit,
  For Heaven is yours at last;
In that one minute's anguish
  Your thousand years have passed."

"MY NEW PITTAYATEES."

ANONYMOUS.

Enter KATTY, *with a gray cloak, a dirty cap, and a black eye; a siere of potatoes on her head, and a " trifle o' sper'ts" in it. KATTY meanders down Patrick Street.*

KATTY.—" *My new pittayatees! My-a-new pittayatees! My new—*"

(Meeting a friend.)

Sally, darlin', is that you?

SALLY.—Throth. it's myself; and what's the matther wid you, Katty?

KAT.—'Deed my heart's bruk, cryin'—" *New pittayatees!*"—cryin' afther that vagabone.

SAL.—Is it Mike?

KAT.—Throth, it's himself indeed.

SAL.—And what is it he done?

KAT.—Och! he ruined me with his—" *New pittayatees!*"—with his goin's-an. Yis, my darlint; he kem home th' other night, blazin' blind dhrunk, cryin' out— " *New pittay-a-tees!*"—roarin' and bawlin'. that you'd think he'd rise the roof aff o' the house.

" Bad luck attend you; bad cess to you, you pot-wallopin' varmint," says he (maynin' me, if you plaze), " wait till I ketch you, you sthrap, and it's I'll give you your fill iv "—" *New pittayatees!*"—" your fill iv a licking, if ever you got it," says he.

So, with that, I knew the villian was *mulvathered.**

Musha! wait till you hear the ind o' my—" *New pittayatees!*"—o' my throubles, and it's then you'll open your eyes—" *My new pittayatees!*"

Well, as he was comin' up-stairs (knowin' how it ud be,) I thought it best to take care o' my—" *My new pittayatees!*"—to take care o' myself; so with that I put the bowlt an the door, betune me and danger, and kep' listnin' at the keyhole; and sure enough, what should I hear but—" *New*

---

* Intoxicated.

pittayatees!"—but the vagabone gropin' his way round the cruked turn in the stair, and tumblin' afther into the hole in the flure an the landin', and whin he come to himself he gev a thunderin' thump at the door. "Who's there?" says I; says he—"*New pittayatees!*"—"Let me in," says he, "you vagabone." (swarein' by what I wouldn't min-tion), "or by this and that, I'll *massacray* you," says he, "within an inch o'"—"*New pittayatees!*"—"within an inch o' your life," says he. "Mikee, darlint," says I, sooth-erin him—"*New pittayatees!*"—with a tindher word, so says I, "Mikee, you villain, you're disguised," says I, "you're disguised, dear."

"You lie," says he, "you impident sthrap, I'm not dis-guised," says he, "I'll make you know the differ," says he.

Oh! I thought the life id lave me when I heered him say the word; and with that I put my hand an—"*My new pittayatees!*"—an the latch o' the door, to purvint it from slippin; and he ups and he gives a wicked kick at the door, and says he, "If you don't let me in this minit," says he, "I'll be the death o' your"—"*New pittayatees!*"—"o' yourself and your dirty breed," says he. Think o' that, Sallie, dear, to abuse my relations!

Dirty breed, indeed! By my sowkins, they're as good as his any day in the year, and was never behoulden to—"*New pittayatees!*"—to go a beggin' to the mendicity for their dirty—"*New pittayatees!*"—their dirty washin's o' pots, and sarvints' lavins, and dog's bones.

Well, at the word, "dirty breed," I knew full well the bad dhrop was up in him—and, faith, it's soon and suddint he made me sensible av it, for the first word he said was—"*New pittayatees!*"—the first word he said was to put his shoulder to the door, and in he bursted the door, fallin' down in the middle o' the flure, cryin' out—"*New pittay-atees!*"—cryin' out, "Bad luck attind you," says he, "how dar' you refuse to lit me into my own house, you sthrap, agin the law o' the land?" says he, scramblin' up on his pins agin, as well as he could; and, as he was risin', says I—"*New pittayatees!*"—says I to him, (screechin' out loud, that the neighbors in the flure below might hear me, "Mikee, my darlint," says I.

"Keep the pace, you vagabone," says he; and with that, he hits me a lick av a—"*New pittayatees!*"—a lick av a stick he had in his hand, and down I fell (and small blame to me), down I fell on the flure, cryin'—"*New pittayatees!*" —cryin out, "Murther! murther!"

As I was risin, my jew'l, he was going to sthrek me agin; and with that I cried—"*New pittayatees!*"—I cried out, "Fair play, Mikee," says I, "don't sthrek a man down;" but he wouldn't listen to rayson, and was goin' to hit me agin, when I put up the child that was in my arms betune me and harm. "Look at your babby, Mikee," says I. "Oh," says I, "Mikee, darlint, don't sthrek the babby;" but, my dear, before the word was out o' my mouth, he sthruk the babby. (I thought the life id lave me.) And, iv coorse, the poor babby, that never spuk a word, began to cry—"*New pittayatees!*"—began to cry, and roar, and bawl, and no wondher.

And, my jew'l, the neighbors in the flure below, hearin' the scrimmage, kem runnin' up the stairs, cryin' out—"*New pittayatees!*"—cryin' out, "Watch, watch! Mikee M'Evoy," says they, "would you murther your wife, you villain?" "What's that to you?" says he; "isn't she my own?" says he, "and if I plaze to make her feel the weight o' my" —"*New pittayatees!*"—"the weight o' my fist, what's that to you?" says he; "it's none o' your business, anyhow, so keep your tongue in your jaw, and 'twill be betther for your"—"*New pittayatees!*"—"'twill be betther for your health, I'm thinkin'," says he; and with that he looked cruked at thim, and squared up to one o' thim (a poor definceless craythur, a tailor). But the tailor's wife (and, by my sowl, it's she that's the sthrapper), says she, "Let *me* at him," says she; "it's I that used to give a man

a lickin' every day in the week ; and she wint bally-
raggin him ; and, by gor, they all tuk patthern afther her,
and abused him, my dear, to that degree, that I vow the
very dogs in the sthreet wouldn't lick his blood. And with
that, one and all, they begun to cry—" *New pittayatees !*"
—and they just tuk him up by the scruff o' the neck, and
threw him down the stairs ; every step he'd take, you'd
think he'd brake his neck, thank goodness, and so I got
rid o' the ruffin ; and then they left me cryin'—" *New pittayatees !*"—cryin' afther the vagabone—though the angels
knows well he wasn't deservin' o' one precious drop that
fell from my two good-lookin eyes ; and, oh ! but the condition he left me in. And a purty sight it id be, if you
could see how I was lyin' in the middle o' the flure, cryin'
—" *New pittayatees !*"—cryin' and roarin', and the poor
child, with his eye knocked out, in the corner cryin'—
" *New pittayatees !*"—and, indeed, every one in the place
was cryin'—" *New pittayatees !*"—and divil a thing had I
to put inside my face, nor a dhrop to dhrink, barrin a few
—" *New pittayatees !*"—a few grains o' tay, and the ind iv a
quarther o' sugar, and my eyes as big as your fist, and as
black as the pot (savin' your presence). But I'll not brake
your heart any more, Sally, dear—" *New pittayatees !*"—
Good-bye, Sally, darlint, good-bye—" *New pittay-a-tees !*"

MARY ANN'S WEDDING.

AS RELATED BY MRS. JONES.   ANONYMOUS.

" We were all preparing," said Mrs. Jones, " to go to the
wedding. I was going, father was going, the gals were
going, and we were going to take the baby ; but come to
dress the baby, could not find the baby's shirt. I'd laid a
clean one out of one of the drawers on purpose. I know'd
jist where I had put it ; but come to look for it 'twas
gone.

" 'For mercy's sake,' says I, 'gals,' says I, 'has any on yo seen that baby's shirt ?'

" Of course none of 'em had seen it; and I looked, and looked, and looked again, but 'twant nowhere to be found. 'It's the strangest thing in all nature,' says I, ' here I had the shirt in my hand not mor'n ten minutes ago, and now it's gone, and nobody can tell where. I never seed the beat. 'Gals,' said I, ' do look around, can't ye?' But fretting wouldn't find it; so I gave it up, and I went to the bureau, and fished up another shirt, and put it onto the baby, and at last we were ready for a start.

" Father harnessed up a double team—we drove the old white mare then, and the gals and all was having a good time, going to see Mary Ann married, but somehow I couldn't git over that shirt ! 'Twant the shirt so much; but to have anything spirited away from under my face and eyes so, 'twas provokin'!

'What ye thinking about, mother ?' says Sophrony ; 'What makes you look so sober ?' says she.

'I'm pestered to death, thinking about that ere shirt. One of you must have took it, I am sartin,' says I.

'Now, ma,' says Sophrony, ' you needn't say that,'— and as I'd laid onto her a good many times, she was beginning to get vexed, and so we had it back and forth, and all about that baby's shirt, till we got to the wedding.

" Seeing company kinder put it out of mind, and I was getting good-natured again, though I could not help saying to myself every few minutes, 'What could have become of that shirt ?' till at last they stood up to be married, and I forgot all about it.

" Mary Ann was a real modest creature, and was mor'n half frightened to death when she came into the room with Stephen, and the minister told them to jine hands. She first gave her left hand to Stephen. 'Your other hand,' says the minister; and poor Steve, he was so bashful, too, he didn't know what he was about ; he thought 'twas his mistake, and that the minister meant him, so he gave Mary Ann his left hand. That wouldn't do, any way, a left-handed marriage all around; but by this time they didn't know what they were about, and Mary Ann joined her right hand to his left, then her left with his right, then both their hands again, until I was all of a fidget, and tho't they would never get fixed.

"Mary Ann looked as red as a turkey, and to make matters worse, she began to cough, to turn it off, I suppose, and called for a glass of water. The minister had just been drinking, and the tumbler stood right there, and I was so nervous, and in such a hurry to see it all over with, I ketched up the tumbler and run with it to her, for I thought to goodness she was going to faint. She undertook to drink—I don't know how it happened, but the tumbler slipped, and gracious me, if between us we didn't spill the water all over the collar and dress.

" I was dreadfully flustered, for I thought it looked as though it was my fault, and the first thing I did was to out with my handkerchief, and give it to Mary Ann; it was nicely done up, and she took it. The folks had held in pretty well up to this time, but then such a giggle and laugh as there was—I didn't know what had given them such a start, till I looked and seen that *I'd given Mary Ann that baby's shirt!*"

Here Mrs. Jones, who is a very fleshy woman, undulated and shook like a mighty jelly with her mirth, and it was some time before she could proceed with her narrative.

" Why," said she, with tears of laughter running down her cheeks, " I'd tucked it into my dress for a 'kerchief. That came from being absent-minded and in a fidget."

" And Mary Ann and Stephen—were they married after all ?"

" Dear me, yes," said Mrs. Jones, " and it turned out to be the gayest wedding that I ever attended."

" And the baby's shirt, Mrs. Jones ?"

"La me," said Mrs Jones, " how young folks do ask questions. Everybody agreed I ought to make Mary Ann a present on't."

"Well, Mrs. Jones ?"

"Well," said Mrs. Jones, " twant long 'fore she had a use for it. And that's the end of the story."

AN INQUIRING YANKEE.

ANONYMOUS.

A well-known citizen of Hartford, Ct., a few days ago had taken his seat in an afternoon train for Providence, when a small, weazen-faced, elderly man, having the appearance of a well-to-do farmer, came into the car, looking for a seat. The gentleman good-naturedly made room for him by his side, and the old man looked him over from head to foot.

" Going to Providence ?" he said at length.

"No, sir," the stranger answered, politely, "I stop at Andover."

" I want to know! I belong out that way myself. Expect to stop long ?"

" Only over night, sir."

A short pause.

" Did you cal'late to put up at the tavern ?"

" No, sir; I expect to stop at a private house."

"Private house, eh ? Mebbe at old Jones's?"

" I am not acquainted with him. If you must know, I am going to Mr. Skinner's."

"What, Job Skinner? Deacon Job lives in a little brown house on the pike ? Or mebbe it's his brother's? Was it Tim Skinner, Squire Tim's, where you was going?"

"Yes," said the gentleman, smiling; "it was Squire Tim's."

"Dew tell if you are goin' there to stop over night. Any connection of his'n ?"

"No, sir."

"Well, now that's curus! The old man ain't got into any trouble nor nothing, has he?" lowering his voice; "ain't goin' to serve a writ on him, be you?"

"Oh, no; nothing of the kind."

"Glad on't. No harm in askin', I s'pose. I reckon Miss Skinner's some connection of yourn?"

"No," said the gentleman. Then seeing the amused expression on the faces of two or three acquaintances in the neighboring seats, he added, in a confidential tone:

"I am going to see Squire Skinner's daughter."

"Law sakes!" said the old man, his face quivering with curiosity. That's it, is it? I want to know? Going to see Mirandy Skinner, be ye? Well, Mirandy's a nice gal —kind o' humly and long-favored, but smart tew work, they say; and I guess you're about the right age for her, too. Kep' company together long."

"Never saw her in my life, sir."

"How you talk! Somebody's gin her a recommend, I s'pose, and you're goin' clear out there to take a squint at her! Wa'al, I must say there's as likely gals in Andover as Mirandy Skinner. I've got a family of growed-up darters myself. Never was married afore, was ye? Don't see no weed on your hat."

"I have been married about fifteen years, sir. I have a wife and five children." And then, as the long-restrained mirth of the listeners to this dialogue burst forth at the old man's open-mouthed astonishment, he hastened to explain: "I am a doctor, my good friend, and Squire Skinner called at my office this morning to request my professional services for his sick daughter. As I am not able to return this evening, you see I am obliged to accept Mr. Skinner's hospitality for the night."

"Wa'al now!" And the old bore waddled off into the next car.

THE THREE BELLS.

J. G. WHITTIER.

Beneath the low-hung night cloud
  That raked her splintering mast,
The good ship settled slowly,
  The cruel leak gained fast.

Over the awful ocean
  Her signal guns pealed out.
Dear God! was that thy answer
  From the horror round about?

A voice came down the wild wind,
  "Ho! ship ahoy!" its cry;
"Our stout Three Bells of Glasgow
  Shall lay till daylight by!"

Hour after hour crept slowly,
  Yet on the heaving swells
Tossed up and down the ship-lights,
  The lights of the Three Bells!

And ship to ship made signals,
  Man answered back to man,
While oft, to cheer and hearten,
  The Three Bells nearer ran;

And the captain from the taffrail
  Sent down his hopeful cry,
"Take heart! Hold on!" he shouted,
  "The Three Bells shall lay by!"

All night across the waters
  The tossing lights shone clear;
All night from reeling taffrail
  The Three Bells sent her cheer.

And when the dreary watches
  Of storm and darkness passed,
Just as the wreck lurched under,
  All souls were saved at last.

Sail on, Three Bells, forever,
　　In grateful memory sail !
Ring on, Three Bells of rescue,
　　Above the wave and gale !

Type of the Love eternal,
　　Repeat the Master's cry,
As tossing through our darkness
　　The lights of God draw nigh !

———————— •♦• ————————

LOVE IN A BALLOON.

READ BY J. M. BELLEW.　　　LITCHFIELD MOSELEY.

Some time ago I was staying with **Sir George Flasher**, with a great number of people there—all kinds of amusements going on. Driving, riding, fishing, shooting, everything, in fact. Sir George's daughter, Fanny, was often my companion in these expeditions, and I was considerably struck with her, for she was a girl to whom the epithet "stunning" applies better than any other that I am acquainted with. She could ride like Nimrod, she could drive like Jehu, she could row like Charon, she could dance like Terpsichore, she could row like Diana, she walked like Juno, and she looked like Venus. I've even seen her smoke.

Oh, she was a stunner! you should have heard that girl whistle, and laugh—you should have heard her laugh. She was truly a delightful companion. We rode together, drove together, fished together, walked together, danced together, sang together; I called her Fanny, and she called me Tom. All this could have but one termination, you know. I fell in love with her and determined to take the first opportunity of proposing. So one day when we were out together, fishing on the lake, I went down on my knees amongst the gudgeons, seized her hand, pressed it to my waistcoat, and in burning accents entreated her to become my wife.

" Don't be a fool," she said.   " Now drop it, do, and put
me a fresh worm on."

" Oh, Fanny !" I exclaimed ; " don't talk about worms
when marriage is in question.   Only say—"

" I tell you what it is, now," she replied, angrily, " if you
don't drop it I'll pitch you out of the boat."

Gentlemen, I did not drop it, and I give you my word of
honor, with a sudden shove she sent me flying into the
water ; then seizing the sculls, with a stroke or two she put
several yards between us, and burst into a fit of laughter
that fortunately prevented her from going any further.   I
swam up and climbed into the boat.   " Jenkins," said I to
myself, " revenge ! revenge !"   I disguised my feelings.   I
laughed—hideous mockery of mirth—I laughed, pulled to
the bank, went to the house and changed my clothes.
When I appeared at the dinner-table, I perceived that
every one had been informed of my ducking.   Universal
laughter greeted me.   During dinner Fanny repeatedly
whispered to her neighbor and glanced at me.   Smothered
laughter invariably followed.   " Jenkins !" said I, " revenge !"   The opportunity soon offered.   There was to
be a balloon ascent from the lawn, and Fanny had tor-
mented her father into letting her ascend with the aeronaut.   I instantly took my plans ; bribed the aeronaut to
plead illness at the moment when the machine should have
risen ; learned from him the management of the balloon,
though I understood that pretty well before, and calmly
awaited the result.   The day came.   The weather was fine.
The balloon was inflated.   Fanny was in the car.   Everything was ready, when the aeronaut suddenly fainted.   He
was carried into the house, and Sir George accompanied
him.   Fanny was in despair.

" Am I to lose my air expedition ?" she exclaimed, looking over the side of the car ; " some one understands the
management of this thing, surely ?   Nobody !   Tom !" she
called out to me, " you understand it, don't you ?"

"Perfectly," I answered.

"Come along, then," she cried; "be quick, before papa comes back."

The company in general endeavored to dissuade her from her project, but of course in vain. After a decent show of hesitation, I climbed into the car. The balloon was cast off, and rapidly sailed heavenward. There was scarcely a breath of wind, and we rose almost straight up. We rose above the house, and she laughed and said, "How jolly!"

We were higher than the highest trees, and she smiled, and said it was very kind of me to come with her. We were so high that the people below looked mere specks, and she hoped that I thoroughly understood the management of the balloon. Now was my time.

"I understand the going up part," I answered; "to come down is not so easy," and I whistled.

"What do you mean?" she cried.

"Why, when you want to go up faster, you throw some sand overboard," I replied, suiting the action to the word.

"Don't be foolish, Tom," she said, trying to appear quite calm and indifferent, but trembling uncommonly.

"Foolish!" I said; "oh, dear no, but whether I go along the ground or up in the air I like to go the pace, and so do you, Fanny, I know. Go it, you cripples!" and over went another sand-bag.

"Why, you're mad, surely," she whispered, in utter terror, and tried to reach the bags, but I kept her back.

"Only with love, my dear," I answered, smiling pleasantly; "only with love for you. Oh, Fanny, I adore you! Say you will be my wife."

"I gave you an answer the other day," she replied; "one which I should have thought you would have remembered," she added, laughing a little, notwithstanding her terror.

"I remember it perfectly," I answered, "but I intend to have a different reply to that. You see those five sandbags. I shall ask you five times to become my wife. Every time you refuse I shall throw over a sand-bag—so, lady fair, as the cabmen would say, reconsider your decision, and consent to become Mrs. Jenkins."

"I won't," she said; "I never will; and let me tell you that you are acting in a very ungentlemanly way to press me thus."

"You acted in a very ladylike way the other day, did you not," I rejoined, "when you knocked me out of the boat?" She laughed again, for she was a plucky girl, and no mistake—a very plucky girl. "However," I went on, "it's no good arguing about it—will you promise to give me your hand?"

"Never!" she answered; "I'll go to Ursa Major first, though I've got a big enough bear here, in all conscience. Stay! you'd prefer Aquarius, wouldn't you?"

She looked so pretty that I was almost inclined to let her off. (I was only trying to frighten her, of course—I knew how high we could go safely, well enough, and how valuable the life of Jenkins was to his country), but resolution is one of the strong points of my character, and when I've begun a thing I like to carry it through; so I threw over another sand-bag, and whistled the Dead March in Saul.

"Come, Mr. Jenkins," she said suddenly, "come, Tom, let us descend now, and I'll promise to say nothing whatever about all this."

I continued the execution of the Dead March.

"But if you do not begin the descent at once I'll tell papa the moment I set foot on the ground."

I laughed, seized another bag, and, looking steadily at her, said: "Will you promise to give me your hand?"

"I've answered you already," was the reply.

Over went the sand, and the solemn notes of the Dead March resounded through the car.

"I thought you were a gentleman," said Fanny, rising up in a terrible rage from the bottom of the car, where she had been sitting, and looking perfectly beautiful in her wrath. "I thought you were a gentleman, but I find I was mistaken. Why, a chimney-sweeper would not treat a lady in such a way. Do you know that you are risking your own life as well as mine by your madness?"

I explained that I adored her so much that to die in her company would be perfect bliss, so that I begged she would not consider my feelings at all. She dashed her beautiful hair from her face, and standing perfectly erect, looking like the Goddess of Anger or Boadicea—if you can imagine that personage in a balloon—she said, "I command you to begin the descent this instant!"

The Dead March, whistled in a manner essentially gay and lively, was the only response. After a few minutes' silence I took up another bag, and said:

"We are getting rather high; if you do not decide soon we shall have Mercury coming to tell us that we are trespassing—will you promise me your hand?"

She sat in sulky silence in the bottom of the car. I threw over the sand. Then she tried another plan. Throwing herself upon her knees, and bursting into tears, she said:

"Oh, forgive me for what I did the other day. It was very wrong, and I am very sorry. Take me home, and I will be a sister to you."

"Not a wife?" said I.

" I can't! I can't!" she answered.

Over went the fourth bag, and I began to think she would beat me after all, for I did not like the idea of going much higher. I would not give in just yet, however. I whistled for a few moments, to give her time for reflection, and then said: " Fanny, they say that marriages are made in heaven—if you do not take care, ours will be solemnized there."

I took up the fifth bag. "Come," I said, "my wife in life, or my companion in death. Which is it to be?" and I petted the sand-bag in a cheerful manner. She held her

face in her hands, but did not answer. I nursed the bag
in my arms, as if it had been a baby.

"Come, Fanny, give me your promise." I could hear
her sobs. I'm the softest-hearted creature breathing, and
would not pain any living thing, and I confess she had
beaten me. I forgave her the ducking; I forgave her for
rejecting me. I was on the point of flinging the bag back
into the car, and saying, "Dearest Fanny, forgive me for
frightening you. Marry whomsoever you wish. Give your
lovely hand to the lowest groom in your stables—endow
with your priceless beauty the chief of the Pauki-wanki
Indians. Whatever happens, Jenkins is your slave—your
dog—your footstool. His duty, henceforth, is to go whither-
soever you shall order, to do whatever you shall command."
I was just on the point of saying this, I repeat, when Fanny
suddenly looked up, and said, with a queerish expression
upon her face :

"You need not throw that last bag over. I promise to
give you my hand."

"With all your heart ?" I asked, quickly.

"With all my heart," she answered, with the same
strange look.

I tossed the bag into the bottom of the car, and opened
the valve. The balloon descended. Gentlemen, will you
believe it ?—when we had reached the ground, and the
balloon had been given over to its recovered master, when
I had helped Fanny tenderly to the earth, and turned towards her to receive anew the promise of her affection and
her hand—will you believe it ?—she gave me a box on the
ear that upset me against the car, and running to her
father, who at that moment came up, she related to him
and the assembled company what she called my disgrace-
ful conduct in the balloon, and ended by informing me that
all of her hand that I was likely to get had been already
bestowed upon my ear, which she assured me had been
given with all her heart.

"You villain!" said Sir George, advancing toward me with a horse-whip in his hand. "You villain! I've a good mind to break this over your back."

"Sir George," said I, "villain and Jenkins must never be coupled in the same sentence; and as for the breaking of this whip, I'll relieve you of the trouble," and snatching it from his hand, I broke it in two, and threw the peices on the ground. "And now I shall have the honor of wishing you a good morning. Miss Flasher, I forgive you;" and I retired. Now I ask you whether any specimen of female treachery equal to that has ever come within your experience, and whether any excuse can be made for such conduct?

MRS. BROWN ON THE STATE OF THE STREETS.

ARTHUR SKETCHLEY.

Talk about weather! I never did in all my born days know nothin' like it was the week afore last; you're froze up one moment and all of a glow the next.

As to this house we're a-living in, they calls it a simmy detached, as it's my opinion they was obliged to build it up again next door or it would never have stood by itself, as it is not much stronger than a egg-shell, as the sayin' is. The draught under that kitchen-door it was as give it me, the cold as I've got, for I felt it all the while as I was a-makin' that weal and ham pie, as is a thing as Brown's partial to, and I makes it myself with a flaky crust, though some will have it as a short one is right, which in my opinion goes best with fruit. As to puttin' a bit of bad butter in pie-crust, it's my idea of a sin as is downright filthy to the taste and unwholesome to a delicate stomach like Brown's, though you wouldn't think it to look at him, but no one knows where the shoe pinches but them as is bilious, as the sayin' is.

I certainly did feel a chill, and pr'aps it might have been

through them dratted boys as I give twopence each to for
to clear away the snow. As a feller comes round with a
paper, as he said was the westry's orders as I should clean
up the front of my house. I says, "Then I'll thank the
westry for to turn out and clean the road for me, as I can't
get across, not if it was to save my life, through bein' ankle-
deep, and poor Mrs. Atkins that bad as I wanted for to go
to, through me havin' promised, and only the corner of the
street." So he says, "You may be carried across easy on
a barrow," as I see meant jeers.

So I says, "When I wants to be carried I'll get a steady
donkey, and pr'aps you might be handy." "Well," says
he, "I should recommend a dromedary." I wasn't a-going
to waste my time a-talkin' to such as him, all the more as
I felt a-creepin' all down my back, as is a sure sign of chills
with me, as has throwed me on a sick bed afore now, and
was the death of poor old Mrs. Thornley, as kept the "Blue
Lion" in Horsleydown, and never recovered a-fallin' asleep
one Saturday night whilst a-soakin' her feet, and never
woke up till they was froze hard in the foot-pan, through
the cold bein' that violent below zero as froze the Thames
up with a ox roasted whole, as I've heard my dear mother
say was shameful waste, through the roughs a-tearin' of it
to bits in their open hands though blue and quivery, as is
not wholesome in my opinion, though it should be done
with the gravy in, as gives proper nutriment.

Well, as I was sayin', I give them boys twopence a-piece,
and lent them the fire-shovel for to scrape off them frozen
lumps, as is that dangerous, as well I've known through
a-treadin' on one, as twisted my ankle and down I went,
and shouldn't have minded it so much if it hadn't been for
poor old Mr. Gibbins, next door but two, as had stepped
out for the beer hisself and two new-laid eggs, though I
should say no more new-laid than I am. Well, he had the
beer in one hand and the eggs in the other, with a white
worsted comforter and long ends, as he did ought to have

tucked in somewhere, but left a-hangin'. He was a-walkin' along by my side, a remarkin' about the weather and
such like, when I treads on the bit of frozen snow, and nat'-
rally clutches at anythin' for to save myself, and as bad
luck would have it, seized hold of his ends of his comforter,
and give him that drag as his 'eels slipped from under him,
though list around his shoes, as didn't prove no protec-
tion. Up goes his hand with the beer all in my face and
blinds me, but I heard a crash, and there he was a-welterin'
in his new-laid eggs, and a-sayin' as his back was broke.

So I says, "Kick, 'cos if you can kick your back's all
right," and kick he did, and he had no occasion for to ketch
me on the shin so violent, me a-stoopin' for to help him up,
a-feelin' grateful to him for breakin' my fall, as the sayin
is, but he kep' his bed for weeks. But the cold as I caught
was a caution, as you don't ketch me out in the snow agin
if I knows it.

SHOO FLIES.

ANONYMOUS.

Dose efenin clouds vas sedding fast,
    As a young mans droo der tillage past,
Shkatin along der shtorm und hail,
    Mit dese vords tied py his coat dail—Shoo Flies.

Oh, dond gone out such a nite like dose,
    His mudder cried, you vill got froze ;
Dot Shack Frost he vill nib your ear,
    She oney said so mit a shneer—Shoo Flies.

Come pack, come pack, der olt man said,
    Of you dond look oud you vill peen dead :
Come pack, und py der fire sid,
    Ha, ha ! I dond vas afraid a bit—Shoo Flies.

Schon Henry, der young maid said,
    Come here und eat dis biece of bread ;
He yoost looked down und hofe a sigh,
    I vas a hunki poy mit a klass eye— Shoo Flies.

Higher und higher dot young mans vent,
   For der shtorms he dond did care a cent ;
He ripped der shnow off his left ear,
   Und dese vords vas heard shtill und clear—Shoo Flies.

In aboud a veek, or maype more,
   Der peobles heard an awful roar,
Dot sounded loud und far und wide,
   Von vay up of der moundain side—Shoo Flies.

Dwo mens vas out a shoodin shnibes,
   Und vhile dhey shtobbed to shmoke der bibes,
Und ven dhey habbened to look around,
   Dhey saw dot shticken von der ground—Shoo Flies.

DISCOURSE BY THE REV. MR. BOSAN.

EDWARD EGLESTON.

[I can never picture to you the rich red nose, the see-sawing gestures, the nasal resonance, the suiffle, the melancholy minor key, and all that.]

"You see, my respective hearers, my respective hearers—ah, you see—ah, as how—ah, as my tex'—ah, says that the ox—ah, knoweth his owner—ah, and—ah the ass—ah, his master's crib—ah, a-h-h ! Now, my respective hearers—ah, they're a mighty sight of resemblance—ah, atwixt men—ah, and oxen—ah, bekase—ah, you see, men—ah, is mighty like oxen—ah. For they's a tremengious defference—ah, atwixt defferent oxen—ah, jest as thar is atwext defferent men—ah; fer the ox knoweth—ah, his owner—ah, and the ass—ah, his master's crib—ah. Now, my respective hearers—ah"—[the preacher's voice here grew mellow, and the succeeding sentences were in the most pathetic and lugubrious voice] "you all know—ah, that your humble speaker—ah, has got—ah, jest the best yoke of steers—ah, in this township—ah. They ain't no sech steers as them air two of mine—ah, in this whole kedentry —ah. Them crack oxen over at Clifty—ah, ha'nt a patchin' to mine—ah. Fer the ox knoweth his owner—ah, and the ass—ah, his master's crib—ah.

Now, my respective hearers—ah, they's a right smart sight of defference—ah, atwext them air two oxen—ah, jest like they is atwext defferent men—ah. Fer—ah "—[here the speaker grew earnest, and sawed the air from this to the close in a most frightful way]—"fer—ah, you see—ah, when I go out—ah, in the mornin'—ah, to yoke—ah, up—ah, them air steers—ah, and I says—ah 'Wo, Berry—ah ! *Wo, Berry—ah !!* WO, BERRY — AH !!!' why, Berry—ah, jest stands stock still—ah, and don't hardly breathe—ah, while I put on the yoke—ah, and put in the bow—ah, and put in the key—ah, fer, my brethering—ah, and sistering—ah, the ox knoweth his owner—ah, and the ass—ah, his master's crib—ah. Hal-le-lu-ger—ah ! But — ah, my hearers — ah, but—ah, when I stand at t'other eend of the yoke—ah, and say, 'Come, Buck—ah ! *Come, Buck—ah !!* COME, BUCK—AH !!! COME, BUCK ·—AH !!!!' why, what do you think—ah ? Buck—ah, that ornery ole Buck, ah, 'stid of comin' right along—ah, and puttin' his neck under—ah, acts jest like some men—ah, what is fools—ah. Buck—ah, jest kinder sorter stands off —ah, and kinder sort puts his down—ah, this ere way—ah, and kinder looks looks mad—ah, and says, ' Boo-oo-oo-OO —ah."

WITHOUT THE CHILDREN.

ANONYMOUS.

Oh, the weary, solemn silence
Of a house without the children ;
Oh, the strange, oppressive stillness,
    Where the children come no more.
Ah ! the longing of the sleepless
For the soft arms of the children,
Ah ! the longing for the faces
    Peeping through the opening door—
    Faces gone for evermore !

ing how he could manage to get introduced into genteel
society for the first time, when his eyes rested on Signor
Billsmethi's announcement, which, it immediately struck
him, was just the very thing he wanted; for he should not
only be able to select a genteel circle of acquaintance at
once, out of the five-and-seventy pupils at four-and-six-
pence a quarter, but should qualify himself at the same
time to go through a hornpipe in private society with perfect ease to himself, and great delight to his friends. So
he stopped the advertisement—an animated sandwich
composed of a boy between two boards—and having pro-
cured a very small card with the Signor's address indented
thereon, walked straight at once to the Signor's house—
and very fast he walked too, for fear the list should be
filled up, and the five-and-seventy completed before he got
there. The Signor was at home, and what was still more
gratifying, he was an Englishman! Such a nice man—
and so polite! The list was not full, but it was a most
extraordinary circumstance that there was only just one
vacancy, and even that one would have been filled up that
very morning, only Signor Billsmethi was dissatisfied with
the reference, and, being very much afraid that the lady
wasn't select, wouldn't take her.

"And very much delighted I am, Mr. Cooper," said
Signor Billsmethi, "that I did *not* take her. I assure you,
Mr. Cooper—I don't say it to flatter you, for I know you're
above it—that I consider myself extremely fortunate
in having a gentleman of your manners and appearance,
sir."

"I am very glad of it too, sir," said Augustus Cooper.

"And I hope we shall be better acquainted, sir," said
Signor Billsmethi.

"And I'm sure I hope we shall too, sir," responded
Augustus Cooper. Just then, the door opened, and in
came a young lady, with her hair curled in a crop all over
her head, and her shoes tied in sandals all over her ankles.

" Don't run away, my dear," said Signor Billsmethi; for the young lady didn't know Mr. Cooper was there when she ran in, and was going to run out again in her modesty, all in confusion-like. " Don't run away, my dear," said Signor Billsmethi, " this is Mr. Cooper—Mr. Cooper, of Fetter Lane. Mr. Cooper, my daughter, sir — Miss Billsmethi, sir, who, I hope, will have the pleasure of dancing many a quadrille, minuet, gavotte, country dance, fandango, double hornpipe and faringaholkajingo with you, sir. She dances them all, sir; and so shall you, sir, before you're a quarter older, sir."

And Signor Billsmethi slapped Mr. Augustus Cooper on the back, as if he had known him a dozen years—so friendly;—and Mr. Cooper bowed to the young lady, and the young lady curtseyed to him, and Signor Billsmethi said they were as handsome a pair as ever he'd wish to see; upon which the young lady exclaimed, " Lor, pa!" and blushed as red as Mr. Cooper himself—you might have thought they were both standing under a red lamp at a chemist's shop; and before Mr. Cooper went away it was settled that he should join the family circle that very night —taking them just as they were—no ceremony nor nonsense of that kind—and learn his positions in order that he might lose no time, and be able to come out at the forthcoming ball.

Well, Mr. Augustus Cooper went away to one of the cheap shoemakers' shops in Holborn, where gentlemen's dress-pumps are seven-and-sixpence and men's strong walking just nothing at all, and bought a pair of the regular seven-and-sixpenny, long-quartered town-mades, in which he astonished himself quite as much as his mother, and sallied forth to Signor Billsmethi's. There were four other private pupils in the parlor: two ladies and two gentlemen. Such nice people! Not a bit of pride about them. One of the ladies in particular, who was in training for a Columbine, was remarkably affable; and she and

Miss Billsmethi took such an interest in Mr. Augustus Cooper, and joked and smiled, and looked so bewitching, that he got quite at home, and learned his steps in no time. After the practicing was over, Signor Billsmethi, and Miss Billsmethi, and Master Billsmethi, and a young lady, and the two ladies, and the two gentlemen, danced a quadrille—none of your slipping and sliding about, but regular warm work, flying into corners, and diving among chairs, and shooting out at the door—something like dancing! Signor Billsmethi in particular, notwithstanding his having a little fiddle to play all the time, was out on the landing every figure, and Master Billsmethi, when everybody else was breathless, danced a hornpipe, with a cane in his hand and a cheese-plate on his head, to the unqualified admiration of the whole company. Then Signor Billsmethi insisted, as they were so happy, that they should all stay to supper, and proposed sending Master Billsmethi for the beer and spirits, whereupon the two gentlemen swore, "strike 'em wulgar if they'd stand that;" and were just going to quarrel who should pay for it, when Mr. Augustus Cooper said he would, if they'd have the kindness to allow him—and they *had* the kindness to allow him; and Master Billsmethi brought the beer in a can, and the rum in a quart-pot. They had a regular night of it; and Miss Billsmethi squeezed Mr. Augustus Cooper's hand under the table, and Mr. Augustus Cooper returned the squeeze and returned home too, at something to six o'clock in the morning, when he was put to bed by main force by the apprentice, after repeatedly expressing an uncontrollable desire to pitch his revered parent out of the second-floor window, and to throttle the apprentice with his own neck-handkerchief.

Weeks had worn on, and the seven-and-sixpenny town-mades had nearly worn out, when the night arrived for the grand dress ball at which the whole of the five-and-seventy pupils were to meet together for the first time that season, and to take out some portion of their respective four-and-sixpences in lamp-oil and fiddlers. Mr. Augustus Cooper had ordered a new coat for the occasion—a two-pound-tenner from Turnstile. It was his first appearance in public; and, after a grand Sicilian shawl-dance by fourteen young ladies in character, he was to open the quadrille department with Miss Billsmethi herself, with whom he had become quite intimate since his first introduction. It *was* a night! Everything was admirably arranged. The sandwich boy took the hats and bonnets at the street door; there was a turn-up bedstead in the back parlor, on which Miss Billsmethi made tea and coffee for such of the gentlemen as chose to pay for it, and such of the ladies as the gentlemen treated; red port-wine negus and lemonade were handed round at eighteen-pence a head; and in pursuance of a previous engagement with the public house at the corner of the street, an extra pot-boy was laid on for the occasion. In short, nothing could exceed the arrangements, except the company. Such ladies! Such pink silk stockings! Such artificial flowers! Such a number of cabs! No sooner had one cab set down a couple of ladies, than another cab drove up and set down another couple of ladies, and they all knew, not only one another, but the majority of the gentlemen into the bargain, which made it all as pleasant and lively as could be. Signor Billsmethi, in black tights, with a large blue bow in his button-hole, introduced the ladies to such of the gentlemen as were strangers; and the ladies talked away—and laughed they did—it was delightful to see them.

As to Mr. Augustus Cooper's share in the quadrille, he got through it admirably. He was missing from his partner, now and then, certainly, and discovered on such occasions to be either dancing with laudable perseverance in another set, or sliding about in perspective, without any definite object; but generally speaking, they managed to shove him through the figure, until he turned up in the right

place. Be this as it may, when he had finished, a great
many ladies and gentlemen came up and complimented
him very much, and said they had never seen a beginner
do anything like it before; and Mr. Augustus Cooper was
perfectly satisfied with himself, and everybody else into
the bargain; and "stood" considerable quantities of spir-
its-and-water, negus and compounds, for the use and be-
hoof of two or three dozen very particular friends, selected
from the select circle of five-and-seventy pupils.

Now, whether it was the strength of the compounds, or
the beauty of the ladies, or what not, it did so happen that
Mr. Augustus Cooper encouraged, rather than repelled,
the very flattering attentions of a young lady in brown
gauze over white calico, who had appeared particularly
struck with him from the first; and when the encourage-
ments had been prolonged for some time, Miss Billsmethi
betrayed her spite and jealousy thereat by calling the
young lady in brown gauze a "creetur," which induced the
young lady in brown gauze to retort, in certain sentences
containing a taunt founded on the payment of four-and-six-
pence a quarter, which reference Mr. Augustus Cooper, being then and there in a state of considerable bewilderment,
expressed his entire concurrence in. Miss Billsmethi, thus
renounced, forthwith began screaming in the loudest key
of her voice, at the rate of fourteen screams a minute; and
being unsuccessful, in an onslaught on the eyes and face,
first of the lady in gauze and then of Mr. Augustus Cooper,
called distractedly on the other three-and-seventy pupils to
furnish her with oxalic acid for her own private drinking;'
and, the call not being honored, made another rush at Mr.
Cooper, and then had her stay-lace cut, and was carried
off to bed. Mr. Augustus Cooper, not being remarkable
for quickness of apprehension, was at a loss to understand what all this meant, until Signor Billsmethi explained
it in a most satisfactory manner, by stating to the pupils
that Mr. Augustus Cooper had made and confirmed divers

promises of marriage to his daughter on divers occasions, and had now basely deserted her; on which, the indignation of the pupils became universal; and as several chivalrous gentlemen inquired rather pressingly of Mr. Augustus Cooper, whether he required anything for his own use, or, in other words, whether he "wanted anything for himself," he deemed it prudent to make a precipitate retreat. And the upshot of the matter was, that a lawyer's letter came next day, and an action was commenced next week; and that Mr. Augustus Cooper, after walking twice to the Serpentine for the purpose of drowning himself, and coming twice back without doing it, made a confidante of his mother, who compromised the matter with twenty pounds from the till; which made twenty pounds four shillings and sixpence paid to Signor Billsmethi, exclusive of treats and pumps. And Mr. Augustus Cooper went back and lived with his mother, and there he lives to this day; and as he has lost his ambition for society, and never goes into the world, he will never see this account of himself, and will never be any the wiser.

DER GOOT LOOKIN SHNOW.

ANONYMOUS.

Oh, dot shnow, dot goot lookin shnow,
Vhich makes von der shky out, on tings below;
Und yoost on der hause vhere der shingles vas grow,
You come mit some coldness, vherefer you go;
    Valtzin und pblayin und zinging along,
    Goot lookin shnow, you dond cood done wrong.
Efen of you make on some oldt gal's scheek,
It makes notting tifferent, ofer das shendlesom freak.
Goot lookin shnow, von der glouds py der shky,
You vas bully mit cold vedder, und bully von high.

Oh, dot shnow, dot goot lookin shnow,
Yoost dis vay und dot you make vhen you go;

Fhlyin aroundt, you got matness mit fun,
Und fhreeze makes der nose of efery von ;
   Lafein, runnin, mit gwickness go py,
    Yoost shtobbin a leedle, den pooty gwick fhly ;
Und efen der togs, dot ras out in der vet,
Vood shnab at der bieces vhich makes on dhere hedt.
Der peobles vas grazy, und caddles vood crow
Und say how you vas, you goot lookin shnow.

Und so gwick you vas dhere, und der vedder did shnow,
Dhey shpeak out in dones so shweeder as low,
Und der shleigh-riders, too, vas gone py in der lite,
You dond cood saw dhem, dill quite out of site.
   Schwimmen, shkimmen, fhlirdin dhey go
    Recht on der tob of dot goot lookin shnow.
Dot shnow vas vhite glean vhen it comes der shky down,
Und yoost so muddy like mud, vhen it comes of der
    town,
To been valked on py more as dwo hoondret fife feet,
Dill gwick, vas yoost lookin so phlack like der shtreet.

Vell, I vas yoost lookin vonce so goot like dot shnow,
But I tumbled me off, und vay I did go ;
Nicht so glean, like der mut dot growed on der shtreet,
I vas sheraped von der poots off, of der peobles I meet.
   Dinkin und shworin, I like of I die,
    To been shtiff like a mackerel mit no von to buy,
Vhile I trink me some lager to got a shquare meal,
I vas afraid von der ghosts mine pody vood shteal.
Got in Himmel, how ish dot ? Vas I gone down so low,
Vhen I vonce vas so vhiteness like dot goot lookin
    shnow ?

Yah, for dhrue, I vas told you, I vas vonce pure like
   dot shnow,
Mit blaindy of lofe, von mine heart out vas grow ;
I dink von dhem efery von, und dhey dink von me too,
Und I vas humpugged mit fhladeries, dot's yoost vot
    dhey do.
   Mine Fadder, Mudder, Gabruder der same,

Vas loose me some sympadies, und forget vonce
    mine name.
Und dot raskals who comes of me in der tarkness py nite,
Vood gone more as a plocks to got out of mine site.
Der coat von mine lecks, und poots of mine toe,
Vas not gleaner as doze of dot goot lookin shnow.

It vas gweer it shood been dot dot goot lookin shnow
Vood make on a pad mans mit no vhere to go;
Und how gweer it vood been, vhen yoost pehindt tay,
Ofer der hail und das vind mit mine pody vood pblay,
    Hobbin, skibben, und me dedt like an eel—
    Mine mat vas got oop, nefer a vord cood I shpeil,
To been zeen py der peobles who vas valk ofer der town,
Who vas dickled mit pbleasures, of der shnow vas come
    down,
I yoost lay der ground, und gone died mit a woe,
Mit a pedgwilts und billows, von der goot lookin shnow.

THE CELEBRATED JUMPING FROG.

WITH PERMISSION OF THE AUTHOR.   MARK TWAIN.

There was a feller here once by the name of Jim Smiley,
who was the curiosest man about always betting on anything that turned up you ever see, if he could get anybody
to bet on the other side; and if he couldn't, he'd change
sides. Any way that suited the other man would suit him—
any way just so's he got a bet, he was satisfied. He was
always ready and laying for a chance.

Well, this hyer Smiley had rat-tarriers, and fighting-
cocks, and tom-cats and all them kind of things, till you
couldn't rest, and you couldn't fetch nothing for him to bet
on but he'd match you. He ketched a frog one day, and
took him home, and said he cal'klated to edercate him; and
so he never done nothing for three months but set in his
back yard and learn that frog to jump. And you bet you

he *did* learn him, too. He'd give him a little punch behind, and the next minute you'd see that frog whirling in the air like a doughnut—see him turn one summerset, or may be a couple if he got a good start, and come down flat-footed and all right, like a cat. He got him up so in the matter of catching flies, and kept him in practice so constant, that he'd nail a fly every time as far as he could see him. Smiley said all a frog wanted was education, and he could do most anything—and I believe him. Why, I've seen him set Dan'l Webster down here on this floor—Dan'l Webster was the name of the frog—and sing out, " Flies, Dan'l, flies !" and quicker'n you could wink, he'd spring straight up, and snake a fly off'n the counter there, and flop down on the floor again as solid as a gob of mud, and fall to scratching the side of his head with his hind foot, as indifferent as if he hadn't no idea he'd been doin' any more'n any frog might do. You never see a frog so modest and straightfor'ard as he was, for all he was so gifted. And when it come to fair and square jumping on a dead level, he could get over more ground at one straddle than any animal of his breed you ever see. Jumping on a dead level was his strong suit, you understand ; and when it come to that, Smiley would ante up money on him as long as he had a red. Smiley was monstrous proud of his frog, and well he might be, for fellers that had traveled and been everywheres all said that he laid over any frog that ever *they* see.

Well, Smiley kept the beast in a little lattice box, and he used to fetch him down town sometimes and lay for a bet. One day a feller—a stranger in the camp, he was—come across him with his box, and says:

" What might it be that you've got in the box ?"

And Smiley says, sorter indifferent like, " It might be a parrot, or it might be a canary, may be, but it ain't—it's only jest a frog."

And the feller took it, and looked at it careful and turned

it round this way and that, and says, "H'm—so 'tis. Well, what's *he* good for?"

"Well," Smiley says, easy and careless, "He's good enough for *one* thing, I should judge—he can outjump any frog in Calaveras county."

The feller took the box again, and took another long, particular look, and give it back to Smiley, and says, very deliberate, "Well, I don't see no p'ints about that frog that's any better'n any other frog."

"May be you don't," Smiley says; "may be you understand frogs, and may be you don't understand 'em; may be you've had experience, and may be you ain't only a amature, as it were. Anyways, I've got my opinion, and I'll risk forty dollars that he can outjump anything in Calaveras county."

And the feller studied a minute, and then says, kinder sad like, "Well, I'm only a stranger here, and I ain't got no frog; but if I had a frog I'd bet you."

And then Smiley says, "That's all right—that's all right —if you'll hold my box a minute, I'll go and get you a frog." And so the feller took the box, and put up his forty dollars along with Smiley's, and set down to wait.

So he set there a good while, thinking and thinking to hisself, and then he got the frog out and pried his mouth open and took a teaspoon and filled him full of quail shot —filled him pretty near up to his chin—and set him on the floor. Smiley he went to the swamp and slopped around in the mud for a long time, and finally he ketched a frog, and fetched him in, and give him to this feller, and says:

"Now, if you're ready, set him alongside of Dan'l, with his fore-paws jest even with Dan'l's, and I'll give the word." Then he says, "One, two, three—jump!" and him and the feller touched up the frogs from behind, and the new frog hopped off, but Dan'l give a heave, and hysted up his shoulders, so, like a Frenchman, but it wasn't no use—he couldn't budge; he was planted as solid as an anvil, and he couldn't no more stir than if he was anchored out. Smiley was a good deal surprised, and he was disgusted too, but he didn't have no idea what the matter was, of course.

The feller took the money and started away, and when he was going out at the door he sorter jerked his thumb over his shoulders, this way, at Dan'l, and says again, very deliberate, " Well, *I* don't see no p'ints about that frog that's any better'n any other frog."

Smiley he stood scratching his head and looking down at Dan'l a long time, and at last he says, "I do wonder what in the nation that frog throw'd off for—I wonder if there ain't something the matter with him—he 'pears to look mighty baggy, somehow." And he ketched Dan'l by the nap of the neck and lifted him up and says, " Why, blame my cats if he don't weigh five pound !" and turned him upside down, and he belched out a double handful of shot. And then he see how it was, and he was the maddest man—he set the frog down and took out after that feller, but he never ketched him.

———————— ◆◆◆ ————————

THE "LOST CHORD."

ADELAIDE PROCTOR.

Seated one day at the organ,
  I was weary and ill at ease,
And my fingers wandered idly
  Over the noisy keys.

I do not know what I was playing,
  Or what I was dreaming then ;
But I struck one chord of music,
  Like the sound of a great Amen !

It flooded the crimson twilight,
  Like the close of an angel's psalm,
And it lay on my fevered spirit,
  With a touch of infinite calm.

It quieted pain and sorrow,
  Like love overcoming strife ;
It seemed the harmonious echo
  From our discordant life.

It linked all perplexed meanings
  Into one perfect peace,
And trembled away into silence,
  As if it were loth to cease.

I have sought, but I seek it vainly,
  That one lost chord divine,
That came from the soul of the organ,
  And entered into mine.

It may be that Death's bright angel
  Will speak in that chord again ;
It may be that only in heaven
  I shall hear that grand Amen.

A TALE OF A LEG.

THOMAS MILLER.

Ben Brust was driving his sheep from Newark. Ben
had a fine leg of Northamptonshire mutton slung over his
shoulder, and ever as he drove his sheep along, and got
them nicely together, he turned to admire the joint, and
by a jerk of his arm brought it at the front. "Hev it
boiled," said Ben ; "sup of prime broth, but broth fills one
so soon. It's prime baked over a lot of nice mealy tatoes,
it gives the tatoes sich a flavor. Roasted's better—but,
laws! it meeks me so hungry while turning it, and I half
fill me we' sops in the pan. And he again examined it,
took hold of the shank and felt its weight, then threw it
once more over his shoulder. The fat almost frizzled in the
sun, for the morning was unusually hot. How nice it will
eat—prime red gravy! England's a glorious country! there's
no sich legs of mutton in the world beside, there isn't a leg
like this in foreign parts abroad. It's a blessed country.

But I begin to want my lunch. Or should I stay and make a good dinner at Besthorpe? I think I will, he gives capital shilling dinners. He says he loses two shillings by me every time. I dare say he don't get much. But, laws! everybody don't eat alike; and I dare say, what we' one and another, it pays very well indeed. Who the dickens is yon coming? Why, I declare it's my wife's cousin. Dash him, if he sees this mutton he'll want to fall bones on it! He's sich a fellow for fresh meat."

"Sweet leg of mutton there, Ben," said cousin William, glutting his gaze upon it, as if he would have eaten it with his eyes. "What a nice relish a slice round would but give a pint of ale! I made but a poor breakfast. I never saw a prettier leg than that, Ben."

"It's a real good un," answered Ben, hitching it farther back, "and I mean to hev it done for Sunday's dinner."

"I don't mind going back we' you," said the hungry-looking cousin. "I should enjoy a bit of that mutton on Sunday, Ben, that I should."

"It would be all the better for being hung up a day or two longer," said Ben, who had seen cousin William eat once, "and if I should change my mind, and not hev it cooked on Sunday, it would be a disappointment to you."

"Why, for that matter," answered the persevering cousin, "I could stay as long as it would keep good."

*   *   *   *   *   *   *

"I'll tell you what I'll do," said Ben; "if you'll pay for th' ale, I'll stand a dinner for you at Besthorpe. They charge a shilling, and if you eat a stone of meat, they charge no more. You'll see how I'll teck the landlord in, for he's often grumbled at giving a dinner for a shilling; but we'll sarve him out to-day. Are you in good trim?"

"Capital," said cousin William; "I'm good for half-a-crown's worth, anyhow."

"Then we'll do him, by Jove!" said Ben, rubbing his

hands with delight; "for I'm in beautiful order. He shall hev someat to grumble about this time. I think you and I, cousin, can put as much under our jackets, as any two men in England."

They soon arrived at Besthorpe, and put up at the old "Black Bell."

* * * * * * *

The sheep were put into a neighboring paddock, and Ben began to inquire after dinner.

"It's only just down," said the landlord, looking very hard at cousin William's long jaws, for the host had some skill in the physiognomy of a good trencherman, and he wished his guests had traveled a little farther. "It'll be an hour and a half before it's ready. Hadn't you better go on to Newton?—you'll about get there in time."

"No, thank you," said Ben, winking at his cousin, "we can wait till dinner's ready; the sheep want a bit of a rest." Then calling to the servant-girl, he said, "Here, Mary, just hang this leg of mutton up in a cool place until I go."

The girl obeyed; and as the landlord threw his sharp eye upon it, he said, "It's a prime leg that, Ben; but I think we shall have as good a one to-day."

"Roasted?" said Ben.

"Yes; I'll just see how they are getting on with it," said the landlord, and he went into the back kitchen.

"Roast leg of mutton," said Ben, nudging the cousin with his elbow; "my eyes, William, won't we see the bone before we've done we' it! We'll teck him in."

"We will," answered cousin William, his mouth already watering. "I'll astonish you to-day, Ben."

"We'll make him gape," said Ben, "and eat such a meal as he'll niver forget. Only a shilling, my boy! I'm good for three pounds."

"So am I," answered William, "besides bread and potatoes. Laws! I wish it was but ready."

* * * * * * *

It seemed a long while to wait; but after the first hour there came such a rich smell of roast mutton from the back kitchen, that even Ben and the cousin sat patiently to inhale it, and snuffed up the fragrance with delight, until their appetites rose to "hunger heat."

"Should just like one sop," said Ben. "Laws, what a delicious smell."

"It would spoil your enjoying the last pound," answered William. "I like to start with a clear course. I think I can eat half of it. Just throw the window up, Ben; if I hev this smell much longer, I shall be rushing into the kitchen and fetching it off the hook."

"Dinner's ready," said the landlord, and Ben and the cousin had well-nigh tumbled over each other, in the hurry to reach the parlor; they had not time to think of time.

It was really a fine leg of mutton, and the dish of new potatoes looked beautiful—the landlord had dug them out of his garden. They would have been sufficient for half-a-dozen ordinary people. A new brown loaf stood in the bread-basket.

Ben made a hole in the middle of the leg at the first cut, such as two men, with a fair appetite, might be supposed to leave after they have dined.

Cousin William devoured the largest mouthfuls, but Ben seemed to make the most progress—to take it easier, somehow. He cut his meat in smaller pieces, and ate two to his cousin's one—Ben had excellent teeth. A potato vanished at every mouthful—not one was cut—they seemed to go down whole. "Don't spare it," said Ben, having finished his first huge plateful. "Just the same to pay if we eat it all! Beautiful, isn't it?"

"Ah! quite heavenly," answered the cousin, casting a loving glance at the joint, then helping himself to another tremendous slice, and adding, "Eating's hard work, Ben;" and he took off his neckcloth and smock-frock and threw them on the floor. Ben ate on, and seemed not to put himself out of the way. He was like a man who, being perfectly master of his trade, feels no doubt of finishing his task in first-rate style, and goes on easily and leisurely ; while the cousin, scarcely so perfect a hand, seemed to make a labor of it.

"It looks very queer now," said Ben, laying down his knife and fork, and taking a close survey of the joint, which looked like a bottle with nearly the whole centre gone, and only the bottom and neck left. "He'll not save a fortune out of us, I think."

"He'll remember our shilling dinner the longest day he has to live." And Ben glanced at the remainder of the leg and smiled—the sight of it pleased him, for it looked almost all bone. "It weighs six pounds lighter than it did," said Ben, "I'll warrant it ;" and his fat sides shook with delight. Then he laughed outright as he thought how they had taken the host in.

"Eating takes away one's appetite after we've swallowed the first two pounds," said William.

"It does," answered Ben. "I think a man, according to his size, eats the least of anything. Look what a truss of hay a horse can get through. Now I think we ought to eat as much accordingly; then a leg of mutton for one man would be a fair meal. Laws, cousin! lay down four or five pound of meat beside me—then look at my size— why, it seems like nowt !"

"No more it don't," replied the cousin.

*   *   *   *   *   *   *

Cousin William took up the last potato and cut it in two. It was the first one that had been halved. He dipped it in salt and gravy, and had difficulty to swallow it. He was full to the very throat. They had eaten like famished wolves.

"Now, then, we'll be jogging on the road," said William; "and I'll pull the bell, to see what's to pay. The two shillings for dinner you're to stand, Ben. I'll pay for the ale."

"All right," answered Ben, and the landlord entered the room. They both cast down their eyes, for (to do them justice) they felt half-ashamed of looking either at the landlord or the mangled skeleton that lay on the dish.

"I'm glad to see you've made sich a famous dinner," said the landlord, smiling.

"We've done very fairly indeed," replied Ben, now looking up under such encouragement. "What's to pay?"

"There's nothing to pay, Ben," answered the host; "potatoes, bread, ale and cooking you're welcome to, and I'm glad to get off so cheap. The leg of mutton was your own, Ben, and I hope it was done to your liking!"

"What?" said Ben, not fully comprehending the host's meaning; "you don't mean to say that we've been eating that leg of mutton I brought!"

"The very same," answered the host, laughing. "I put it down to roast myself."

Ben stared at the landlord in silence, and, after a long pause, he said, "Why, it cost me six shillings. It's a regular swindle," continued Ben, "and I'll hev an action-at-law against you. Here you pretend to give a man a dinner for a shilling, and set before him his own joint that cost six shillings, which he eats up and loses five by it; I'll never use your house again. What do I care about your few potatoes, your bit of bread and drop of ale? I'll have my leg of mutton, if I get it out of your bones."

Cousin William could scarcely keep his seat for laughing; he shook from head to foot, as he exclaimed, "So I've dined off that prime leg after all. Ben, you're done this time."

"I niver was so teeken in before in my life," said Ben. "Next time I dine anywhere, and hev a joint we' me, I'll keep it tied round my shoulder all the while I eat. Dash your wig, landlord, you've done me this time, but I'll be even we' you yet!"

THAT WEST-SIDE DOG, OR WILLIAM NYE IN CHICAGO.

B. F. WILKIE.

There is a family out on the west-side who had a visit one day from a strange dog. He walked in while they were at breakfast, gave them a friendly shake of his tail, and then sat down and waited expectantly for a bone, just as though he had always lived there.

He was not a handsome dog. His father must have been a mighty mean-looking dog, and his mother must have looked meaner than his father, while he inherited all their mean looks, and had picked up a few additional ones on his own account. He was short-legged, with great splay feet that turned out, a big body, a head like a big, dirty lump of dough, and a mouth that opened as far back as an oyster's.

He was given a bone and requested to put out, which he proceeded not to do by being suddenly possessed with the idea that there was some lurking danger in the coal-house, which only he was competent to master. Then he went for rats behind the house, and then he proceeded to open on some boys who were playing tag on a vacant lot. He did all these things to prove that he was a valuable dog. But the thing didn't win. He was finally chased into the street, and around two blocks.

A half an hour later, that same dog walked into the kitchen, wagging his tail as if he wished to invite attention to the fact that he had been engaged in arduous labor for the benefit of the family, and would take another bone for his reward. For three days was that dog kicked out, broom-sticked out, mop-sticked out, while his retreat was harassed by old shoes, bricks, pieces of stove-wood, and chunks of coal; but it was all of no use. He always left on such occasions with an appearance of the most abject terror, and would be back in ten minutes with a sunny smile on his open mouth, and a friendly wag in his tail, as if he was rejoiced to see everybody, and he knew everybody was equally rejoiced to see him.

Having thrown a couple of cords of wood at him, and a ton or so of coal, the woman of the house, who is a great strategist, and abounding in resources, resolved to economize in fuel and to try something else. With this view, she hunted up an old tea-kettle and a piece of stout twine. Inside the kettle were put tin things, so that when the kettle was shaken it was a musical instrument of very high power. And then William Nye—that was his name—was invited into the sitting-room. He was rather amazed at such unwonted condescension, but, supposing it the reward for having just throttled a pet cat belonging to a little girl next door, he came in with the air of a conqueror.

And then to William's tail the young woman proceeded to attach the piece of twine, with a double and a half hitch. Mr. Nye, looking upon the matter as a decoration for his gallantry in the cat business, took the process with great equanimity. When it was all hitched, William was pointed to the other door, and insinuatingly invited to " sick 'im !" as if there were another cat or two.

William was a willing dog, and so he up and got, to "sick 'im." He proceeded to start for the door, and, in doing so, hauled taut the piece of twine, whose other end, it may be remarked, had been attached with great care to the tea-kettle. This strain excited Mr. Nye's curiosity, and he turned himself about, and smelt first of the hitch on his tail, and then transferred his investigations to the tea-kettle. He seemed to discover nothing very suspicious, and, supposing everything right, he resolved to make up for lost time, and made a vigorous lunge after the hypothetical cats. This brought the tea-kettle with a heavy impact against the rear-guard of Mr. Nye's column. The result was a panic.

It had been expected that when Mr. Nye took up his march, it would be through the kitchen door, thence into the street, thence straight ahead in a direct line for Calumet or Bridgeport. But the parlor door happened to be open, and Mr. Nye shot through it.

It was a thrilling affair, and lasted some time. William laid down his ears, and commenced making the circuit of the parlor at a rate so rapid that one couldn't tell whether it was the dog running away with the tea-kettle or the tea-kettle running away with the dog. The first eight times around he knocked down the etagere, and smashed in the lower panes of the book-case. The next eleven times around, he knocked down three flower-pots, broke a molding off the sofa, and smashed three costly vases. Every time he went around he made a big "dent" in each leg of the piano, until, at the last, they loooked like sticks of cord-wood.

In all, with his ears flat down, his tongue out eighteen inches, and his mouth open like a carpet-sack, he went around till he had knocked off all the plastering within two feet of the floor, chipped all the furniture, and then he made a bolt through the window, smashing a large pane of glass, went through the gate, and thence down the street, rattling and clattering as though he were a runaway tin-pedler's cart.

And that's the last that was ever seen of William Nye by that west-side family. All that could be said of him was that, like sorrow, he had been, and left his traces there.

HOW DENNIS TOOK THE PLEDGE.

ANONYMOUS.

A Limerick Irishman named Dennis, addicted to strong drink, was often urged by his friends to sign the pledge, but with no avail, until one day they read to him from a newspaper an account of a man who had become so thoroughly saturated with alcohol, that, on attempting to blow out a candle, his breath ignited, and he was instantly blown to.atoms. Dennis' face showed mingled horror and contrition, and his friends thought that the long-desired moment of repentance was at hand.

"Bring me the book, boys, bring me the book! Troth, his breath took fire, did it? Sure I'll niver die that death, anyhow;" said Dennis, with the most solemn countenance imaginable. "Hear me now, boys, hear me now. I, Dennis Finnegan, knowin' my great weakness, deeply sinsible of my past sins, an' the great danger I've been in, hereby take me solemn oath that, so long as I live, under no provocation whativer, will I—*blow out a candil agin!*"

THE FISHERMAN'S SUMMONS.

ANONYMOUS.

The sea is calling, calling!
　Wife, is there a log to spare?
Fling it down on the hearth and call them in,
The boys and girls with their merry din,
I am loth to leave you all just yet;
In the light and the noise I might forget
　The voice in the evening air.

The sea is calling, calling,
　Along the hollow shore;
I know each nook in the rocky strand,
And the crimson weeds on the golden sand,
And the worn old cliff where the sea-pinks cling,
And the winding caves where the echoes ring—
　I shall wake them never more.

How it keeps calling, calling,
　It is never a night to sail;
I saw the "sea-dog" over the height,
As I strained through the haze my failing sight,
And the cottage creaks and rocks, well nigh
As the old "Fox" did in the days gone by,
　In the moan of the rising gale.

Yet it is calling, calling;
  It is hard on a soul, I say,
To go fluttering out in the cold and the dark,
Like the bird they tell us of, from the ark,
While the foam flies thick on the bitter blast,
And the angry waves roll fierce and fast,
  Where the black buoy marks the bay.

  Do you hear it calling, calling?
  And yet, I am none so old.
At the herring fishery, but last year,
No boat beat mine for tackle and gear,
And I steered the cobble past the reef,
When the broad sail shook like a withered leaf,
  And the rudder chafed my hold.

  Will it never stop calling, calling?
  Can't you sing a song by the hearth—
A heartsome stave of a merry glass,
Or a gallant fight, or a bonny lass?
Don't you care for your grand-dad just so much
Come near, then, give me a hand to touch,
  Still warm with the warmth of earth.

  You hear it calling, calling?
  Ask her why she sits and cries.
She always did when the sea was up,
She would fret, and never take bit or sup,
When I and the lads were out at night,
And she saw the breakers cresting white
  Beneath the low black skies.

  But then, in its calling, calling,
No summons to soul was sent.
Now—well, fetch the parson, find the book,
It is up on the shelf there, if you look;
The sea has been friend, and fire, and bread;
Put me where it will tell of me, lying dead,
  How it called, and I rose and went.

BADGER'S DEBUT AS HAMLET.

READ BY J. M. BELLEW.   LITCHFIELD MOSELEY.

"That's something like a bill," said Jobson, the manager, holding it against the wall, and addressing me as I entered his sanctum.   It read as follows:

, Reopening of the Theatre Royal, Slushington.   Under the sole management of Mr. Leonardo Jobson.

Engagement of the celebrated American Tragedian, Mr. Titus B. Badger, (from the principal theatres of the United States, California, New Zealand, the Sandwich Islands, the Carribees and Timbuctoo), who will appear in his great impersonation of Hamlet, as performed by him for 1231 nights with the greatest success.

The entire press of the two hemispheres has unanimously pronounced this gentleman to be the only successor to Edmund Kean.

He will be supported by a powerful Company, selected from the principal Metropolitan Theatres.

After which will be presented an entirely New and Original Farce, entitled "Skedaddling."

Notwithstanding the enormous expense of this engagement, there will be no advance in the prices.

"That's something like a bill," again said Jobson, stepping back a few paces in order more fully to admire it. "What do you think of it, eh?"

I had picked up a slight acquaintance with the manager, who was—to use the mildest term possible—a theatrical adventurer, with as many aliases as there are letters in the alphabet; one of those sharp individuals whose trickiness brings the stage into disrepute.

"A very taking poster," I replied.

"Think so?" said he.   "There's one fault in it—Badger's name isn't half *large* enough.   You wouldn't believe the difference that an inch or two of type makes to a tragedian.   Supposing I leave that bill as it is, nobody will think anything of Badger. Give him *two*-inch letters, people will glance at the name, and pass on; increase them to *four*, and they'll wonder who Badger is; put him in *twelve*-inch type, and we shan't know where to seat the people. I'm having some posters done now with letters four feet high, and nothing on them but 'BADGER;' and if they don't draw in the public my name's not—Bless me! if I know what my name is!"

"I should not have thought it," I replied.

"Shouldn't you? Why, if we had Phelps down here, and only gave him ordinary type, I don't believe we should have fifty people in the house."

"Indeed! But who is Badger?" I asked. "I never heard of him."

"No more has anybody else. But we're going to have a dress rehearsal directly, and you shall see him."

"Does he come from America?"

"Not a bit of it. He's a stage-struck young idiot from the Bow-road, who's never been farther west than Pimlico. His name's Tibbetts, and he's clerk to a shoemaker in the city. He fancies he has a genius for tragedy, and has paid me twenty pounds to allow him to appear here. Fact! My company never costs me anything for salaries. I always make 'em pay me for the privilege of performing. It suits my pocket, it pleases them, and so neither of us grumble. Mugford!" This was to one of the carpenters.

"Thir," said Mugford, who suffered from a lisp.

"Have you finished those skulls yet—Yorick's and the other two?"

"Yeth, Mithter Jobthon, thir. I've bought three big thwede turnipth, and I've covered 'em over with brown paper, and I think they'll do, thir."

"Very well."

Exit Mugford and enter Ikey.

"Now, Ikey, what do you want?"

"Please sir, we can't get no earth for Hamlick's grave,

so you'll have to do with a bag o' silver sand; and please, sir, the rehearsal bell's a-ringing."

"That'll do. Now, sir, follow me, if you please," and the manager led the way onto the stage.

"Ah, Mr. Badger, allow me to introduce you to this gentleman—Mr. Badger, Mr. Robinson. Proud to make two eminent men acquainted with each other. Mr. Badger, sir," said Jobson, turning to me—"Mr. Badger is a young man brimming over with talent—genius, sir, positive genius. All fire, sir—all fire."

Perhaps his having been all fire accounted for his scarcity of flesh. He was an overgrown, shambling lad, of about twenty, with a cast in one eye, a snub nose, red hair, a wide mouth, and an unpleasant smile.

"'Ope I see you well, sir," said Badger, grinning sheepishly, and sliding a damp paw into my hand.

"Well, Mr. Badger, I suppose you're going to astonish us all down here."

"I 'ope so, sir."

"I hope so too," I rejoined.

"Now, then, clear the stage for the rehearsal!" said Jobson. "Where are you all?—King! Queen! Hamlet! Polonius! Rosencrantz! Guildenstern! Horatius! Marcellus! Bernardo!"

"Here!" "Here!" "Here! Mr. Jobson."

"Tompkins! run up to the flies with some nails and the glue-pot, and tinker up that castle-wall a bit; and Ikey! pull up that sky, and let the moon down two or three feet lower. Hi! what's that smoke? What are you burning in that moon—eh?"

"Kerosene, sir."

"Put it out! put it out directly! I won't have a kerosene moon. I won't have a drop of kerosene in the place. Burn candle-ends."

"Right, sir."

"Mr. Dawbs! Mr. Dawbs! where *is* Mr. Dawbs?"

" Here, sir."

" What's the meaning of all those holes in that horizon-cloth—eh ?"

" They're stars, sir."

"Stars, sir ! stars ! Why, some of your stars are bigger than the moon ; they're not stars, they're comets ! meteors, sir ! meteors ! Cover 'em over directly !"

" Certainly, sir," said the crestfallen Dawbs ; and the rehearsal commenced.

In the opening scene I heard fragments being given thus :

King. Though yet of a—Hamlet, our dear ber-rother's death
The mem'ry be ger-reen ; and that it is befitted
To bear our a—hearts in ger-rief, and our whole Kingdom
To be contracted by one ber-row of woe, &c.

Queen. (with a strong Scotch accent). Gude Hamlet, cast thee
        neeghted coolor off,
An' let theen 'ee look like a friend on Dinmork ;
Do not for eever wi' thee vailed lids
Seek for the nooble feyther in the doost.
Thee knawest 'tis common, a' that leeves must dee,
Passin' thraw nature to eternit*ee*.
Wha' seem ye then to fret about 'un, mon ?

Hamlet (jerkily). Seems, madam. Nay, *hit his*.
Hi know not seems.
It ain't alone my *hinky* cloke, good mother,
Nor customary suits of *sollum* black,
Nor windy perspiration nor forced breath ;
But *Hi* 'are that within which passeth show.
These 'ere the trappings *hand* the suits o' woe.

" Green !" interrupted Jobson, " see that those two egg-boxes for the throne steps are painted red before we rehearse again."

And having seen as much of the rehearsal as I wanted, I bade Jobson " Good morning," and left the theatre.

Monday evening arrived in due course, and the Theatre Royal, Slushington, was crowded. Badger was much ap-

plauded on his appearance; but as soon as he found himself before the audience, his voice became totally inaudible.
At length a gentleman in the gallery shouted, "Speak up,
undertaker!" which had the effect of increasing his ner-
vousness to such an extent, that Hamlet's part in the
Ghost scene became merely a piece of dumb show; during
which the grumblings of the "gods," at first "not loud, but
deep," ripened into an angry roar, and culminated in a
clamor for "Hot Codlings," or "Tipetywichit," intermin-
gled with cries of "Go home," and "Bravo, Shakespeare."
Badger, however—who, it soon became evident, had had
recourse to a stimulant—plodded on somewhat after this
fashion :

   Hamlet. 'Tis now the very witchin' hour hof night,
When churchyards yawn, and 'ell itself breathes out
Contagion to this world. Now—now
   Prompter (at wing). Now could I drink hot blood.
   Hamlet. Now could I drink 'ot blood,
And do a bit o' business that the day
Would quake to look on.
Oh 'art, lose not thy nature, let not *h*ever
The soul o' Nero henter this firm bosom, &c.

In the churchyard scene, Badger made a great, but un-
expected hit. In declaiming the famous speech—

   What is he whose grief bears such an hemphasis?
   Whose phase of sorrow
  · Conjures the wondering stars, and makes them stand
   Like wonder-wounded 'earers. This *h*is *Hi !*
   'Amlet, the Dane—

He kept backing step by step, until—forgetting its prox-
imity—he missed his footing, and turned a back somer-
sault into Ophelia's grave, burying himself so effectually
that the two grave-diggers had to extricate him from his
living tomb, amid roars of laughter from the audience. In
this mishap he also lost his black wig, and played the remainder of the tragedy in his own red hair.

But the climax was reached in the last scene; when,

having killed Laertes, Hamlet wrests the poisoned cup from the attendant's hand. In flinging it away it hit the dead Laertes on the nose; whereupon, that gentleman—who was of a fiery temperament—sprang up, and striding to Hamlet, asked "Whether he did that on purpose? as, if so, he felt inclined to give him something for himself." Here the other performers interfered; and Laertes having been coaxed to die again peaceably, the tragedy was suffered to proceed. The curtain had barely fallen on "Hamlet," before some half score scene-shifters and carpenters, headed by Green, came running onto the stage. After a short pause, Green—who was an Irishman—pulled off his cap, and making a low bow, said:

"Plaze yer honors, axing yer honors' pardon—I should be afther saying, Ladies and Gintlemen—the manager—bad 'cess to him—has been and gone and boulted with the resates, and he's forgotten to pay us our wages. Sure an' its hard loines for me mates an' me, as has got twelve small childern—mostly under the age o' four—to pervide for, to be done out of our airnings in this way by a thafe as he is. Och! bad luck to ould Jobson; as I'd be afther wishin' him to his face if he was here now. And, plaze yer honors, I'm half ashamed to ax ye; but one o' the bhoys will stand by the door with the cap, and if so be as ye've got a few coppers to spare, we shall all feel very grateful to ye." Here the speaker was answered by a smart shower of small coin on the stage. "Hooray! for yer honors' ginerous hearts. Good luck to ye, and may ye live for iver, and die at a grane old age. Kape up the supply, gintlemen, and don't be afraid as we shall complain o' the throuble o' pickin' 'em up. May the blissins o' the missis and the young 'uns be upon ye, and thank ye for me; and may ye niver be afther knowin' what it is to feel the wants of a penny."

And this was the finish of Badger's *debut*.

HOW HEZEKIAH STOLE THE SPOONS.

ANONYMOUS.

In a quiet little Ohio village, many years ago, was a tavern where the stages always changed, and the passengers expected to get breakfast. The landlord of the said hotel was noted for his tricks upon travelers, who were allowed to get fairly seated at the table, when the driver would blow his horn (after taking his "horn"), and sing out, "Stage ready, gentlemen!"—whereupon the passengers were obliged to hurry out to take their seats, leaving a scarcely tasted breakfast behind them, for which, however, they had to fork over fifty cents! One day, when the stage was approaching the house of this obliging landlord, a passenger said that he had often heard of the landlord's trick, and he was afraid they would not be able to eat any breakfast.

"What!—how? No breakfast!" exclaimed the rest.

"Exactly so, gents, and you may as well keep your seats and tin."

"Don't they expect passengers to breakfast?"

"Oh, yes! they expect you to it, but not to *eat* it. I am under the impression that there is an understanding between the landlord and the driver, that for sundry and various drinks, &c., the latter starts before you can scarcely commence eating."

"What on airth are you all talking about? Ef you calkelate I'm going to pay four-and ninepence for my breakfast, and not get the valee on't, you're mistaken," said a voice from a back seat, the owner of which was one Hezekiah Spaulding—though "tew hum" they call him "Hez" for short. "I'm goin' to get my breakfast here, and not pay nary red cent till I do."

"Then you'll be left."

"Not as you knows on, I guess I won't."

"Well, we'll see," said the other, as the stage drove up

to the door, and the landlord, ready " to do the hospitable," says—

" Breakfast just ready, gents! Take a wash, gents?
Here's water, basins, towels, and soap."

After performing the ablutions, they all proceeded to
the dining-room, and commenced a fierce onslaught upon
the edibles, though Hez took his time. Scarcely had they
tasted their coffee, when they heard the unwelcome sound
of the horn, and the driver exclaim—" Stage ready!" Up
rise eight grumbling passengers, pay their fifty cents, and
take their seats.

" All on board, gents?" inquires the host.

" One missing," said they.

Proceeding to the dining-room, the host finds Hez very
coolly helping himself to an immense piece of steak, the
size of a horse's hip.

" You'll be left, sir! Stage going to start!"

" Wall, I hain't got nothin' agin it," drawls out Hez.

' Can't wait, sir—better take your seat."

" I'll be gall-darned ef I dew, nother, till I've got my
breakfast! I paid for it, and I am goin' to get the valee
on't; and ef you calkelate I hain't, you are mistaken."

So the stage did start, and left Hez, who continued his
attack upon the edibles. Biscuits, coffee, &c., disappeared
before the eyes of the astonished landlord.

" Say, squire, them there cakes is 'bout eat—fetch on
another grist on 'em. You " (to the waiter), " 'nother cup
of that ere coffee. Pass them eggs. Raise your own pork,
squire? This is 'mazin' nice ham. Land 'bout here toler-
able cheap, squire? Hain't much maple timber in these
parts, hev ye? Dew right smart trade, squire, I calkelate?" And thus Hez kept quizzing the landlord until he
had made a hearty meal.

" Say, squire, now I'm 'bout to conclude paying my de-
vowers tew this ere table, but jest give us a bowl of bread
and milk to top off with; I'd be much obleeged tew ye."

So out go the landlord and waiter for the bowl, milk, and bread, and set them before him.

"Spoon, tew, ef you please.'"

But no spoon could be found. Landlord was sure he had plenty of silver ones lying on the table when the stage stopped.

"Say, dew ye? dew ye think them passengers is goin' to pay ye for a breakfuss and not git no *compensashun?*"

"Ah! what? Do you think any of the passengers took them?"

"Dew I *think?*" No, I don't think, but I'm sartin. Ef they are all as green as yew 'bout here, I'm going to locate immediately, and tew wonst."

The landlord rushes out to the stable, and starts a man off after the stage, which had gone about three miles. The man overtakes the stage, and says something to the driver, in a low tone. He immediately turns back, and on arriving at the hotel, Hez comes out, takes his seat, and says—

"How are yew, gents? I'm rotted glad to see yew."

"Can you point out the man you think has the spoons?" asked the landlord.

"P'int him out? Sartinly I ken. Say, squire, I paid yew four-and-ninepence for a breakfuss, and I calkelate *I got the valee on't!* You'll find them spoons in the coffee-pot."

"Go ahead! All aboard, driver."

The landlord stared.

PADDY'S DREAM.

ANONYMOUS.

I have often laughed at the way an Irish help we had at Barnstaple once fished me for a glass of whiskey. One morning he says to me—"Oh, yer honor," says he, "I had a great drame last night intirely—I dramed I was in

Rome, tho' how I got there is more than I can tell; but
there I was, sure enough; and as in duty bound, what does
I do but go and see the Pope. Well, it was a long journey,
and it was late when I got there—too late for the likes of
me; and when I got to the palace I saw priests, and
bishops, and cardinals, and all the great dignitaries of the
Church a coming out; and sais one of them to me, ' How
are ye, Pat Moloney?' sais he; 'and that spalpeen yer
father, bad luck to him, how is he?' It startled me to
hear me own name so suddent, that it came mighty nigh
waking me up, it did. Sais I, ' Your riverence, how in the
world did ye know that Pat Moloney was me name, let
alone that of me father?'—'Why, ye blackguard,' sais he,
'I knew ye since ye was knee-high to a goose, and I knew
yer mother afore ye was born.'—'It's good right yer honor
has then to know me,' sais I.—'Bad manners to ye,' sais
he, 'what is it ye are afther doing here at this time o'
night?'—'To see his Holiness the Pope,' sais I.—'That's
right,' sais he; 'pass on, but leave yer impudence with
yer hat and shoes at the door.' Well, I was shown into a
mighty fine room where his Holiness was, and down I went
on me knees. 'Rise up, Pat Moloney,' sais his Holiness;
'ye're a broth of a boy to come all the way from Ireland to
do yer duty to me; and it's dutiful children ye are, every
mother's son of ye. What will ye have to drink, Pat?'
(The greater a man is, the more of a rael gintleman he is,
yer honor, and the more condescending.)—'What will ye
have to drink, Pat?' sais he.—'A glass of whiskey, yer
Holiness,' sais I, 'if it's all the same to ye.'—'Shall it be
hot or cold?' sais he.—'Hot,' sais I, 'if it's all the same,
and gives ye no trouble.'—'Hot it shall be,' sais he; 'but
as I have dismissed all me servants for the night, I'll just step
down below for the tay-kettle;'—and wid that he left the
room, and was gone for a long time; and jist as he came
to the door again he knocked so loud the noise woke me
up, and, be jabers! I missed me whiskey entirely! Be-

dad, if I had only had the sense to say 'Nate, yer Holiness,' I'd a had me whiskey sure enough, and never known it warn't all true, instead of a drame." I knew what he wanted, so I poured him out a glass. "Won't it do as well now, Pat?" said I. "Indeed it will, yer honor," says he, "and me drame will come true, after all. I thought it would, for it was mighty natural at the time, all but the whiskey."

VICTUALS AND DRINK.

MOTHER GOOSE FOR OLD FOLKS.   ANONYMOUS.

"There once was a woman, and what do you think?
She lived upon nothing but victuals and drink;
Victuals and drink were the chief of her diet,
And yet this poor woman scarce ever was quiet."

And were you so foolish as really to think
That all she could want was her victuals and drink?
And that while she was furnished with that sort of diet,
Her feeling and fancy would starve and be quiet?

Mother Goose knew far better, but thought it sufficient,
To give a mere hint that the fare was deficient;
For I do not believe she could ever have meant
To imply there was reason for being content.

Yet the mass of mankind is uncommonly slow
To acknowledge the fact it behooves them to know;
Or to learn that a woman is not like a mouse,
Needing nothing but cheese, and the walls of a house.

But just take a man,—shut him up for a day;
Get his hat and his cane—put them snugly away,
Give him stockings to mend, and three sumptuous meals,
And then ask him at night—if you dare—how he feels!
Do you think he will quietly stick to the stocking,
While you read the news, and don't care about talking?"

Oh, many a woman goes starving, I ween,
Who lives in a palace, and fares like a queen;
Till the famishing heart and the feverish brain
Have spelled out to life's end the long lesson of pain.

Yet stay! To my mind an uneasy suggestion
Comes up, that there may be two sides to the question;
That, while here and there proving inflicted privation,
The verdict must often be, "willful starvation,"
Since there *are* men and women would force one to think
They *choose* to live only on victuals and drink.

O restless and craving, unsatisfied hearts,
Whence never the vulture of hunger departs.
How long on the husks of your life will ye feed,
Ignoring the soul and her famishing need?

Bethink you, when lulled in your shallow content,
'Twas to Lazarus only the angels were sent;
And 'tis he to whose lips but earth's ashes are given,
For whom the full banquet is gathered in heaven!

------ ◆◆◆ ------

HOW JAKE SCHNEIDER WENT BLIND.

ANONYMOUS.

In Germantown, near Philadelphia, several years ago, a native, simple-minded Dutchman, named Jacob Schneider, kept a liquor and lager-bier saloon. Jacob was not only fond of drinking lager with his customers, but would not refuse either corn-juice, red-eye, or Jersey lightning, when asked to imbibe thereof in a social way—the customer, of course, paying an extra half-dime for Jacob's drink. One would not suppose that this friendly habit could, by any possibility, bring trouble and vexation upon honest Jacob, but it did, as we shall presently show.

One eventful night it was observed that Schneider had shut up his saloon and gone home full an hour earlier than usual. Being asked, next day, what was the matter, he told the following droll story :

"I shut up mine blace pecause I vas mat as ter tyfel, and vas humpugged into der pargain. I'll tell you 'pout it. Yer see, dree or four young sheamps gomes into mine saloon, and one says to me, ' Yacob, you got some fresh lager ?' I says ' yaas,' and I draws der lager ; anoder von says he vants gards, and I prings de gards, and da blays gards. Pimeby noder says, ' Yacob, old poy, let's have some ret-eye ; and mind you, Yacob, pring an extra glass for yourself.' Vell den, I prings der pottle of ret-eye, and da drinks two dree dimes, and I drinks mit 'em two dree dimes ; and I gets so tauf trunk dat I lies down on der pench and goes to shleep. Ven I vakes up, der room ish dark as der tyfel, put I hears der young chaps calling der gards ; von says, ' bass !' nodder says, ' left power !—right power !' den nodder von, he says, ' uker'd !' and shwears like a drooper. Da vas all blaying at der taple, shust as da vas ven I goes to shleep, but mine eyes vas nix—I could shust see notting at all—the room vas bitch dark. So I dinks I vas plind, and I feel pad, and I cry out, ' O, mine Gott ! I p'lieve I'm shtruck plind !'—Den der young chaps leaves der table and gomes vhere I vas, and makes p'leeve da very sorry. One says, ' Poor Yacob ! you no can see— vat vill der poor man's vamerly do !' Nodder call me poor cuss, and says I no pusiness to trink noding stronger dan lager. I got mat den—mat as dunder—and I says to him, ' Vy, den, you vants me to drink it mit you ? I p'leeve you put shtuff in der liquor to make me plind !' Den he laughs at me, and says I needn't trink if I didn't pe a mind to. Shust den von little poy gomes to der door mit a lantern, and I finds out der drick da vas blaying me—I see shust as goot as ever ! Der rascals had plow out der lights, and make p'leeve play uker to vool me ! I told 'em 'twas all humpug, and they petter glear out, for I vouldn't light up no more. Dat's vat mine shaloon vas shut up for."

AURELIA'S UNFORTUNATE YOUNG MAN.

MARK TWAIN.

The facts in the following case came to me by letter from a young lady who lives in the beautiful city of San José; she is perfectly unknown to me, and simply signs herself "Aurelia Maria," which may possibly be a fictitious name. But no matter, she, poor girl, is almost heart-broken by the misfortunes she has undergone, and so confused by the conflicting counsels of misguided friends and insidious enemies, that she does not know what course to pursue in order to extricate herself from the web of difficulties in which she seems almost hopelessly involved. In this dilemma she turns to me for help, and supplicates for my guidance and instruction with a moving eloquence that would touch the heart of a statue. Hear her sad story:

She says that when she was sixteen years old she met and loved, with all the devotion of her passionate nature, a young man from New Jersey, named Williamson Breckinridge Caruthers, who was some six years her senior. They were engaged, with the free consent of their friends and relatives, and for a time it seemed as if their career was destined to be characterized by an immunity from sorrow beyond the usual lot of humanity. But at last the tide of fortune turned; young Caruthers became infected with small-pox of the most virulent type, and when he recovered from his illness, his face was pitted like a waffle-mould, and his comeliness gone forever. Aurelia thought to break off the engagement at first, but pity for her unfortunate lover caused her to postpone the marriage-day for a season, and give him another trial.

The very day before the wedding was to have taken place, Breckinridge, while absorbed in watching the flight of a balloon, walked into a well and fractured one of his legs, and it had to be taken off above the knee. Again Aurelia was moved to break the engagement, but again love triumphed, and she set the day forward and gave him another chance to reform.

And again misfortune overtook the unhappy youth. He lost one arm by the premature discharge of a Fourth-of-July cannon, and within three months he got the other pulled out by a carding machine. Aurelia's heart was almost crushed by these latter calamities. She could not but be deeply grieved to see her lover passing from her by piecemeal, feeling, as she did, that he could not last forever under this disastrous process of reduction, yet knowing of no way to stop its dreadful career; and in her tearful despair she almost regretted, like brokers who hold on and lose, that she had not taken him at first, before he had suffered such alarming depreciation. Still her brave soul bore her up, and she resolved to bear with her friend's unnatural disposition yet a little longer.

Again the wedding-day approached, and again disappointment overshadowed it; Caruthers fell ill with the erysipelas, and lost the use of one of his eyes entirely. The friends and relatives of the bride, considering that she had already put up with more than could be reasonably expected of her, now came forward and insisted that the match should be broken off; but after wavering awhile, Aurelia, with a generous spirit that did her credit, said she had reflected calmly on the matter, and could not discover that Breckinridge was to blame.

So she extended the time once more, and he broke his other leg.

It was a sad day for the poor girl when she saw the surgeons reverently bearing away the sack whose uses she had learnt by previous experience, and her heart told her the bitter truth that some more of her lover was gone. She felt that the field of her affections was growing more and more circumscribed every day, but once more she frowned down her relatives and renewed her betrothal.

Shortly before the time set for the nuptials another dis-

aster occurred. There was but one man scalped by the
Owens River Indians last year. That man was Williamson
Breckinridge Caruthers, of New Jersey. He was hurrying
home with happiness in his heart, when he lost his hair forever, and in that hour of bitterness he almost cursed the mistaken mercy that had spared his head.

At last Aurelia is in serious perplexity as to what she
ought to do. She still loves her Breckinridge, she writes,
with true womanly feeling—she still loves what is left of
him, but her parents are bitterly opposed to the match,
because he has no property and is disabled from working,
and she has not sufficient means to support both comfort-
ably. "Now what should she do?" she asks with painful
and anxious solicitude.

It is a delicate question; it is one which involves the
lifelong happiness of a woman, and that of nearly two-
thirds of a man, and I feel that it would be assuming too
great a responsibility to do more than make a mere suggestion in the case. How would it do to build to him?
If Aurelia can afford the expense, let her furnish her mu-
tilated lover with wooden arms and wooden legs, and a
glass eye and a wig, and give him another show; give him
ninety days, without grace, and if he does not break his
neck in the meantime, marry him and take the chances.
It does not seem to me that there is much risk, any way,
Aurelia, because if he sticks to his infernal propensity for
damaging himself every time he sees a good opportunity,
his next experiment is bound to finish him, and then you
are all right, you know, married or single. If married, the
wooden legs and such other valuables as he may possess
revert to the widow, and you see you sustain no actual loss
save the cherished fragment of a noble but unfortunate
husband, who honestly strove to do right, but whose extraordinary instincts were against him. Try it, Maria!
I have thought the matter over carefully and well, and it
is the only chance I see for you. It would have been a

happy conceit on the part of Caruthers if he had started
with his neck and broken that first; but since he has seen
fit to choose a different policy, and string himself out as
long as possible, I do not think we ought to upbraid him
for it if he has enjoyed it. We must do the best we can
under the circumstances, and try not to feel exasperated
at him.

MRS. BROWN ON MODERN HOUSES.

ARTHUR SKETCHLEY.

Houses, indeed! I calls 'em reg'lar ram-shackle nut-
shells, run-up rubbish, where you can't drive a nail with
safety, nor hang up a picter with comfort.

Certainly they was elegant outside, with their white
fronts and 'andsome windows to look at; but I never see
such glass to look through, as made things seem that
drawed out as you didn't know the postman from the pot-
boy.

As to anythin' a-fittin', there wasn't a window-frame as
didn't shake like earthquakes with me only a-walkin' across
the room; and as to the Butlers, as lives next door but
three, they give a evenin' party as brought the floor in.

They invited me and Brown, as didn't wish for to go,
bein' one as don't hold with no goin's out through a-takin
of his pipe quiet in the front kitchen, as is a pretty room,
bein' meant for a sittin'-room; not as ever I fancied it,
havin' a mouldy smell, and bein' frequent overflowed in
the spring tides.

Why ever they calls 'em spring I can't think, for we was
very near floated out twice the week afore last, and No-
vember no one can't call spring.

I'm sure the shock as that Mrs. Giddins give me I never
shall forget, as is a wrong-headed woman as ever I had in
my house, though I will say clean and honest.

It was the day after that gal left us I'd give warnin' to,

through her a-sayin' as she'd rather starve than eat cold mutton, as was good enough for me.

So I had Mrs. Giddins in for half-a-day to tidy up the place ready for the young woman as was a-comin' that evenin'. When I come down after puttin' on my cap for tea, I says to her: "Mrs. Giddins, I want you to go up into the lumber room," as is over my bed-room, a sort o' a cupboard in the slant of the roof, as I'd put away some boxes in, "and pull me out a black portmanty, as I wanted to get somethin' out on." Up she goes, all of a bustle.

I says, "Tread light," through a-knowin' as there wasn't no floor but lath and plasters to that cupboard. "All right," says she.

So I hearin' her a rummagin' and a pullin' the things about, calls out, "Can't you find it?" She says, "If you'd come and hold the candle I could get it out," as was jammed and crammed tight in the corner.

Up I goes and takes the candle, and there we was a-standin' in that cupboard as is nothin' but beams. I was standin' on a beam, and Mrs. Giddins in front on me, a-haulin' at that portmanty like mad. Well, she gives it a pull with all her force, as made it come out all of a sudden like.

The jerk as she give it throwed her back agin me, as tipped me off the beam onto the lath and plaster, and through I goes with that crash as made me think the house was all about our ears.

I struggles natural, as any one would, and, ketchin' hold of Mrs. Giddins, pulls her through too.

Well, there we was through the ceilin', with our legs a-danglin' in my bed-room, and that caught as we couldn't get up, Mrs. Giddins a-screamin' like wild as she was murdered, with the candle knocked out, and we might have been there till now, only as luck would have it, Brown came in earlier than I expected. But, law bless you, he could do nothin' for ever so long for laughin', and when he did draw us up, if he didn't say Mrs. Giddins were an old fool, and me another, for not knowin' better than to tread on lath and plaster, as is a downright disgrace for floorin'.

FARM-YARD SONG.

J. T. TROWBRIDGE.

Over the hill the farm-boy goes,
His shadow lengthens along the land,
A giant staff in a giant hand;
In the poplar tree, above the spring,
The katydid begins to sing:
    The early dews are falling.
Into the stone-heap darts the mink;
The swallows skim the river's brink;
And home to the woodland fly the crows,
When over the hill the farm-boy goes,
    Cheerily calling—
    "Co', boss! co', boss! co'! co'! co'!"
Farther, farther over the hill,
Faintly calling, calling still—
    "Co', boss! co', boss! co'! co'!"

Into the yard the farmer goes,
With grateful heart, at the close of day:
Harness and chain are hung away;
In the wagon-shed stand yoke and plow;
The straw's in the stack, the hay in the mow,
    The cooling dews are falling.
The friendly sheep his welcome bleat,
The pigs come grunting to his feet,
And the whinnying mare her master knows,
When into the yard the farmer goes,
    His cattle calling—
    "Co', boss! co', boss! co'! co'! co'!"
While still the cow-boy, far away,
Goes seeking those that have gone astray—
    "Co', boss! co', boss! co'! co'!"

Now to her task the milkmaid goes,
The cattle come crowding through the gate,
Lowing, pushing, little and great;
About the trough, by the farm-yard pump,
The frolicksome yearlings frisk and jump,
    While the pleasant dews are falling;
The new milch heifer is quick and shy,
But the old cow waits with tranquil eye;
And the white stream into the bright pail flows,
When to her task the milkmaid goes,
    Soothingly calling,—
"So, boss! so, boss! so! so! so!"
The cheerful milkmaid takes her stool,
And sits and milks in the twilight cool,
    Saying, "So, so, boss! so! so!"

To supper at last the farmer goes,
The apples are pared, the paper read,
The stories are told, then all to bed.
Without, the crickets' ceaseless song
Makes shrill the silence all night long;
    The heavy dews are falling.
The housewife's hand has turned the lock,
Drowsily ticks the kitchen clock;
The household sinks to deep repose,
But still in sleep the farm-boy goes,
    Singing, calling—
"Co', boss!" co', boss! co'! co'! co'!"
And oft the milkmaid, in her dreams,
Drums in the pail with the flashing streams,
    Murmuring, "So, boss! so!"

——————•◆•——————

MURPHY'S MYSTERY OF THE PORK-BARREL.

ANONYMOUS.

"Murphy, what's the meaning of mystery? Faith, I was reading the paper, and it said 'twas a mystery how it was done."

"Well," said Murphy, "Pat, I'll tache ye. Ye see, when

I lived with my father, a little gossoon, they gave me a parthy, and me mother wint to market to buy somethin' for the parthy to ate, and among the lot of things she bot a half-barrel of pork, ye see. Well, she put it down in the cellar, bless her sowl, for safe keeping, till the parthy come on, do ye see. Well, when the parthy come on, me mother sint me down to the cellar to get some of the pork, do ye see; well, I wint down to the barrel and opened it, and fished about, but not a bit of pork could I find; so I looked around the barrel to see where the pork was, and found a rat-hole in the bottom of the barrel, where the pork had all run out and left the brine standing, do ye see."

"Hould on, Murphy! wait a bit; now tell me how could all the pork get out ov the barrel, and lave the brine standing?"

"Well, Pat," said Murphy, "that's what I'd like to know myself, do you see; there's the mystery."

THE PRAYER-SEEKER.

JOHN G. WHITTIER.

Along the aisle where prayer was made,
A woman, all in black arrayed,
Close veiled, between the kneeling host,
With gliding motion of a ghost,
Passed to the desk and laid thereon
A scroll which bore these words alone
       Pray for me!

Back from the place of worshiping
She glided like a guilty thing;
The rustle of her draperies, stirred
By hurrying feet, alone was heard;
While, full of awe, the preacher read,
As out into the dark she sped—
       "Pray for me!"

Back to the night from whence she came,
To unimagined grief or shame!

Across the threshold of that door
None knew the burden that she bore;
Alone she left the written scroll,
The legend of a troubled soul—
     Pray for me!

Glide on, poor ghost of woe or sin!
Thou leav'st a common need within;
Each bears, like thee, some nameless weight,
Some misery inarticulate,
Some secret sin, some shrouded dread,
Some household sorrow all unsaid—
     Pray for us!

Pass on!   The type of all thou art,
Sad witness to the common heart!
With face in veil, and seal on lip,
In mute and strange companionship,
Like thee we wander to and fro,
Dumbly imploring as we go—
     Pray for us!

Ah, who shall pray? since he who pleads
Our want perchance hath greater needs!
Yet they who make their loss the gain
Of others, shall not ask in vain,
And Heaven bends low to hear the prayer
Of love from lips of self-despair—
     Pray for us!

In vain remorse and fear and hate
Beat with bruised hands against a fate
Whose walls of iron only move
And open to the touch of love;
He only feels his burdens fall,
Who, taught by suffering, pities all—
     Pray for us!

He prayeth best who leaves unguessed
The mysteries of another's breast—

Why cheeks grow pale, why eyes o'erflow,
Or heads are white, thou need'st not know.
Enough to note by many a sign
That every heart hath needs like thine—
Pray for us!

AN EXTRAORDINARY PHENOMENON.

ANONYMOUS.

It was on a moonlight night that Pennypacker, while walking by the riverside at Norristown, came across Jones standing on the bank, in a condition of intoxication, gazing stupidly into the water. When Jones saw Pennypacker he said to him:

"Mizzer Bennyback'r, 'm very glad you've come. I've been stan'in' here c'nsiderin' a moz extraordinary ph'nom'non."

"What is it, Jones?"

"Moz extr'ordinary ph'nom'non th't ever came under my obzervation, Mr. Bennybacker—the moz extr'ordinary."

"What is the nature of the phenomenon, Mr. Jones?"

"I zay, Mizzer Bennybacker, id'uez very way extr'ordinary. D'you obzerve that?"

Then Jones gazed and pointed into the water, putting his head on one side and then on the other. Then he would draw back, as if to get the phenomenon in a new light, and finally he doubled up both fists and attempted to look through them, and all the time he kept muttering to himself:

"Very 'stonishing zircumstance altogether. Moz remark'ble freak ov nature idz ever bin my lod t'p'zerve. Can't cound for id upon any theory whadever."

"Well, Mr. Jones, what is it that surprises you?"

"Mizzer Bennybacker, cas' y'r eye down there. D' you 'pzerve anythin' of a 'strordinary nature?"

"No, Jones, nothing; there is nothing unusual there that I can see."

"Thadz moz extr'ordinary zirgumstanz ov all. Don' you perzeive the moon down there, Mizzer Bennybacker?" said Jones, pointing to the water.

"Certainly I do."

"Well, Mizzer Bennybacker, dozzen it strige you as moz incompre'ns'ble ph'nom'non, now?"

"Of course not."

"Well, Mizzer Bennybacker, you may be drunk ur you may be zober, but in all my 'xperienze I never before found m'zelf vorty thousan' miles 'bove the moon. Id's an incompre'nsible zirgumstanz, Mizzer Bennybacker, how you au' I sh'd uv god up here an' the moon down there without our being 'ware of the fagd, when I'm perfectly certain I'm not stan'nin on my head."

Then Pennypacker led Jones calmly home and put him to bed, and he slept off his surprise at the extraordinary phenomenon.

———————————

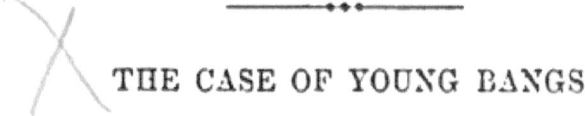

THE CASE OF YOUNG BANGS.

MAX ADELER.

When Mr. Bangs, the elder, returned from Europe, he brought with him from Geneva, a miniature musical-box, long and very narrow, and altogether of hardly greater dimensions, say, than a large pocket-knife. The instrument played four cheerful little tunes, for the benefit of the Bangs family, and they enjoyed it very much. Young William Bangs enjoyed it to such an extent that one day, just after the machine had been wound up ready for action, he got to sucking the end of it, and in a moment of inadvertence it slipped, and he swallowed the whole concern. The only immediate consequence of the action was that a harmonic stomach-ache was at once organized upon the interior of William Bangs, and he experienced a restless-

ness which he well knew would defy the soothing tenden-
cies of peppermint, and make a mockery of paregoric.

And William Bangs kept his secret in his own soul and
in his stomach, also determined to hide his misery from
his father, and to spare the rod to the spoiled child—
spoiled, at any rate, as far as his digestive apparatus was
concerned.

But that evening, at the supper table, W. Bangs had
eaten but one mouthful of bread, when strains of wild, mysterious music were suddenly wafted from under the table.
The entire family immediately groped around upon the
floor, trying to discover whence the sounds came, although
William Bangs sat there filled with agony and remorse and
bread and tunes, and desperately asserted his belief that
the music came from Mary Ann, who might perhaps be
playing upon the harp or the dulcimer in the cellar. He
well knew that Mary Ann was unfamiliar with the harp,
and that to her the dulcimer was as much an insolvable
problem as it would have been to a fishing-worm. But
he was frantic with anxiety to hide his guilt. Thus it is
that one crime leads to another.

But he could not disguise the truth forever, and that
very night, while the family was at prayers, William Bangs
all at once got the hiccups, and the music-box started off
without warning, with "A Life on the Ocean Wave, and a
Home on the Rolling Deep," with variations. Whereupon
the paternal Bangs arose from his knees and grasped
William kindly but firmly by his hair and shook him up,
and inquired what he meant by such conduct. And William threw out a kind of a general idea to the effect that
he was practicing something for a Sunday-school celebration, which old Bangs intimated was a singularly thin
explanation.

Then they tried to get up that music-box, and every
time they would seize young William by the legs and shake
him over the sofa-cushion, or would pour some fresh vari-

ety of emetic down his throat, the harmonium within
would give some fresh spurt, and joyously grind out "Listen to the Mocking Bird," or "Thou'lt Never Cease to
Love."

So they abandoned the attempt, and were compelled to
permit that musical-box to remain within the sepulchral
recesses of the epigastrium of William Bangs.   To say that
the unfortunate victim of the disaster was made miserable
by his condition, would be to express in the feeblest manner the state of his mind.   The more music there was in
his stomach, the wilder and more chaotic became the dis-
cord in his soul.   Just as likely as not it would occur that
while he lay asleep in bed in the middle of the night, the
melody-works within would begin to revolve, and would
play "Home, Sweet Home," for two or three hours, unless
the peg happened to slip, when the cylinder would switch
back again to "A Life on the Ocean Wave, and a Home on
the Rolling Deep," and would rattle out that tune with variations and fragments of the scales, until William Bangs'
brother would kick him out of bed in wild despair, and sit
on him in a wild effort to subdue the serenade, which,
however, invariably proceeded with fresh vigor when sub-
jected to unusual pressure.

And when William Bangs went to church it frequently
occurred that, in the very midst of the most solemn portion
of the sermon, he would feel a gentle disturbance under the
lowest button of his jacket, and presently, when everything
was hushed, the undigested engine would give a preliminary buzz, and then reel off " Listen to the Mocking Bird,"
and " Thou'lt Never Cease to Love," and scales and exercises, until the clergyman would stop and glare at William
over his spectacles, and whisper to one of the deacons.

Then the sexton would suddenly tack up the aisle and
clutch the unhappy Mr. Bangs by the collar, and scud
down the aisle again to the accompaniment of " A Life on
the Ocean Wave, and a Home on the Rolling Deep."

But the end came at last, and the miserable offspring of the senior Bangs found peace. One day, while he was sitting in school, endeavoring to learn his multiplication table to the tune of " Home, Sweet Home," his gastric juice triumphed. Something or other in the music-box gave way all at once, the springs were unrolled with alarming force, and William Bangs, as he felt the fragments of the instrument hurled right through and among his vitals, tumbled over on the floor and expired.

At the *post-mortem* examination they found several pieces of " Home, Sweet Home " in his liver, while one of his lungs was severely torn by a fragment of " A Life on the Ocean Wave."

Small pieces of " Listen to the Mocking Bird " were removed from his heart and breast-bone, and three brass pegs of " Thou'lt Never Cease to Love " were found firmly driven into his fifth rib.

They had no music at the funeral. They lifted the machinery out of him, and buried him quietly in the cemetery. Whenever the Bangses buy musical boxes now, they get them as large as a piano, and chain them to the wall.

A MULE RIDE IN FLORIDA.

ANONYMOUS.

The boys insisted that I needed relaxation. My health required it. I had a pretty fair article of health, I thought, enough to last me as long as I lived. But I must accumulate a stock for future use. The south was the place to get it. And riding was healthy. The sand is too deep to ride, except on horseback, and so I thought I would take a ride. I applied to the livery man for a horse. He had one. He looked sorrowfully at me, as though he pitied me. Did I ever ride a mule ? I never had. He had as good riding horses as were ever saddled, but if I wanted a " Rock Me to

Sleep, Mother" style of a ride, I would take a mule. I don't consider myself a first-class judge of mules. I had some vague notions in regard to them ; supposed they would do a large amount of work with a very little feed, and were immortal. I had read of one being driven over the same route *by the same boy,* for eighty-seven years, and he was a young mule yet.

Bring forth the mule. The mule was brought. He was a meek looking cuss—a perfect "Uriah Heep" of a mule, so far as "umbleness" was concerned. At least that was the view I took of him. He was saddled, and I mounted. For a mile or two he paced beautifully. I thought those old monks I had read about knew what they were doing when they traveled on mules. I had a high respect for their judgment. Just then my mule began to show symptoms—symptoms of what I did not know. I found out. Dropping his head between his legs, his heels described a parabolic curve, or some other infernal curve, in the air, and I got off and sat on the ground. I got off over his head, and I did it quick. I'm not so old, but I can get off an animal of that kind as quick as a boy. Then I looked at the mule, to see if he was hurt. He didn't appear to be. Then I inquired around, to see how I was. I reported an abrasion on the left hip, and a contusion on the lower end of my back. Then I thought I would pronounce a left-handed blessing on that mule, and on his forefathers and foremothers before him, and his children after him. But I didn't. I wondered if he would stand fire. If I had had a pistol, I would have put the muzzle to his ear, and tried him. Not that I was hostile toward him, but I was afraid somebody might take a ride on him some day and get hurt. But I had no pistol, so that benevolent and sanguinary idea was frustrated. Then I got up and shook the dust off my feet, and brushed the sand off my trowsers, as a testimony against that place. Then I led the mule carefully home, and stated my case to the livery man. But

when I looked that he should offer to send for a doctor,
or a Samaritan, to do me up in a rag, and pour olive oil
and champagne on my bruises, he only laughed. And his
man that he had to help him laid down on a bench and
laughed—and I stood holding the mule—then I laughed.
It was ridiculous. But I've learned a little wisdom. Next
time I ride on horseback it will be a different kind of beast
from a begn. *mlass*.

DHREE SHKADERS.

ANONYMOUS.

Dhree shkaders vent ofer mit Cendral Park,
   Vent ofer vhen der moon he vas high,
Und efery von feel so gay like a lark,
   As dhey dink von dhere gals dhey vood sigh.
      Und shents must shkade vhen der vasser vas
      Bud dhey doud vood dook dose maits along
      To dot Cendral Park mit der cidy out.

Dhree maedchens yoost shtob in a barlor togedder,
   Und tanz und zing vhen der moon he vas high,
Und efery leedle vhile looked out mit der redder,
   Vhile der plack glouds valked ofer der shky.
      Vhen shendlemans shkade der vinds ofden blows,
      Yoost der same as dot nite a shtorm he arose,
      Dot trofe dose shkaders mit der cidy quick pack.

Dhree olt coats vas hung mit a rack py der hall,
   Und each shkader vas habby like eny young shpark,
Vhile der maedchens vas lafin und huggin dhem all;
   Dose shkaders dot comes so quick pack mit der Park.
      For shendlemans shkade und maedchens may vait,
      But dot nite der gals plessed fordune und fate,
      Dot der vedder vas so pad der door out, und dhem
        fellers vas come recht avay quick pack dhey can
        mit dhere lofes dot vas vaitin of dhey shood been on
        dhere houses mit 'em.

DICK & FITZGERALD,

PUBLISHERS, NEW YORK.

, The Publishers, upon receipt of the price, will send any of the following ooks by mail, POSTAGE FREE, to any part of the United States. In ordering ooks, the full name, post office, county and State should be plainly written.

Dick's Encyclopedia of **Practical Receipts and Processes.**

Containing over 6,400 Receipts; embracing thorough information, in plain language, applicable to almost every possible industrial and domestic requirement. The scope of this work is different from any other book of the kind. The contents of the Encyclopedia are collated from works on the various subjects by authors of eminence in their respective branches, divested of technicalities, simplified and illustrated by diagrams, where necessary, so as to make the whole plain and intelligible to the uninitiated. This work presents a complete and indispensable book for the household, farm, garden, &c.; including instructions as to what to do and how to do it, in case of all accidents, contingencies, and ailments of daily life. It also affords a valuable Book of Reference for the Druggist, enabling him to make up a number of "Sundries," especially Toilet Soaps, Dentifrices, Cosmetics, and Perfumery; also specific Medicines and Remedies derived from the practice of eminent Physicians, or from various European officinal sources; thus forming a useful and desirable adjunct to the United States Pharmacopœic. It enables the Grocer to prepare his own Flavoring Extracts, Vinegar, and a host of other articles, cheaper and better than he can purchase them; and to test the quality of some of the Goods that he buys and sells. To the Liquor Dealer it gives the best and latest methods of treating and improving his liquors; of preparing Cordials, &c.; of making, managing, and bottling all kinds of Wines, Cider, &c.,—it lays before the workman the results obtained by the experiments and experience of the masters of his trade. In fact it is almost useless to attempt an enumeration of the advantages of this work, as there is scarcely a branch of Industry that may not derive information and profit from its pages. The Index of this work occupies 42 three-column pages, in small type. 600 pages, royal octavo, cloth.
Price ....**$5.00.**
Bound in half calf, extra..**$7.50.**
☞ Full descriptive circular of the above sent, by mail, free.

The **Parlor Stage.** A Collection of Drawing-room Proverbs,

Charades and Tableaux Vivants. By Miss S. A. Frost. The authoress of this attractive volume has performed her task with skill, talent, and wo might say, with genius; for the Acting Charades and Proverbs are really minor dramas of a high order of merit. There are twenty-four of them, and fourteen *Tableaux*, all of which are excellent. The characters are admirably drawn, well contrasted, and the plots and dialogues deeply interesting. 352 pages, small evo, cloth, gilt side and back, beveled edges. Price $1.50

Wilson's **Book of Recitations and Dialogues.** With Instruc-

tions in Elocution and Declamation. Containing a choice selection of Poetical and Prose Recitations and Original Colloquies. Designed as a Reading Book for Classes, and as an Assistant to Teachers and Students in preparing Exhibitions. By Floyd B. Wilson, Professor of Elocution. The Colloquies are entirely original. Paper covers. Price............30 cts.
Bound in boards, cloth back ....50 cts.

The Parlor Magician; *or, One Hundred Tricks for the Drawing-Room,* containing an Extensive and Miscellaneous Collection of Conjuring and Legerdemain; Sleights with Dice, Dominoes, Cards, Ribbons, Rings, Fruit, Coin, Balls, Handkerchiefs, etc., all of which may be performed in the Parlor or Drawing-Room, without the aid of any apparatus; also embracing a choice variety of Curious Deceptions, which may be performed with the aid of simple apparatus; the whole illustrated and clearly explained with 121 engravings. Paper Covers. Price........................30 cts. Bound in boards, with cloth back..................................50 cts.

Book of Riddles and Five Hundred Home Amusements. Containing a Choice and Curious Collection of Riddles, Charades, Enigmas, Rebuses, Anagrams, Transpositions, Conundrums, Amusing Puzzles, Queer Sleights, Recreations in Arithmetic, Fireside Games and Natural Magic, embracing Entertaining Amusements in Magnetism, Chemistry, Second Sight and Simple Recreations in Science for Family and Social Pastime, illustrated with sixty Engravings. Paper covers. Price..............30 cts. Bound in boards, with cloth back..................................50 cts.

Book of Fireside Games. Containing an Explanation of the most Entertaining Games suited to the Family Circle as a Recreation, such as Games of Action, Games which merely require attention, Games which require memory, Catch Games, which have for their objects Tricks or Mystification, Games in which an opportunity is afforded to display Gallantry, Wit, or some slight knowledge of certain Sciences, Amusing Forfeits, Fireside Games for Winter Evening Amusement, etc. Paper covers. Price..30 cts. Bound in boards, with cloth back..................................50 cts.

Parlor Theatricals; *or, Winter Evenings' Entertainment.* Containing Acting Proverbs, Dramatic Charades, Acting Charades, or Drawing-Room Pantomimes, Musical Burlesques, Tableaux Vivants, etc.; with Instructions for Amateurs; how to Construct a Stage and Curtain; how to get up Costumes and Properties; on the "Making up" of Characters; Exits and Entrances; how to arrange Tableaux, etc. Illustrated with Engravings. Paper covers. Price..................................30 cts. Bound in boards, cloth back..50 cts.

The Book of 500 Curious Puzzles. Containing a large collection of entertaining Paradoxes, Perplexing Deceptions in numbers, and Amusing Tricks in Geometry. By the author of "The Sociable," "The Secret Out," "The Magician's Own Book." Illustrated with a great variety of Engravings. This book commands a large sale. It will furnish fun and amusement for a whole winter. Paper covers. Price...............30 cts. Bound in boards, with cloth back..................................50 cts.
The above five books are compiled from the "Sociable" and "Magician's Own."

The American Boys' Book of Sports and Games. A Repository of In and Out-Door Amusements for Boys and Youth. Illustrated with nearly 700 engravings, designed by White, Herrick, Weir and Harvey, and engraved by N. Orr. This is, unquestionably, the most attractive and valuable book of its kind ever issued in this or any other country. It has been three years in preparation, and embraces all the sports and games that tend to develop the physical constitution, improve the mind and heart, and relieve the tedium of leisure hours, both in the parlor and the field. The Engravings are all in the finest style of art, and embrace eight full-page ornamental titles, illustrating the several departments of the work, beautifully printed on tinted paper. The book is issued in the best style, being printed on fine sized paper, and handsomely bound. Extra cloth, gilt side and back, extra gold. Price...................... ....$3 50 Extra cloth, full gilt edges, back and side,.........................$4 00

Howard's Book of Conundrums and Riddles. Containing over 1,400 Witty Conundrums, Queer Riddles, Perplexing Puzzles. Ingenious Enigmas, Clever Charades, Curious Catches, and Amusing Sells, original and newly dressed. This splendid collection of curious paradoxes will afford the material for a never-ending feast of fun and amusement. Any person, with the assistance of this book, may take the lead in entertaining a company and keeping them in roars of laughter for hours together. It is an invaluable companion for a Pic-nic, or Summer Excursion of any kind, and is just the thing to make a fireside circle merry on a long winter's evening. There is not a poor riddle in the book, the majority being fresh and of the highest order. Paper cover, price..................30 cts. Bound in boards, cloth back, price.....................50 cts.

Frost's Book of Tableaux and Shadow Pantomimes. Containing a choice collection of Tableaux or Living Pictures, embracing Moving Tableaux, Mother Goose Tableaux, Fairy Tale Tableaux, Charade and Proverb Tableaux; together with directions for arranging the stage costuming the characters, and forming appropriate groups. By Miss S. Annie Frost. To which is added a number of Shadow Acts and Pantomimes, with complete stage instructions. 180 pages, paper cover...30 cts. Bound in boards, cloth back..........................50 cts.

Laughing Gas. An Encyclopædia of Wit, Wisdom, and Wind. By Sam Slick, Jr. Comically illustrated with 100 original and laughable Engravings, and nearly 500 side-extending Jokes, and other things to get fat on; and the best thing of it is, that everything about the book is new and fresh—all new—new designs, new stories, new type—no comic almanac stuff. Price..........................25 cts.

The Egyptian Dream Book and Fortune-Teller. Containing an Alphabetical List of Dreams, and numerous methods of Telling Fortunes, including the celebrated Oraculum of Napoleon Bonaparte. Illustrated with explanatory diagrams. 16mo, boards, cloth back. Price...40 Cts.

Ned Turner's Black Jokes. A collection of Funny Stories, Jokes, and Conundrums, interspersed with Witty Sayings and Humorous Dialogues. As given by Ned Turner, the Celebrated Ethiopian Delineator and Equestrian Clown. Price....................10 cts.

Book of 1,000 Tales and Amusing Adventures. Containing over 300 Engravings, and 450 pages. This is a magnificent book, and is crammed full of narratives and adventures. Price..........$1 50

The Game of Whist. Rules, Directions, and Maxims to be observed in playing it. Containing, also, Primary Rules for Beginners, Explanations and Directions for Old Players, and the Laws of the Game. Compiled from Hoyle and Matthews. Price.....................12 cts.

10,000 Wonderful Things. Comprising the Marvellous and Rare, Odd, Curious, Quaint, Eccentric, and Extraordinary, in all Ages and Nations, in Art, Nature, and Science, including many Wonders of the World, enriched with hundreds of authentic illustrations. 16mo, cloth, gilt side and back. Price.........................$1 50

Ned Turner's Clown Joke Book. Containing the best Jokes and Gems of Wit, composed and delivered by the favorite Equestrian Clown and Ethiopian Comedian, Ned Turner. 18mo. Price................10 cts.

Sam Slick in Search of a Wife. 12mo.
Paper cover. Price...75 cts.
Bound cloth $1 25

Cards of Courtship.

Arranged with such apt Conversations that you will be enabled to ask the momentous question categorically, in such a delicate manner that the girl will not suspect what you are at. These cards may be used, either by two persons, or they will make lots of fun for an evening party of young people. There are fourteen question cards, and twenty-eight answers—forty-two in all. Each answer will respond differently to every one of the questions. The person holding the questions either selects or draws one out, as he pleases. The answer is given by shuffling the answer cards, and then throwing one of them down promiscuously. It may be a warm and loving, a non-committal, a genial assenting, a cold denying, an evasive, or even a coquettishly uncertain answer—for they are all there, besides others which it is difficult to classify. When used in a party, the question is read aloud by the lady receiving it—she shuffles and hands out an answer—and that also must be read aloud by the gentleman receiving it. The fun thus caused is intense. Put up in handsome card cases, on which are printed directions. Price........30 cts.

Love-Making Made Easy.

By Love-Letter Cards. We have just printed a new and novel Set of Cards which will delight the hearts of young people susceptible of the tender passion. These consist of forty-two cards—twenty-one pink, or yellow, and the same number of white ones. Each white card has printed on it a love-letter to a lady, and each of the colored ones has her reply. The letters and replies are all different, and no formality of style, or namby-pambyism, will be found in any of them. All are written in a modern familiar tone, with plain and candid declarations of love—warmly or moderately expressed, or delicately hinted at, as the case may be, and some of them boldly popping the momentous question to the fair recipient. The answer cards are equally terse, candid and to the point.
N. B.—These cards may be also successfully used for models (either wholly or in part) in writing to lovers or sweethearts. Put up in handsome cases on which are printed directions. Price...............................**30 cts.**

Fortune-Telling Cards.

Solutions of uncertain and intricate questions relative to love, luck, lotteries, matrimony, business matters, journeys, and future events generally, are here given in a direct, piquant, and satisfactory manner. They have been carefully worked out on genuine astrological and geometrical principles, by planetarium, and in figures, triangles and curves, and are so arranged that each answer will respond to every one of the questions which may be put. There are fourteen printed questions and twenty-eight answer cards. If none of the questions should suit your case, you can ask any other you please, and the proper answer will come. These cards will also afford a fund of amusement in a party of young people. Each package is enclosed in a card-case, on which are printed directions for using the cards. Price...**30 cts.**

Leap-Year Cards.

To enable any lady to pop the question to the chosen one of her heart. This set of cards is intended more to make fun among young people than for any practical utility. There are twenty-one pink or yellow cards, and the same number of white ones—forty-two in all. On each of the colored cards is a printed letter from a lady to a gentleman, wherein the fair one declares her love, or pops the question in a humorously sentimental manner. The letters all differ in style, and in the mode of attack. The twenty-one answers, on white cards, is where the fun comes in. Put up in handsome cases, on which are printed directions...........30 cts

Souillard's Book of Practical Receipts.

For the use of Families, Druggists, Perfumers, Confectioners, Patent Medicine Factors, and Dealers in Soaps and Fancy Articles for the Toilet. Compiled with great care from receipts now in use by the most popular houses in France and the United States. By F. A. Souillard, practical chemist. Paper cover. Price...25 cts

Brudder Bones' Book of Stump Speeches and Burlesque Orations. Also containing Humorous Lectures, Ethiopian Dialogues, Plantation Scenes, Negro Farces and Burlesques, Laughable Interludes and Comic Recitations, interspersed with Dutch, Irish, French and Yankee Stories. Compiled and edited by JOHN F. SCOTT. This book contains some of the best hits of the leading negro delineators of the present time, as well as mirth-provoking jokes and repartees of the most celebrated End-Men of the day, and specially designed for the introduction of fun in an evening's entertainment. Paper covers. Price................................30 cts.
Bound in boards, illuminated...50 cts.

Frost's Original Letter-Writer. A complete collection of Original Letters and Notes, upon every imaginable subject of Every-Day Life, with plain directions about everything connected with writing a letter. Containing Letters of Introduction, Letters on Business, Letters answering Advertisements, Letters of Recommendation, Applications for Employment, Letters of Congratulation, of Condolence, of Friendship and Relationship, Love Letters, Notes of Invitation, Notes Accompanying Gifts, Letters of Favor, of Advice, and Letters of Excuse, together with an appropriate answer to each. The whole embracing three hundred letters and notes. By S. A. FROST, author of "The Parlor Stage," "Dialogues for Young Folks," etc. To which is added a comprehensive Table of Synonyms alone worth double the price asked for the book. This work is not a rehash of English writers, but is entirely practical and original, and suited to the wants of the American public. We assure our readers that it is the best collection of letters ever published in this country. Bound in boards, cloth back, with illuminated sides. Price...50 cts.

Inquire Within *for Anything you Want to Know; or, Over* 3,700 *Facts for the People.* "Inquire Within" is one of the most valuable and extraordinary volumes ever presented to the American public, and embodies nearly 4,000 facts, in most of which any person will find instruction, aid and entertainment. It contains so many valuable recipes, that an enumeration of them requires *seventy-two columns of fine type for the index.* Illustrated. 436 large pages. Price........................$1 50

The Sociable; *or, One Thousand and One Home Amusements.* Containing Acting Proverbs, Dramatic Charades, Acting Charades, Tableaux Vivants, Parlor Games and Parlor Magic, and a choice collection of Puzzles, etc., illustrated with nearly 300 Engravings and Diagrams, the whole being a fund of never-ending entertainment. By the author of the "Magician's Own Book." Nearly 400 pages, 12 mo. cloth, gilt side stamp. Price..$1 50

Martine's Hand-Book of Etiquette and Guide to True Politeness. A complete Manual for all those who desire to understand good breeding, the customs of good society, and to avoid incorrect and vulgar habits. Containing clear and comprehensive directions for correct manners, conversation, dress, introductions, rules for good behavior at Dinner Parties and the table, with hints on wine and carving at the table; together with Etiquette of the Ball and Assembly Room, Evening Parties, and the usages to be observed when visiting or receiving calls; deportment in the street and when travelling. To which is added the Etiquette of Courtship and Marriage. Bound in boards, with cloth back. Price...............50 cts.
Bound in cloth, gilt side...75 cts.

Day's American Ready-Reckoner, containing Tables for rapid calculations of Aggregate Values, Wages, Salaries, Board, Interest Money, &c., &c. Also, Tables of Timber, Plank, Board and Log Measurements, with full explanations how to measure them, either by the square foot (board measure), cubic foot (timber measure), &c. Bound in boards. Price..50 cts.
Bound in cloth...75 cts.

Spencer's Book of Comic Speeches and Humorous Recitations.

A collection of Comic Speeches and Dialogues, Humorous Prose and Poetical Recitations, Laughable Dramatic Scenes and Burlesques, and Eccentric Characteristic Soliloquies and Stories. Suitable for School Exhibitions and Evening Entertainments. Edited by ALBERT J. SPENCER. This is the best book of Comic Recitations that has ever been published, and commands a large sale on account of its real merit. It is crammed full of Comic Poetry, Laughable Lectures, Irish and Dutch Stories, Yankee Yarns, Negro Burlesques, Short Dramatic Scenes, Humorous Dialogues, and all kinds of Funny Speeches.

Paper covers. Price..30 cts.
Bound in boards, cloth back...50 cts.

Marache's Manual of Chess.

Containing a description of the Board and the Pieces, Chess Notation, Technical Terms with diagrams illustrating them, Relative Value of the Pieces, Laws of the Game, General Observations on the Pieces, Preliminary Games for Beginners, Fifty Openings of Games, giving all the latest discoveries of Modern Masters, with best games and copious notes. Twenty Endings of Games, showing easiest ways of effecting Checkmate. Thirty-six ingenious Diagram Problems, and Sixteen curious Chess Stratagems. To which is added a Treatise on the Games of Backgammon, Russian Backgammon and Dominoes, the whole being one of the best Books for Beginners ever published. By N. MARACHE, Chess Editor of "Wilkes' Spirit of the Times."

Bound in boards, cloth back. Price..................................50 cts.
Cloth, gilt side...75 cts.

Martine's Sensible Letter Writer;

Being a comprehensive and complete Guide and Assistant for those who desire to carry on Epistolary Correspondence; Containing a large collection of model letters, on the simplest matters of life, adapted to all ages and conditions,

EMBRACING,

Business Letters;
Applications for Employment, with Letters of Recommendation, and Answers to Advertisements;
Letters between Parents and Children;
Letters of Friendly Counsel and Remonstrance;
Letters soliciting Advice, Assistance and Friendly Favors;
Letters of Courtesy, Friendship and Affection;
Letters of Condolence and Sympathy;
A Choice Collection of Love Letters, for Every Situation in a Courtship;
Notes of Ceremony, Familiar Invitations, etc., together with Notes of Acceptance and Regret.

The whole containing 300 Sensible Letters and Notes. This is an invaluable book for those persons who have not had sufficient practice to enable them to write letters without great effort. It contains such a variety of letters, that models may be found to suit every subject. Bound in boards, with illuminated cover and cloth back, 207 pages. Price...........50 cts.
Bound in cloth ....75 cts.

The Perfect Gentleman.

A book of Etiquette and Eloquence. Containing Information and Instruction for those who desire to become brilliant or conspicuous in General Society, or at Parties, Dinners, or Popular Gatherings, etc. It gives directions how to use wine at table, with Rules for judging the quality thereof, Rules for Carving, and a complete Etiquette of the Dinner Table, including Dinner Speeches, Toasts and Sentiments, Wit and Conversation at Table, etc. It has also an American Code of Etiquette and Politeness for all occasions. Model Speeches, with Directions how to deliver them. Duties of the Chairman at Public Meetings. Forms of Preambles and Resolutions, etc. It is a handsomely bound and gilt volume of 335 pages.

Price..$1 50

Hillgrove's Ball-room Guide and Complete Dancing-master. Containing a plain treatise on Etiquette and Deportment at Balls and Parties, with valuable hints on Dress and the Toilet, together with full explanations of the Rudiments, Terms, Figures and Steps used in Dancing, including clear and precise instructions how to dance all kinds of Quadrilles, Waltzes, Polkas, Redowas, Reels, Round, Plain and Fancy Dances, so that any person may learn them without the aid of a teacher; to which is added, easy directions for calling out the Figures of every dance, and the amount of Music required for each. The whole illustrated with 176 descriptive engravings and diagrams. By Thomas Hillgrove, Professor of Dancing.

Bound in cloth, with gilt side and back. Price......................$1 00
Bound in boards, cloth back..75 cts.

Wright's Book of 3,000 American Receipts; or, Light-House of Valuable Information. Containing over 3,000 Receipts in all the Useful and Domestic Arts—including Cooking, Confectionery, Distilling, Perfumery, Chemicals, Varnishes, Dyeing, Agriculture, etc. Embracing valuable secrets that cannot be obtained from any other source. No exertion or expense has been spared to make this work as comprehensive and accurate as possible. Many Receipts will be found in it that have never before appeared in print in this country. Some idea may be formed of its value in the latter respect, when it is stated that the compiler has been for many years engaged in collecting rare and valuable Receipts from numerous languages besides the English. This is by far the most valuable American Receipt Book that has ever been published.

12mo., cloth, 359 pages. Price.....................................$1 50

The Modern Pocket Hoyle. Containing all the Games of Skill and Chance, as played in this country at the present time; being an "authority on all disputed points." By "Trumps." This valuable manual is all original, or thoroughly revised, from the best and latest authorities, and includes the laws and complete directions for playing one hundred and eleven different games, comprising Card games, Chess, Checkers, Dominoes, Backgammon, Dice, Billiards, and all the Field Games. 388 pages.

Paper covers. Price...50 cts
Bound in boards, cloth back..75 cts.
Bound in cloth, gilt side and back.....................................$1 25

Richardson's Monitor of Free-Masonry. A Complete Guide to the various Ceremonies and Routine in Free-Mason's Lodges, Chapters, Encampments, Hierarches, etc., in all the Degrees, whether Modern, Ancient, Ineffable, Philosophical or Historical. Containing, also, the Signs, Tokens, Grips, Pass-words, Decorations, Drapery, Dress, Regalia and Jewels, in each Degree. Profusely illustrated with Explanatory Engravings, Plans of the Interior of Lodges, etc. By Jabez Richardson, A. M. A book of 185 pages.

Bound in paper covers. Price..75 cts.
Bound and gilt...$1 25

Rarey and Knowlson's Complete Horse-tamer and Farrier. A New and Improved Edition, containing Mr. Rarey's whole Secret of Subduing and Breaking Vicious Horses, together with his Improved Plan of Managing Young Colts, and breaking them to the Saddle, the Harness and the Sulky, with Rules for selecting a good Horse, for Feeding Horses, etc. Also, THE COMPLETE FARRIER; or, Horse Doctor; a Guide for the Treatment of Horses in all Diseases to which that noble animal is liable, being the result of fifty years' extensive practice of the author, John C. Knowlson, during his life an English Farrier of high popularity, containing the latest discoveries in the Cure of Spavin. Illustrated with descriptive Engravings.

Bound in boards, cloth back. Price......................................50 cts

Book of Household Pets. Containing valuable instructions about the Diseases, Breeding, Training and Management of the Canary, Mocking Bird, Brown Thrush, or Thrasher, and other birds, and the rearing and management of all kinds of Pigeons and Fancy Poultry, Rabbits, Squirrels, Guinea Pigs, White Mice, and Dogs; together with a Comprehensive Treatise on the Principle and Management of the Salt and Fresh Water Aquarium. Illustrated with 123 fine wood-cuts.
Bound in boards. Price...50 cts.
Bound in cloth, gilt side...75 cts.

Athletic Sports for Boys. A Repository of Graceful Recreations for Youth, containing clear and complete instructions in Gymnastics, Limb Exercises Jumping, Pole Leaping, Dumb Bells, Indian Clubs, Parallel Cars, the Horizontal Bar, the Trapeze, the Suspended Ropes, Skating, Swimming, Rowing, Sailing, Horsemanship, Riding, Driving, Angling, Fencing and Broadsword. The whole splendidly illustrated with 194 fine wood-cuts and diagrams.
Bound in boards, with cloth back. Price....................75 cts.
Bound in cloth, gilt side...$1 00

The Play-Ground; *or, Out-Door Games for Boys.* A Book of Healthy Recreations for Youth, containing over a hundred Amusements, including Games of Activity and Speed; Games with Toys, Marbles, Tops, Hoops, Kites, Archery, Balls; with Cricket, Croquet and Base-Ball. Illustrated with 124 wood-cuts. Bound in boards. Price.................50 cts.
Bound in cloth, gilt side...75 cts.

The above three books are abridged from the "American Boy's Book of Sports and Games."

The Young Reporter; *or, How to Write Short-Hand.* A complete Phonographic Teacher, intended to afford thorough instruction to those who have not the assistance of an Oral Teacher. By the aid of this work, any person of the most ordinary intelligence may learn to write Short-Hand, and Report Speeches and Sermons in a short time. Bound in boards, with cloth back. Price...50 cts.

Barton's Comic Recitations and Humorous Dialogues. Containing a variety of Comic Recitations in Prose and Poetry, Amusing Dialogues, Burlesque Scenes, Eccentric Orations and Stump Speeches, Humorous Interludes and Laughable Farces. Designed for School Commencements and Amateur Theatricals. Edited by JEROME BARTON. This is the best collection of Humorous pieces, especially adapted to the parlor stage, that has ever been published. Illuminated paper cover. Price.....30 cts.
Bound in boards, with cloth back.................................50 cts.

The Secret Out; *or, One Thousand Tricks with Cards, and other Recreations.* Illustrated with over Three Hundred Engravings. A book which explains all the Tricks and Deceptions with Playing Cards ever known, and gives, besides, a great many new ones—the whole being described so carefully, with engravings to illustrate them, that anybody can easily learn how to perform them. This work also contains 240 of the best Tricks in Legerdemain, in addition to the card tricks. 12mo., 400 pages bound in cloth, with gilt side and back. Price....................$1 50

The American Card Player. Containing clear and comprehensive directions for playing the games of Euchre, Whist, Bezique, All Fours French Fours, Cribbage, Cassino, Straight and Draw Poker, Whisky Poker and Commercial Pitch, together with all the laws of those Games. 150 pages, bound in boards, with cloth back. Price............................ 50 cts.
Bound in cloth gilt side ....75 cts.

The Young Debater and Chairman's Assistant. Contain-

ing instructions how to form and conduct Societies, Clubs and other organ
ized associations. Also, full Rules of Order for the government of their
Business and Debates; together with complete directions How to Compose
Resolutions, Reports and Petitions; and the best way to manage Public
Meetings, Celebrations, Dinners and Pic-Nics. Also instructions in Elocution, with hints on Debate. This book is compiled from our larger work
entitled "The Finger Post to Public Business." To any one who desires
to become familiar with the duties of an Officer or Committee-man in a
Society or Association, this work will be invaluable, as it contains minute
instructions in everything that pertains to the routine of Society Business.
152 pages. Paper cover, price..................................30 cts.
Bound in boards, with cloth back, price..........................50 cts.

Frost's Laws and By-Laws of American Society. A con-

densed but thorough treatise on Etiquette and its usages in America.
Containing plain and reliable directions for deportment on the following
subjects: Letters of Introduction, Salutes and Salutations, Calls, Conversations, Invitations, Dinner Company, Balls, Morning and Evening Parties, Visiting, Street Etiquette, Riding and Driving, Travelling; Etiquette
in Church, Etiquette for Places of Amusement; Servants, Hotel Etiquette;
Etiquette in Weddings, Baptisms, and Funerals; Etiquette with Children,
and at the Card-Table; Visiting Cards, Letter-Writing, the Lady's Toilet,
the Gentleman's Toilet; besides one hundred unclassified laws applicable
to all occasions. Paper cover, price...............................30 cts.
Bound in boards, with cloth back, price..........................50 cts.

How to Cook Potatoes, Apples, Eggs and Fish, Four Hun-

dred Different Ways. The matter embraced in this work consists of the
combined contents of four little books which have obtained immense popularity in France and England, and which have been thoroughly revised and
adapted for American housekeepers by an American cook of great experience. The work especially recommends itself to those who are often em-
barrassed for want of variety in dishes suitable for the breakfast table or,
on occasions where the necessity arises for preparing a meal at short notice.
Paper covers, price..30 cts.
Bound in boards, with cloth back, price..........................50 cts.

Uncle Josh's Trunk-Full of Fun. A portfolio of first-class

Wit and Humor, and never-ending source of Jollity. Containing the rich-
est collection of Comical Stories, Cruel Sells, Side-splitting Jokes, Humorous
Poetry, Quaint Parodies, Burlesque Sermons, New Conundrums and Mirth
Provoking Speeches ever published. Interspersed with Curious Puzzles,
Amusing Card Tricks, and Feats of Parlor Magic. Illustrated with nearly
200 Funny Engravings. This book consists of 64 large octavo pages, and
contains three times as much reading matter and real fun as any other
book of the same price. Illustrated cover, printed in colors, price...15 cts.

The American Housewife and Kitchen Directory. This

valuable book embraces three hundred and seventy-eight receipts for
cooking all sorts of American dishes in the most economical manner, and,
besides these, it also contains a great variety of important secrets for wash-
ing, cleansing, scouring, and extracting grease, paints, stains and iron-
mould from cloth, muslin and linen.
Bound in ornamental paper covers, price..........................30 cts.
Bound in boards, with cloth back, price..........................50 cts.

How to Cook and How to Carve. Giving plain and easily

understood directions for preparing and cooking, with the greatest economy,
every kind of dish, with complete instructions for serving the same. This
book is just the thing for a young Housekeeper. It explains everything
about the art of Cooking. It is worth a dozen of expensive French books.
Paper covers, price..30 cts.
Bound in boards, with cloth back, price..........................50 cts.

Duncan's Masonic Ritual and Monitor; *or, Guide to the Three Symbolic Degrees of the Ancient York Rite, Entered Apprentice, Fellow Craft, and Master Mason.* And to the Degrees of Mark Master, Past Master, Most Excellent Master, and the Royal Arch. By MALCOM C. DUNCAN. Explained and Interpreted by copious Notes and numerous Engravings. It is not so much the design of the author to gratify the curiosity of the uninitiated, as to furnish a Guide to the Younger Members of the Order, by means of which their progress from .ade to grade may be facilitated. It is a well-known fact that comparativel,'few of the fraternity are "Bright Masons," but with the aid of this invaluable Masonic Companion any Mason can, in a short time, become qualified to take the Chair as Master of a Lodge. Nothing is omitted in it that may tend to impart a full understanding of the principles of Masonry. This is a valuable book for the Fraternity, containing, as it does, the MODERN "WORK" of the order. No Mason should be without it. It is entirely different from any other Masonic book heretofore published.
Bound in cloth. Price...$2 50
Leather tucks (Pocket-book Style), with gilt edges. Price........... 3 00

'Trumps'" American Hoyle; *or, Gentleman's Hand-book of Games.* Containing clear and complete descriptions of all the Games played in the United States, with the American Rules for playing them; including Whist, Euchre, Bezique, Cribbage, All-Fours, Loo, Poker, Brag, Piquet, Ecarte, Boston, Cassino, Chess, Checkers, Backgammon, Dominoes, Billiards, and a hundred other Games. This work is designed to be an American authority in all games of skill and chance, and will settle any disputed point. It has been prepared with great care by the editor, with the assistance of a number of gentlemen players of skill and ability, and is not a re-hash of English Games, but a live American book, expressly prepared for American readers. THE AMERICAN HOYLE contains 525 pages, is printed on fine white paper, bound in cloth, with beveled boards, and is profusely illustrated with engravings explaining the different Games.
Price...$2 00

Brisbane's Golden Ready Reckoner. Calculated in Dollars and Cents, being a useful Assistant to Traders in buying and selling various commodities, either wholesale or retail, showing at once the amount or value of any number of articles, or quantity of goods, or any merchandise, either by the gallon, quart, pint, ounce, pound, quarter, hundred, yard, foot, inch, bushel, etc., in an easy and plain manner. To which are added Interest Tables, calculated in dollars and cents, for days and for months, at six per cent. and at seven per cent. per annum, alternately; and a great number of other Tables and Rules for calculation never before in print. By WILLIAM D. BRISBANE, A. M., Accountant, Book-keeper, etc.
Bound in boards, cloth back. Price..................................35 cts.

The Art of Conversation. With remarks on Fashion and Address. By MRS. MABERLY. This is the best book on the subject ever published. It contains nothing that is verbose or difficult to understand, but all the instructions and rules for conversation are given in a plain and common-sense manner, so that any one, however dull, can easily comprehend them. 64 pages octavo, large. Price........................25 cts.

Live and Learn. A Guide for all who wish to Speak and Write correctly. Containing examples of one thousand mistakes of daily occurrence, in speaking, writing and pronunciation.
216 pages, cloth, small octavo. Price.............................75 cts.

Mrs. Crowen's American Lady's Cookery Book. Containing over 1,200 original receipts for preparing and cooking all kinds of dishes. The most popular Cook Book ever published.
12mo., cloth, 474 pages.. $2 00

One Hundred and Thirty Comic Dialogues and Recitations.

Being Barton's Comic Recitations and Humorous Dialogues, and Spencer's Comic Speeches and Dialogues, combined in one volume. This capital book contains an endless variety of Comic Speeches, Humorous Scenes, Amusing Burlesques, and Diverting Dialogues. It embraces French, Dutch, Irish, Ethiopian and Yankee Stories, and from its fruitful pages may be selected enough fun to make any entertainment or exhibition a success. Bound in cloth. Price..$1 50

Burlesque and Musical Acting Charades. By Edmund C.

Nugent. Containing ten Charades, all in different styles, two of which are easy and effective Comic Parlor Operas, with Music and Pianoforte Accompaniments. These Plays require no scenery, and the dialogue is short, witty, and easy to learn. To each Charade will be found an introductory note, containing hints for its performance. Paper cover. Price........30 cts. Bound in boards, cloth back....................................50 cts.

Twenty-Six Short and Amusing Plays for Private Theatri-

cals. Being Howard's Drawing-room Theatricals, and Hudson's Private Theatricals, combined in one volume. This book, as the title implies, contains twenty-six of the best plays that can be selected for a private theatrical entertainment. It contains several amusing plays for one sex only, and is thus adapted for the army, navy, and male or female boarding-schools. It contains plain directions for getting up a good amateur performance. Bound in cloth. Price..$1 50

Frost's School and Exhibition Dialogues. Comprising

Frost's Humorous Exhibition Dialogues, and Frost's Dialogues for Young Folks, combined in one volume. By getting this excellent book, the difficulty in procuring a good dialogue for a school exhibition will be entirely overcome. It contains sixty-one good dialogues of every shade and variety, and from its well-stored pages, may be selected enough original matter to ensure the success of a score of entertainments. Bound in cloth. Price..$1 50

Snipsnaps and Snickerings of Simon Snodgrass. A Collec-

tion of Droll and Laughable Stories. These funny and amusing stories are illustrative of Irish Drolleries and Blarney, Ludicrous Dutch Blunders, Queer Yankee Tricks and Dodges, Southern Fire-Eating Braggadocia, Bombast of Suckerdom, Backwoods Boasting, Humors of Horse-trading, Negro Comicalities, Perilous Pranks of Fighting Men, Frenchmen's Queer Mistakes, Scotch Shrewdness, and other phases of eccentric character that go to make up a perfect and complete Medley of Wit and Humor. It is really and truly the most entertaining collection of Lively, Laughable and Ludicrous Yarns ever presented in a single volume. There is not a dull story in the whole book, and we feel sure that it will give the most ample satisfaction. It is also full of funny engravings. Price..........25 cts.

The Strange and Wonderful Adventures of Bachelor But-

terfly. Showing how his passion for Natural History completely eradicated the tender passion implanted in his breast—also, detailing his Extraordinary Travels, both by sea and land—his Hairbreadth Escapes from fire and cold—his being come over by a Widow with nine small children—his wonderful Adventures with the Doctor and the Fiddler—his being Swallowed by a Whale, and then afterwards restored to his friends—his capture by Algerine Pirates—his being Frozen nearly to Death, and then Roasted Alive; and his firm endurance of these and other Perils of a most extraordinary nature. The whole illustrated by about 200 engravings. This book is printed on fine plate paper in the neatest manner, and is the cheapest pictorial work ever issued in America. Price..............................30 cts.

The Book of 1,000 Comical Stories; *or, Endless Repast of Fun.* A rich banquet for every day in the year, with several courses and a dessert. BILL OF FARE: Comprising Tales of Humor, Laughable Anecdotes, Irresistible Drolleries, Jovial Jokes, Comical Conceits, Puns and Pickings, Quibbles and Queries, Bon Mots and Broadgrins, Oddities, Epigrams, etc. Appropriately Illustrated with 300 Comic Engravings. By the author of "Mrs. Partington's Carpet-bag of Fun." Large 12mo., cloth. Price...$1 50

Mrs. Partington's Carpet-bag of Fun. A collection of over one thousand of the most Comical Stories, Amusing Adventures, Side-splitting Jokes, Check-extending Poetry, Funny Conundrums, QUEER SAYINGS OF MRS. PARTINGTON, Heart-rending Puns, Witty Repartees, etc. The whole illustrated by about 150 comic wood-cuts. 12mo., 300 pages, cloth, gilt. Price..............................$1 25
Ornamented paper covers...75 cts.

How to Behave; *or, The Spirit of Etiquette.* A Complete Guide to Polite Society, for Ladies and Gentlemen; containing rules for good behavior at the dinner table, in the parlor, and in the street; with important hints on introduction, conversation, etc.
Price...12 cts.

Dr. Valentine's Comic Metamorphoses. Being the second series of Dr. Valentine's Lectures, with Characters, as given by the late Yankee Hill. Embellished with numerous portraits.
Ornamental paper cover. Price......................................75 cts.
Cloth, gilt..$1 25

Broad Grins of the Laughing Philosopher. Being a Collection of Funny Jokes, Droll Incidents, and Ludicrous pictures. By PICKLE THE YOUNGER. This book is really a good one. It is full of the drollest incidents imaginable, interspersed with good jokes, quaint sayings, and funny pictures. Price...13 cts.

The Knapsack Full of Fun; *or, One Thousand Rations of Laughter.* Illustrated with over 500 comical Engravings, and containing over one thousand Jokes and Funny Stories. By DOESTICKS and other witty writers. Large quarto. Price...............................30 cts.

The Plate of Chowder; *A Dish for Funny Fellows.* Appropriately illustrated with 100 Comic Engravings. By the author of "Mrs. Partington's Carpet-bag of Fun." 12mo., paper cover. Price...25 cts.

How to Talk and Debate; *or, Fluency of Speech Attained without the Sacrifice of Elegance and Sense.*
Price...12 cts.

How to Dress with Taste. Containing Hints on the harmony of colors, the theory of contrast, the complexion, shape or height.
Price...12 cts.

How to Cut and Contrive Children's Clothes at a Small Cost. With numerous and explanatory engravings. Price..........12 cts

The Young Housekeeper's Book; *or, How to Have a Good Living upon a Small Income.* Price...................................12 cts.

The Chairman and Speaker's Guide; *or, Rules for the Orderly Conduct of Public Meetings.* Price..............................12 cts

The Mishaps and Adventures of Obadiah Oldbuck. Wherein are set forth the Crosses, Chagrins, Calamities, Checks, Chills, the Changes, Circumgyrations, by which his Courtship was attended. Showing also, the Issue of his suit, and his Espousal to his Lady Love. This humorous and curious book sets forth with 183 comic drawings, the misfortunes which befell Mr. Oldbuck; and also his five unsuccessful attempts to commit suicide—his hairbreadth escapes from fire, water and famine—his affection for his poor dog, etc. To look over this book will make you laugh and you can't help it. Price...30 cts.

Barber's American Book of Ready-Made Speeches. Containing 150 original examples of humorous and serious Speeches, suitable for the following occasions: Presentation Speeches, Convivial Speeches, Festival Speeches, Addresses of Welcome, Addresses of Congratulation and Compliment, Political Speeches, Dinner and Supper Speeches, for Clubs, Associations, etc.; Trade Banquets, etc.; Off-hand Speeches on a variety of subjects; together with appropriate Replies to each. To which are added, Resolutions of Compliment, Congratulation and Condolence, and a variety of Toasts and Sentiments for Public and Private Entertainments. Paper cover. Price...30 cts.
Bound in boards, cloth back..50 cts.

Allyn's Ritual of Freemasonry. Containing a Complete Key to the following Degrees: Degree of Entered Apprentice; Degree of Fellow Craft; Degree of Master Mason; Degree of Mark Master; Degree of Past Master; Degree of Excellent Master; Degree of Royal Arch; Royal Arch Chapter; Degree of Royal Master; Degree of Select Master; Degree of Super-Excellent Master; Degree of Ark and Dove; Degree of Knights of Constantinople. Degree of Secret Monitor; Degree of Heroine of Jericho; Degree of Knights of Three Kings; Mediterranean Pass; Order of Knights of the Red Cross; Order of Knights Templar and Knights of Malta; Knights of the Christian Mark, and Guards of the Conclave; Knights of the Holy Sepulchre; The Holy and Three Illustrious Order of the Cross; Secret Master; Perfect Master; Intimate Secretary; Provost and Judge; Intendant of the Buildings, or Master in Israel; Elected Knights of Nine; Elected Grand Master; Sublime Knights Elected; Grand Master Architect; Knights of the Ninth Arch; Grand Elect, Perfect and Sublime Mason. Illustrated with 38 copper-plate engravings; to which is added, a Key to the Phi Beta Kappa, Orange, and Odd Fellows' Societies. By Avery Allyn, K. R. C. K. T. K. M., etc. 12mo, cloth. Price...$3 00

Charley White's Joke Book. Being a perfect Casket of Fun, the first and only work of the kind ever published. Containing a full exposé of all the most laughable Jokes, Witticisms, etc., as told by the celebrated Ethiopian Comedian, CHARLES WHITE; with full-page illustrations of his most popular characters. 94 pages. Price.............12 cts.

Black Wit and Darkey Conversations. By CHARLES WHITE. Containing a large collection of laughable Anecdotes, Jokes, Stories, Witticisms, and Darkey Conversations. Illustrated with cuts of the comedian in his best delineations.............................12 cts.

Mother Shipton's Fortune Teller; or, Future Fate foretold by the Planets. Being the 900 Answers of Pythagoras to the Questions of Life's Destiny. Derived from the Mystic Numbers and Letters of the Planets. Containing the Emblematic and Mystical Wheel of Fortune and Fate, beautifully colored. Also, containing the Moon's good and evil influences on Mankind, compiled from the most ancient authorities, by the Astrologer of the 19th Century. 16mo, 115 pages. Illuminated paper cover ....30 cts.

Day's Book-keeping Without a Master. Containing the Rudiments of Book-keeping in Single and Double Entry, together with the proper Forms and Rules for opening and keeping Condensed and General Book Accounts. This work is printed in a beautiful script type, and hence combines the advantages of a handsome style of writing with its very simple and easily understood lessons in Book-keeping. It presents a *fac-simile* of a handsomely written set of account books—on a small scale, it is true, but very neat and pretty. This will enable the learner to improve his hand-writing, while perfecting himself as an expert, or first-class accountant—which is done by frequent practice. The book exhibits all the different forms of Accounts, Balance Sheets, Trial-Balance, Commercial and Monetary Letters, Drafts, Notes, Credits, Orders, Inquiries, Replies, etc., etc., arranged in the script type exactly as they should be written for business purposes. This feature makes the work invaluable as a book of reference. The several pages have explanations at the bottom, to assist the learner, in small type. As a pattern for opening book-accounts it is especially valuable—particularly for those who are not well posted in the art. DAY'S BOOK-KEEPING is the size of a regular quarto Account Book, and is made to lie flat open, for convenience in use. Price................50 Cts.

Blank Books for Day's Book-keeping. We have for sale Books of 96 pages each, ruled according to the patterns mentioned on page 3 of DAY'S BOOK-KEEPING, suitable for practice of the learner, viz.: No. 1—For General Book-keeping, pages 4 and 5; for Cash Account on page 13; for Day Book in Single Entry, pages 15 to 25. No 2—For Condensed Accounts, pages 9 and 10; for Cash Accounts, page 12; for Journal in Double Entry, pages 34 to 43. No. 3—For Ledgers in Double or Single Entry, pages 26 to 44. Price, each...50 Cts.

How to Write a Composition. This original work will be found a valuable aid in writing a composition on any topic. It lays down plain directions for the division of a subject into its appropriate heads, and for arranging them in their natural order, commencing with the simplest theme and advancing progressively to the treatment of more complicated subjects. The use of this excellent hand-book will save the student the many hours of labor too often wasted in trying to write a plain composition. It affords a perfect skeleton of each subject, with its headings or divisions clearly defined, and each heading filled in with the ideas which the subject suggests; so that all the writer has to do, in order to produce a good composition, is to enlarge on them to suit his taste and inclination. Bound in boards, cloth back. Price...............................50 Cts.

Nugent's Burlesque and Musical Acting Charades. Containing ten Charades, all in different styles, two of which are easy and effective Comic Parlor Operas, with Music and Pianoforte Accompaniments. These Plays require no scenery, and the dialogue is short, witty, and easy to learn. To each Charade will be found an introductory note, containing hints for its performance. Paper cover. Price.....................30 Cts. Bound in boards, cloth back.................................50 Cts.

Snipsnaps and Snickerings of Simon Snodgrass. These funny and amusing stories are illustrative of Irish Drolleries, Ludicrous Dutch Blunders, Yankee Tricks and Dodges, Backwoods Boasting, Negro Comicalities, Perilous Pranks of Fighting Men, Frenchmen's Queer Mistakes, and other phases of eccentric character to make a complete Medley of Wit and Humor. Full of funny engravings. Price.....................25 cts.

The Strange and Wonderful Adventures of Bachelor Butterfly. Showing his Hairbreadth Escapes from fire and cold—his being come over by a Widow with nine small children—and his firm endurance of these and other perils of a most extraordinary nature. The whole illustrated by about 200 engravings. Price...................30 cts.

Howard's Recitations, *Comic, Serious* **and** *Pathetic.* Being a collection of fresh Recitations in Prose and Poetry, suitable for Anniversaries, Exhibitions, Sociables and Evening Parties. 180 pages, 16mo. Paper Cover...............30cts. Bound in Boards...........50cts.

Frost's New Book of Dialogues. Being an entirely new and original series of Humorous Dialogues, designed for performance at School Anniversaries **and Exhibitions.** 180 pages. **Paper Covers.........30**cts. Bound in Boards...............................50cts.

Frost's Dialogues for Young Folks. A collection of Original, Moral and Humorous Dialogues, adapted to the use of School and Church Exhibitions, Family Gatherings and Juvenile Celebrations on all occasions. A few of the Dialogues are long enough to form a sort of little drama that will interest more advanced scholars, while short and easy ones abound for the use of quite young children. Paper Cover...............30cts. Bound in Boards, with Cloth Backs, Side in Colors.................50cts.

Frost's Humorous and Exhibition Dialogues. This is a collection of Sprightly Original Dialogues, in Prose and Verse, intended to be spoken at School Exhibitions. Some of the pieces are for boys, some for girls, while a number are designed to be used by both sexes. 180 pages. Paper Covers...............30cts. Bound in Boards...........50cts

French Self-Taught. A new system on the most simple principles for Universal Self-Tuition, with English **Pronunciation of every word.** By FRANZ THIMM. Price.................................25cts.

German Self-Taught. Uniform with "French Self-Taught." By FRANZ THIMM. Price............................... 25cts.

Spanish Self-Taught. Uniform with "French Self-Taught.' By FRANZ THIMM. Price...........................25cts.

Italian Self-Taught. Uniform with "French Self-Taught." By FRANZ THIMM. Price...............................25cts.

Franz Thimm's Modern Languages. Being the above four works bound together in cloth, 16mo. Price........................$1.50

The Banjo, and How to Play It. Containing, in addition to the Elementary Study, a choice collection of Polkas, Waltzes, Solos, Schottisches, Songs, Hornpipes, Jigs, Reels, &c.; with full explanations of both the "Banjo" and "Guitar" styles of execution, and designed to impart a complete knowledge of the Art of Playing the Banjo practically, without the aid of a Teacher. By FRANK CONVERSE, author of the "Banjo without a Master." 16mo. Bound in Boards, with Cloth Back.............50cts.

How to Speak in Public; *or, the Art of Extempore Oratory.* A valuable manual for those who desire to become ready, off-hand speakers. 16mo. Paper Cover...25cts.

How to Shine in Society; *or, the Science of Conversation.* Containing the principles, laws, and general usages of polite society. 16mo. Paper Cover...25cts.

The Athlete's Guide. A hand-book on Walking, Running, and Rowing, giving full instructions for Training, and a Record of all the principal events since the year 1775, with sketches of the lives of the most celebrated Athletes. By W. E. HARDING, Ex-Champion. 18mo, cloth, Price.50cts

Howard's Book of Drawing-Room Theatricals. A collection of twelve short and amusing plays in one act and one scene, specially adapted for private performances; with practical directions, for their preparation and management. Some of the plays are adapted for performers of one sex only. This book is just what is wanted by those who purpose getting up an entertainment of private theatricals: it contains all the necessary instructions for insuring complete success. 180 pages.
Paper cover. Price..30 cts.
Bound in boards with cloth back...............................50 cts.

Judson's Private Theatricals for Home Performance. A collection of Humorous Plays suitable for an Amateur Entertainment, with directions how to carry out a performance successfully. Some of the plays in this collection are adapted for performance by males only, others require only females for the cast, and all of them are in one scene and one act, and may be represented in any moderate sized parlor, without much preparation of costume or scenery. 180 pages.
Paper covers. Price..30 cts.
Bound in boards with cloth back...............................50 cts.

The Art of Dressing Well. By Miss S. A. Frost. This book is designed for ladies and gentlemen who desire to make a favorable impression upon society, and is intended to meet the requirements of any season, place, or time; to offer such suggestions as will be valuable to those just entering society; to brides, for whose guidance a complete trousseau is described; to persons in mourning; indeed, to every individual who pays attention to the important objects of economy, style, and propriety of costume. 188 pages.
Paper covers. Price..30 cts
Bound in boards, cloth back...................................50 cts

How to Amuse an Evening Party. A complete collection of Home Recreations, including Round Games, Forfeits, Parlor Magic, Puzzles, and Comic Diversions; together with a great variety of Scientific Recreations and Evening Amusements. Profusely illustrated with nearly two hundred fine woodcuts. Here is family amusement for the million. Here is parlor or drawing-room entertainment, night after night, for a whole winter. A young man with this volume may render himself the *beau ideal* of a delightful companion at every party. He may take the lead in amusing the company, and win the hearts of all the ladies, and charm away the obduracy of the stoniest-hearted parent, by his powers of entertainment.
Bound in ornamental paper cover. Price........................30 cts.
Bound in boards, with cloth back..............................50 cts.

Martine's Droll Dialogues and Laughable Recitations. By Arthur Martine, author of "Martine's Letter-Writer," etc., etc. A collection of Humorous Dialogues, Comic Recitations, Brilliant Burlesques, Spirited Stump Speeches, and Ludicrous Farces, adapted for School Celebrations and Home Amusement. 188 pages.
Paper covers. Price..30 cts.
Bound in boards, with cloth back..............................50 cts.

Frost's Humorous and Exhibition Dialogues. This is a collection of sprightly original Dialogues, in Prose and Verse, intended to be spoken at School Exhibitions. Some of the pieces are for boys, some for girls, while a number are designed to be used by both sexes. The Dialogues are all good, and will recommend themselves to those who desire to have innocent fun—the prevailing feature at a school celebration. 186 pages.
Paper cover. Price..30 cts.
Bound in boards...50 cts

What Shall We Do To-Night? *or, Social Amusements for Evening Parties.* This Elegant Book affords an almost inexhaustible fund of Amusement for Evening Parties, Social Gatherings, and all Festive Occasions, ingeniously grouped together so as to furnish complete and ever-varying entertainment for *Twenty-six Evenings.* Its repertoire embraces all the best Round and Forfeit Games, clearly described and rendered perfectly plain by original and amusing examples; interspersed with a great variety of Ingenious Puzzles, Entertaining Tricks, and Innocent Sells; new and original *Musical* and *Poetical* Pastimes, Startling Illusions, and Mirth-provoking Exhibitions; including complete directions and text for performing *Charades,* **Tableaux,** *Parlor Pantomimes,* the world-renowned *Punch and Judy, Gallanty Shows,* and original *Shadow Pantomimes;* also, full information for the successful performance of *Dramatic Dialogues* and *Parlor Theatricals,* with a selection of Original Plays, etc., written expressly for this work. It is embellished with over one hundred descriptive and explanatory engravings, and contains 366 pages, printed on fine toned paper, 12mo, bound in extra cloth.....................$2.00

How To Conduct a Debate. A Series of Complete Debates, Outlines of Debates, and Questions for Discussion; with references to the best sources of information on each particular topic. In the Complete Debates, the questions for discussion are defined, the debate formally opened, an array of brilliant arguments adduced on either side, and the debate closed according to Parliamentary usages. The second part consists of Questions for Debate, with heads of arguments, for and against, given in a condensed form for the speakers to enlarge upon to suit their own fancy. In addition to these are a large collection of good Debatable Questions. The authorities, to be referred to for information, being given at the close of every debate throughout the work. By Frederic Rowton. 232 pages, 16mo, paper cover..50 cts.
Bound in boards, cloth back.......................................75 cts.

McBride's Comic Dialogues *for School Exhibitions and Literary Entertainments.* A collection of original Humorous Dialogues, especially designed for the development and display of **Amateur Dramatic Talent,** and introducing a variety of sentimental, **sprightly,** comic, and genuine Yankee characters. By H. Elliott McBride. 16mo, illuminated paper cover...30 cts.
Bound in boards...50 cts.

The Fireside Magician; *or, The Art of Natural Magic made Easy*—being a familiar and scientific explanation of Legerdemain, Physical Amusement, Recreative Chemistry, Diversions with Cards, and of all the minor mysteries of Mechanical Magic, with feats as performed in public by Herr Alexander and Robert Houdin. 132 pages, 16mo, illuminated paper cover...30 cts.
Bound in boards, cloth back.......................................50 cts.

Frost's Original Letter-Writer, *and Laws and By-Laws of American Society Combined.* Being a complete collection of original Letters and Notes upon every imaginable subject of every day life, and a condensed but thorough treatise on Etiquette, and its usages in America. This work includes a dictionary of synonyms especially adapted for the use of correspondents. By S. A. Frost. 16mo, 378 pages, extra cloth, gilt...$1.50

Row's Complete Fractional Ready Reckoner. For buying and selling any kind of merchandise, giving the fractional parts of a pound, yard, etc., from one quarter to one thousand, at any price from one-quarter of a cent to five dollars. By Nelson Row. 36mo, 232 pages. Boards..50 cts.

Brudder Bones' Book of Stump Speeches and Burlesque

Orations. Also containing Humorous Lectures, Ethiopian Dialogues, Plantation Scenes, Negro Farces and Burlesques, Laughable Interludes and Comic Recitations, interspersed with Dutch, Irish, French and Yankee Stories. Compiled and edited by JOHN F. SCOTT. This book contains some of the best hits of the leading negro delineators of the present time, as well as mirth-provoking jokes and repartees of the most celebrated End-Men of the day, and specially designed for the introduction of fun in an evening's entertainment. Paper covers. Price...............................30 cts. Bound in boards, illuminated..........................50 cts.

Frost's Original Letter-Writer. A complete collection of

Original Letters and Notes, upon every imaginable subject of Every-Day Life, with plain directions about everything connected with writing a letter. Containing Letters of Introduction, Letters on Business, Letters answering Advertisements, Letters of Recommendation, Applications for Employment, Letters of Congratulation, of Condolence, of Friendship and Relationship, Love Letters, Notes of Invitation, Notes Accompanying Gifts, Letters of Favor, of Advice, and Letters of Excuse, together with an appropriate answer to each. The whole embracing three hundred letters and notes. By S. A. FROST, author of "The Parlor Stage," "Dialogues for Young Folks," etc. To which is added a comprehensive Table of Synonyms alone worth double the price asked for the book. This work is not a rehash of English writers, but is entirely practical and original, and suited to the wants of the American public. We assure our readers that it is the best collection of letters ever published in this country. Bound in boards, cloth back, with illuminated sides. Price.................................50 cts.

Inquire Within *for Anything you Want to Know ; or, Over*

3,700 *Facts for the People.* "Inquire Within" is one of the most valuable and extraordinary volumes ever presented to the American public, and embodies nearly 4,000 facts, in most of which any person will find instruction, aid and entertainment. It contains so many valuable recipes, that an enumeration of them requires *seventy-two columns of fine type for the index.* Illustrated. 436 large pages. Price.....................$1 50

The Sociable; *or, One Thousand and One Home Amusements.*

Containing Acting Proverbs, Dramatic Charades, Acting Charades, Tableaux Vivants, Parlor Games and Parlor Magic, and a choice collection of Puzzles, etc., illustrated with nearly 300 Engravings and Diagrams, the whole being a fund of never-ending entertainment. By the author of the "Magician's Own Book." Nearly 400 pages, 12 mo. cloth, gilt side stamp. Price..$1 50

Martine's Hand-Book of Etiquette and Guide to True Politeness.

A complete Manual for all those who desire to understand good breeding, the customs of good society, and to avoid incorrect and vulgar habits. Containing clear and comprehensive directions for correct manners, conversation, dress, introductions, rules for good behavior at Dinner Parties and the table, with hints on wine and carving at the table; together with Etiquette of the Ball and Assembly Room, Evening Parties, and the usages to be observed when visiting or receiving calls; deportment in the street and when travelling. To which is added the Etiquette of Courtship and Marriage. Bound in boards, with cloth back. Price..............50 cts. Bound in cloth, gilt side.................................75 cts.

Day's American Ready-Reckoner, containing Tables for

rapid calculations of Aggregate Values, Wages, Salaries, Board, Interest Money, &c., &c. Also, Tables of Timber, Plank, Board and Log Measurements, with full explanations how to measure them, either by the square foot (board measure), cubic foot (timber measure), &c. Bound in boards. Price...50 cts. Bound in cloth...75 cts.

Martine's Letter-writer and Etiquette Combined. For the use of Ladies and Gentlemen. 12mo., cloth, gilt side and back. A great many books have been printed on the subject of etiquette and correct behavior in society, but none of them are sufficiently comprehensive and matter-of-fact enough to suit the class of people who may be called new beginners in fashionable life. This book is entirely different from others in that respect. It explains in a plain, common-sense way, precisely how to conduct yourself in every position in society. This book also contains over 300 sensible letters and notes suitable to every occasion in life, and is probably the best treatise on Letter-writing that has ever been printed. It gives easily understood directions that are brief and to the point. It has some excellent model letters of friendship and business, and its model Love Letters are unequaled. If any lady or gentleman desires to know how to *begin* a love correspondence, this is just the book they want. This volume contains the same matter as "Martine's Hand-book of Etiquette," and "Martine's Sensible Letter-writer," and, in fact, combines those two books bound together in one substantial volume of 373 pages........$1 50

Row's National Wages Tables. Showing at a glance the amount of wages, from half an hour to sixty hours, at from $1 to $37 per week. Also from one-quarter of a day to four weeks, at $1 to $37 per per week. By Nelson Row. By this book, which is particularly useful when part of a week, day, or hour is lost, a large pay-roll can be made out in a few minutes, thus saving more time in making out one pay-roll than the cost of the book. Every employer hiring help by the hour, day or week, should get a copy; and every employee should also obtain one, as it will enable him to know exactly the amount of money he is entitled to on pay-day. 12mo, 80 pages. Half bound......................50 cts.
Cloth..75 cts.
Roan Tuck............•....................................$1.00

The Young Reporter; or, *How to Write Short-Hand.* A complete Phonographic Teacher, intended to afford thorough instruction to those who have not the assistance of an Oral Teacher. By the aid of this work, any person of the most ordinary intelligence may learn to write Short-Hand, and report Speeches and Sermons in a short time. Bound in boards, with cloth back..**50 cts.**

The Yankee Cook Book. *A New System of Cookery.* Containing hundreds of excellent receipts from actual experience in Cooking; also, full explanations in the art of Carving. 126 pages. Illuminated paper cover..30 cts.
Bound in boards, cloth back..50 cts.

Mother Shipton's Oriental Dream Book. Being a reliable Interpretation of Dreams, Visions, Apparitions, etc. Together with a history of remarkable Dreams, proven true as interpreted. Collected and arranged from the most celebrated Masters. 16mo, 118 pages. Illuminated paper cover..30 cts.

Jack Johnson's Jokes for the Jolly. A collection of Astonishing Anecdotes, Weird Witticisms, Side-Splitting Stories, and Mirthful Morsels for the Melancholy. Providing a sure solace for sadness, a balm for the blues, and an active antidote against all aches. 128 pages, 16mo. Illuminated paper cover..25 cts.

Day's Conversation Cards. *A New Original Set,* Comprising Eighteen Questions and Twenty-four Answers, so arranged that the whole of the Answers are Apt Replies to each one of the Eighteen Questions. The Set comprises forty-two Cards in the aggregate, which are put up in a handsome case, with printed directions for use..20 cts.

The American Home Cook Book.

Containing several hundred excellent Recipes. The whole based on many years' experience of an American Housewife. Illustrated with Engravings. All the Recipes in this book are written from actual experiments in Cooking. There are no copyings from theoretical cooking recipes.
Bound in boards, cloth back. Price.................................50 cts.
Bound in paper covers. Price.................................30 cts.

Amateur Theatricals and Fairy-Tale Dramas.

A collection of original plays, expressly designed for Drawing-room performance. By S. A. Frost. This work is designed to meet a want, which has been long felt, of short and amusing pieces suitable to the limited stage of the private parlor. The old friends of fairy-land will be recognized among the Fairy-Tale Dramas, newly clothed and arranged.
Paper covers. Price.................................30 cts.
Bound in boards, with cloth back.................................50 cts.

Parlor Tricks with Cards.

Containing explanations of Tricks and Deceptions with Playing Cards, embracing Tricks with Cards performed by Sleight-of-hand, by the aid of Memory, Mental Calculation and Arrangement of the Cards, by the aid of Confederacy; and Tricks performed by the aid of Prepared Cards. The whole illustrated and made plain and easy, with 70 engravings. This book is an abridgment of our large work, entitled "The Secret Out."
Paper covers. Price.................................30 cts.
Bound in boards, with cloth back.................................50 cts.

Chesterfield's Letter-writer and Complete Book of Etiquette;

or, Concise, Systematic Directions for Arranging and Writing Letters. Also, Model Correspondence in Friendship and Business, and a great variety of Model Love Letters. This work is also a Complete Book of Etiquette. There is more real information in this book than in half a dozen volumes of the most expensive ones.
Bound in boards, with cloth back. Price.................................35 cts.

Frank Converse's Complete Banjo Instructor.

Without a Master. Containing a choice collection of Banjo Solos, Hornpipes, Reels, Jigs, Walk Arounds, Songs, and Banjo Stories, progressively arranged and plainly explained. Bound in boards, with cloth back. Price.......50 cts.

The Magician's Own Book.

Containing several hundred amusing Sleight-of-hand and Card Tricks, Perplexing Puzzles, Entertaining Tricks and Secret Writing Explained. Illustrated with over 500 wood engravings. 12mo., cloth, gilt side and back stamp. Price.........$1 50

North's Book of Love Letters.

With Directions how to write and when to use them, and 120 specimen Letters, suitable for Lovers of any age and condition, and under all circumstances. Interspersed with the author's comments thereon. The whole forming a convenient handbook of valuable information and counsel for the use of those who need friendly guidance and advice in matters of Love, Courtship and Marriage. By Ingoldsby North. This book is recommended to all who are from any cause in doubt as to the manner in which they should write or reply to letters upon love and courtship. The reader will be aided in his thoughts—he will see where he is likely to please and where to displease, how to begin and how to end his letter, and how to judge of those nice shades of expression and feeling concerning which a few mistaken expressions may create misunderstanding. All who wish not only to copy a love letter, but to learn the art of writing them, will find North's book a very pleasant, sensible and friendly companion. It is an additional recommendation that the variety offered is very large. Cloth. Price.................................75 cts.
Bound in boards.................................50 cts.

The Courtship and Adventures of Jonathan Homebred;
or, The Scrapes and Escapes of a Live Yankee. Beautifully Illustrated. 12mo., cloth. This book is printed in handsome style, on good paper, and with amusing engravings.
Price...$1 56

The Wizard of the North's Hand-Book of Natural Magic. Being a series of the Newest Tricks of Deception, arranged for Amateurs and Lovers of the Art. By Professor J. H. ANDERSON, the great Wizard of the North.
Price..25 cts.

The Encyclopædia of Popular Songs. Being a compilation of all the new and fashionable Patriotic, Sentimental, Ethiopian, Humorous, Comic and Convivial Songs, the whole comprising over 400 songs.
12mo., cloth, gilt. Price..$1 25

Tony Pastor's Book of 600 Comic Songs and Speeches. Being an entire collection of all the Humorous Songs, Stump Speeches, Burlesque Orations, Funny Scenes, Comic Duets, Diverting Dialogues, and Local Lyrics, as sung and given by the unrivaled Comic Vocalist and Stump Orator, TONY PASTOR.
Bound in boards, cloth back...$1 00

Yale College Scrapes; or, How the Boys Go It at New Haven. This is a book of 111 pages, containing accounts of all the noted and famous "Scrapes" and "Sprees," of which students at Old Yale have been guilty for the last quarter of a century.
Price..25 cts.

The Comic English Grammar; or, A Complete Grammar of our Language, with Comic Examples. Illustrated with about fifty engravings. Price..25 cts.

The Comical Adventures of David Dufficks. Illustrated with over one hundred Funny Engravings. Large octavo.
Price..25 cts.

Anecdotes of Love. Being a true account of the most remarkable events connected with the History of Love in all Ages and among all Nations. By LOLA MONTEZ, Countess of Landsfeldt.
Large 12mo., cloth. Price...$1 50

Tony Pastor's Complete Budget of Comic Songs. Containing a complete collection of the New and Original Songs, Burlesque Orations, Stump Speeches, Comic Dialogues, Pathetic Ballads, as sung and given by the celebrated Vocalist, TONY PASTOR.
Cloth, gilt. Price...$1 25

The Laughable Adventures of Messrs. Brown, Jones and Robinson. Showing where they went and how they went, what they did and how they did it. With nearly two hundred most thrillingly comic engravings.
Price..30 cts.

De Walden's Ball Room Companion; or, Dancing Made Easy. A collection of the Fashionable Drawing-Room Dances, with instructions for dancing all the figures of "The German." By EMILE DE WALDEN, Professor of Dancing. Bound in boards, cloth back............50 cts.

NEW SONG BOOKS.

This list of Song Books contains all kinds of Songs, embracing Love, Sentimental, Ethiopian, Scotch, Irish, Convivial, Comic, Patriotic, Pathetic, and Dutch Songs, besides a great variety of Stump Speeches, Burlesque Orations, Plantation Scenes, Irish, Dutch, and Yankee Stories, Comic Recitations, Conundrums and Toasts.

BARRY RICHMOND'S MY YOUNG WIFE AND I SONGSTER ......10 Cts.
BARRY ROBINSON'S DON'T YOU WISH YOU WAS ME SONGSTER.10 "
JOHNNY WILD'S WHAT AM I DOING SONGSTER....................10 "
BUELL'S KU-KLUX-KLAN SONGSTER...............................10 "
FRANK KERN'S PRETTY LITTLE DEAR SONGSTER.................10 "
HARRY RICHMOND'S NOT-FOR-JOSEPH SONGSTER..............10 "
DAVE REED'S SALLY-COME-UP SONGSTER....................10 "
THE ROOTLE-TUM TOOTLE-TUM TAY SONGSTER.................10 "
SAM SLICK'S YANKEE SONGSTER.................................10 "
CHAMPAGNE CHARLEY SONGSTER...............................10 "
JENNY ENGEL'S DEAR LITTLE SHAMROCK SONGSTER..........10 "
BILLY EMERSON'S NEW COMIC SONGSTER.....................10 "
BERRY'S LAUGH AND GROW FAT SONGSTER ....10 "
TONY PASTOR'S BOWERY SONGSTER...........................10 "
TONY PASTOR'S WATER-FALL SONGSTER ....10 "
TONY PASTOR'S 4th COMBINATION SONGSTER..................10 "
TONY PASTOR'S OPERA-HOUSE SONGSTER......................10 "
TONY PASTOR'S CARTE DE VISITE SONGSTER..................10 "
TONY PASTOR'S GREAT SENSATION SONGSTER.................10 "
TONY PASTOR'S OWN COMIC VOCALIST........................10 "
TONY PASTOR'S COMIC IRISH SONGSTER......................10 "
TONY PASTOR'S COMIC SONGSTER.............................10 "
TONY PASTOR'S UNION SONGSTER.............................10 "
PADDY'S THE BOY SONGSTER..................................10 "
BONNY DUNDEE SONGSTER.....................................10 "
WILL CARLETON'S DANDY PAT SONGSTER ....10 "
BILLY EMERSON'S NANCY FAT SONGSTER ....10 "
HOOLEY'S OPERA HOUSE SONGSTER...........................10 "
SAM SHARPLEY'S IRON-CLAD SONGSTER.......................10 "
JOE ENGLISH'S COMIC IRISH SONGSTER......................10 "
RODY MAGUIRE'S COMIC VARIETY SONGSTER..................10 "
HARRY PELL'S EBONY SONGSTER..............................10 "
FRANK BROWER'S BLACK DIAMOND SONGSTER.................10 "
FRANK CONVERSE'S OLD CREMONA SONGSTER.................10 "
NELSE SEYMOUR'S BIG SHOE SONGSTER.......................10 "
THE LANIGAN'S BALL SONGSTER..............................10 "
TOM MOORE'S IRISH MELODIES................................10 "
BILLY HOLMES' COMIC LOCAL LYRICS.........................10 "
FATTIE STEWART'S COMIC SONGSTER.........................10 "
CHRISTY'S BONES AND BANJO SONGSTER.....................10 "
GEORGE CHRISTY'S ESSENCE OF OLD KENTUCKY..............10 "
CHRISTY'S NEW SONGSTER AND BLACK JOKER................10 "
THE CONVIVIAL SONGSTER....................................10 "
HEART AND HOME SONGSTER..................................10 "
BOB HART'S PLANTATION SONGSTER..........................10 "
BILLY BIRCH'S ETHIOPIAN SONGSTER.........................10 "
THE SHAMROCK; OR, SONGS OF IRELAND.....................10 "
HARRISON'S COMIC SONGSTER................................10 "
THE CAMP-FIRE SONG BOOK..................................10 "
THE CHARLEY O'MALLEY IRISH SONGSTER ....10 "
FRED MAY'S COMIC IRISH SONGSTER ....10 "
THE LOVE AND SENTIMENTAL SONGSTER....................10 "
THE IRISH BOY AND YANKEE GIRL SONGSTER...............10 "
THE FRISKY IRISH SONGSTER................................10 "
GUS SHAW'S COMIC SONGSTER...............................10 "
WOOD'S MINSTREL SONG BOOK..............................10 "
WOOD'S NEW PLANTATION MELODIES.........................10 "

Spayth's Draughts or Checkers for Beginners. Being a comprehensive Guide for those who desire to learn the Game. This treatise was written by HENRY SPAYTH, the celebrated player, and is by far the most complete and instructive elementary work on Draughts ever published. It is profusely illustrated with diagrams of ingenious stratagems, curious positions, and perplexing problems, and contains a great variety of interesting and instructive Games, progressively arranged and clearly explained with notes, so that the learner may easily comprehend them. With the aid of this valuable Manual, a beginner may soon master the theory of Checkers, and will only require a little practice to become proficient in the Game. Cloth, gilt side. Price..............................**75 cts.**

The Reason Why of General Science. A careful collection of some thousands of Reasons for things, which, though generally known, are imperfectly understood. Being a book of Condensed Scientific Knowledge. It is a complete Encyclopedia of Science; and persons who have never had the advantage of a liberal education may, by the aid of this volume, acquire knowledge which the study of years only would impart in the ordinary course. It explains everything in Science that can be thought of, and the whole is arranged with a full index. A large volume of 346 pages, bound in muslin, gilt, and illustrated with numerous wood-cuts. Price..............................**$1 50**

De Walden's Ball-room Companion; *or, Dancing Made Easy.* A Complete Practical Instructor in the art of Dancing, containing all the fashionable and approved Dances, directions for calling the Figures, etc. By EMILE DE WALDEN, Teacher of Dancing. This book gives instruction in Deportment, Rudiments and Positions, Bows and Courtesies, Fancy Dancing, Quadrilles, Waltzes, Minuets, Jigs, Spanish Dances, Polka, Schottische, Galop, Deux Temps, Danish, Redowa, Varsovienne, Hop, etc., together with all the newest Waltzes and Quadrilles in vogue. It also contains complete directions for all the figures of the celebrated "German" or Cotillion. Bound in boards, cloth back. Price..............................**50 cts.**

The Game of Draughts, or Checkers, *Simplified and Explained.* With practical Diagrams and Illustrations, together with a Checker-Board, numbered and printed in red. Containing the Eighteen Standard Games, with over 200 of the best variations, selected from the various authors, together with many original ones never before published. By D. SCATTERGOOD.
Bound in cloth, with flexible covers. Price..............................**50 cts.**

Courteney's Dictionary of Abbreviations; Literary, Scientific, Commercial, Ecclesiastical, Military, Naval, Legal and Medical. A book of reference—4,000 abbreviations—for the solution of all literary mysteries. By EDWARD S. C. COURTENEY, Esq. This is a very useful book. Everybody should get a copy. Price..............................**12 cts.**

How to Detect Adulteration in Our Daily Food and Drink. A complete analysis of the frauds and deceptions practised upon articles of consumption, by storekeepers and manufacturers; with full directions to detect genuine from spurious, by simple and inexpensive means. Price..............................**12 cts.**

Blunders in Behavior Corrected. A Concise Code of Deportment for both sexes. Price..............................**12 cts.**
"It will polish and refine either sex, and is Chesterfield superseded."— *Home Journal.*

Five Hundred French Phrases. Adapted for those who aspire to speak and write French correctly. Price..............................

www.ingramcontent.com/pod-product-compliance
Lightning Source LLC
Chambersburg PA
CBHW030536040726
47497CB00008B/2472